Gladys Swan

Carnival for the Gods

GLADYS SWAN

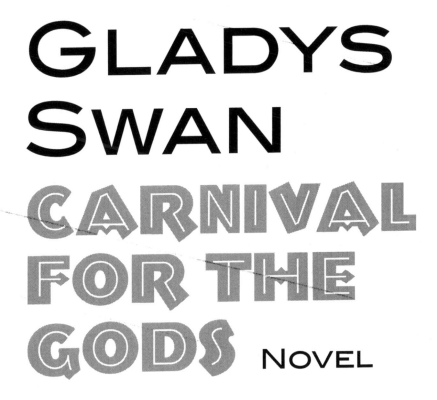 NOVEL

In memory of Richard, my companion through the territory.

Design: Stephan Cuber, diaphan gestaltung, Switzerland
Cover image: Painting by Gladys Swan
Printed by CreateSpace
Available from Amazon.com and other online stores

ISBN 978-1-937247-01-0

1

It was the first time Dusty had ever backhanded her, and it was not just the blow, the pain, the blood from her lip flowing saltily into her mouth that gave Alta the shock: it was the sense that something fatal had struck at the roots of her life. Things would never be the same. It was the edge of Dusty's ring that had cut her lip, a gold ring with a strange little head carved in ivory that he'd bought during a fit of extravagance in Kansas City and said was his good luck and that he'd never part with it. As she stood in the cramped little bathroom, looking into the mirror, teeth all outlined in red as though she'd been eating red-hearted plums or pomegranates, the lip still bleeding, it seemed as though she'd never staunch the flow. This is my life, she thought; this is time leaking away, as it has been doing year upon year. And I'm standing here letting it happen like I was born without a brain.

The whole of the little trailer had shaken with their quarrel, till even words and the clash of voices could not contain the violence. Pansy, the little curly-haired dog she kept, a cross between a poodle and a wire-haired terrier, had taken refuge under the couch and, looking at Alta with brown eyes that seemed full of the light of tragedy, still refused to come out. Dusty meanwhile had thrown himself out of the trailer and into the truck, banging doors all the way, setting up a cloud of dust as he roared off into town, leaving her there alone with the freaks and the animals in the broken-down carnival.

She dabbed at her lip as she tried to calm her feelings. She was looking pretty terrible at the moment. Face blotched, bags under her eyes, broken lip, but she wasn't all that old—forty-seven—and there was still a chance for . . . what? For love, for money?

Money talks—she'd learned that much. It says *yes* and it says *no*. Says, *you owe it to yourself, baby; go on and have it. Be my guest. Says, you're out of luck, sister. Says go to the city and have yourself a ball; says, stay home and starve your gut. Says, turn on the gold-plated faucet, break out the champagne. Says, stay away, lady, you smell bad, and nobody's gonna give you a second look. Says, dream—the sky's the limit. Says, look at the walls peeling. Says, go hang yourself.*

It says, Alta concluded, *you have been with a man who's brought you nothing but trouble and grief, all the while promising you the world.* And where has it landed you? Down in the flatlands with blood on your teeth. Always full of harebrained schemes. And he wasn't half as crazy as the rest of the outfit, only more unreliable.

"I'm sick of this life. Filled up to here." That's how it had begun.

Dusty, sitting at the narrow Formica-topped table with the bench on either side, at which they had shared what might be called their domestic life, was adding up one of his interminable columns of figures. Always trying to turn nothing into something, as Alta had it, to make less come out to be more. "Sick of it." He looked up: "There's no anchor hanging out of your ass."

The truth of this observation left her momentarily speechless—a yawl in a dead wind. Then her fury unlidded, and the fine brew the years had whipped to froth came boiling over, pouring out: the salt was in her mouth, the distillation of years of sweat and tears and gall. All she might have had—all that had gone down the drain.

It was the sandstorm that finally did it to her. Bad enough to have the equipment truck break down in the flattest, most god-forsaken stretch of natural freakishness she'd ever laid eyes on. Like somebody's uninteresting nightmare. A world created out of what any sensible being would've rejected in the first place or else reached for only in the dry heaves of violent boredom: things twisted and sharp and spiny and hard. Some of them reached up and out with arms dried and dead in their attitudes of empty aspiration. They seemed neither plant nor tree, these cacti and Joshua trees; nor alive, these clutches of dry grass and sage brush against a rocky ground that gave off a hard glint. The rocks that rose in the distance looked to have no living thing growing on them. Only telephone poles and the blacktop to show that human beings had been here, mainly, Alta thought, to get through it and on to somewhere else: the sort of place you might consider beautiful only if you didn't have to be there.

It was one of those undistinguished spots of blacktop, miles from the notion of a town, they'd come to a halt in the middle of, when the rear axle of the equipment truck broke down, and their little procession came to an uneven halt, like train cars piling up. There was a dull, angry look in the sky, and they'd no sooner got their vehicles pulled off onto the shoulder than the wind picked up the dust and flung it at them, striking the metal roofs and sides like a flail. It was a good thing they weren't going anywhere, because they couldn't have seen to get there anyway. The sun was eclipsed, the windows dark with dust. And though the doors and windows were shut, so they were nearly stifled inside, the dust sifted through anyway, a fine layer over everything. They drank it in their coffee and ate it with their food.

The animals nearly went crazy. The horses neighed and tried to rear in their trailer. The little elephant stamped and trumpeted. The tiger paced her cage all night. And what with the fray and the clatter, the bay gelding had somehow injured a leg. They needed both a vet and a mechanic, two more bills to pay. So it was no wonder that on this day, in what appeared to be the wreckage of the storm, most of the people in the show pulled out. The operators of the booths— little independent outfits that had hooked with them and would hook on somewhere else. The shooting gallery left, and the lucky spinning wheel, the car races, the coin and ring tossing set-ups—most of the acts and all the games of chance were taking their chances elsewhere.

"Well, you gotta live," Pearl Diamond said when she and Bates, who threw knives at her till her silhouette stood outlined upon the wall and she stepped forth unscathed, were taking off. "Be seeing you," they said to Alta. "No hard feelings." The first to leave, they had put the idea into the common mind, though no doubt somebody else would have thought of it too. Any woman, Alta thought, who trusted a man enough to allow him to throw knives at her was either too dumb or too lucky to have troubles in the world, and she envied her even as she wished her well.

If they hadn't missed the turn-off, probably none of this would have happened. They were supposed to have headed north towards Albuquerque, but they'd missed the sign and hadn't had the sense God gave a turnip to stop and look at a map. Before they knew it, they'd gone fifty miles out of their way.

If you hadn't ... And how are we going to get out of this godforsaken place? Money and blame. Bitch, bitch, bitch. As if a man hasn't got enough troubles... Whose idea was it to...? As if you never made a mistake ... Money and blame. I could've made fifty to your one, and we'd both be better off. Brick bats flying back and forth. Pulling your weight ... Whose weight? ... Fed up with your ... Because of you, goddammit. You gave me nothing, not even a child... Couldn't plant anything in that belly of yours except a fart ... I should've got me a better man to try.

The blood had dried on her lip. Tentatively she touched the spot, then turned from the mirror. *I could've been ...* Not been—was. *Was* one of the best damn trapeze artists in the business. The two of them together: Gold Dust and Dream Girl. The dream had turned to dust —hah! Ashes to ashes: Gold Dust to Dusty, what a joke. The two of them one great act, till the moment suddenly came, maybe by a slip of the foot and one miss in midair too many, by too dizzying a glance down below, Dusty seemed to lose his nerve, wanted to settle for a life on the ground, but with higher ambitions: a show of his own. At the time when they could've had top billing in "The Greatest Show on Earth," Dusty chased his dream of something grander yet, circus and carnival together, triumphantly called "The Carnival for the Gods." Earth wasn't enough for him.

He was headed into the clouds, into the skyscape of the forever possible, the shape of things to come. They'd play all the big cities, bringing back the days when everybody went to the circus. Giant celebrations in the heart of every city.

But the idea never really got off the ground. It was too vast for anybody but Dusty to believe in for very long. The force of his enthusiasm—he could talk people into anything and they would follow him around with puppy-like loyalty—held them for awhile. But starvation was a powerful eye-opener. The shine wore off and off they went. And now they were down to the rag, taggle and bob that had stayed because they had nowhere else to go.

There had been better days: when she was up on the high wire, and her body was a flash of motion as she swung, hanging by her heels, across the top of the tent, the faces below like rows of light bulbs, her body light as a firefly in her blue body suit. All alone up there, no nets below, with the tight thrill that was the joy bred of danger. The tingle in the blood. God, how she loved it! It was the years that had brought her down to earth. She'd nearly killed herself once in a fall. She'd lost her timing, her body had gotten heavy despite all her efforts. The pull of gravity, the reluctance of the flesh. And all the while Dusty trying to put together his misbegotten scheme.

She put some water in the kettle to boil and took out a jar of Sanka. She didn't like the taste much, but even with the heat it was something to put into your mouth and swallow. Something to look into and stir your spoon around in while you sat. She spooned out the instant, poured in the water and sat ruminating, waiting for the coffee to cool, gazing into the dark liquid. Time out. It allowed you to sit down right in the midst of life while somewhere else people were killing each other or having babies or getting the mortgage foreclosed or carrying on a family quarrel that would leave seven people sworn enemies for life. Set a cup of coffee in front of you and none of it mattered, at least for the moment; otherwise you were out scratching and biting and clawing because the world was an obstacle you had to strike out at.

She was full of yearning, but she didn't know what for. When she had had money, she bought clothes, strange fanciful outfits that could have taken her to another age and fashion, or to a costume party. She loved bodices decorated with pearls and sequins and fringes that shimmied when you walked and rhinestones that danced the light. She loved bright colors: reds that could have come from the throat of a trumpet and pinks and oranges and purples that peeled your eyeball back to the optic nerve. She had trousers and a turban made of cloth of gold, and tops all embroidered. Even now, when she took tickets she sometimes dressed up as the Queen of Sheba or a priestess of the moon in a gown, her special creation that shimmered between gold and silver, set off by a crown of rhinestones with a fan of feathers rising from the back. But nobody paid any special attention. She had the stuff all packed in the closet. And Dusty wanted her to get rid of all that rubbish, just taking up space, but it would have been like stripping off her own skin. Yet she knew she'd never wear them anymore. Most of them were too tight anyway.

No, money wasn't good for anything. It was good to spend when you had it, but then you tossed aside what you had bought as so much junk. Dusty still had his ring—so much for the luck it had brought him.

As for love, that was even worse. Had she loved Dusty, she wondered, or had she just wanted a man who dreamed big, was headed for the clouds?

He couldn't even give her a child.

Small wonder he had time to put the makings in her belly, considering where his head always was: scheming and dreaming and adding up columns of figures and charting their course around the country and talking half the night away, too excited even to make love. And though there were ups as well as downs at the beginning, things now were headed in one direction only. It didn't seem to occur to him that they were all washed up. The gaggle of folks they'd picked up was the rout, the survivors who hadn't quite gone over the edge, not the glittering argosy he'd always had in mind. A man with a dream was a madman.

Love. Much worse than money. A giant and a midget who fought and were inseparable. An animal trainer who was convinced a woman lived inside his tiger, the only woman he'd ever wanted. Idly, she wondered if anybody had ever tried fucking a tiger. She'd heard about doing it with cows and sheep and dogs. Probably even with trees, provided you weren't so unlucky as to strike upon a bee hive inside. For all of which, she thought, you'd have to be pretty damn desperate. But a tiger. Even if you could get one to stand still for it, there was something in the nature of a cat that ought to make you a bit leery. You couldn't put your dependence on them. But then the trainer, Sam, was nuts too. Love was too much. It created bizarre obsessions. It was a form of drunkenness and self-abuse. They threatened you with blindness if you twiddled your own organs, or with impotence or insanity. But they should've been smarter than that. Love itself was blind and impotent, insane, and ate the heart away until it was white and leprous and scarred beyond all telling. Never trust it, she thought.

Every once in a while when she needed to feel a little pride in herself, she got dolled up and ran off to have an affair with a truck driver or salesman or drifter who was looking for a little diversion. Men she didn't count on seeing again and usually didn't—or, if she did, the interest had passed. She used to like the thrill in the blood of having a new man, but even that had got old. She didn't trust it anymore, no more than she trusted a greenback. No, neither love nor money had taken her anywhere—just left her here tasting her own blood.

She wanted vaguely to kill somebody, but there wasn't anybody handy and certainly nobody worth the trouble. If it wasn't love and it wasn't money. . . . The blood was beating in her veins. It went on beating and beating. Blood, sweat and tears—maybe *they* were real. She found the water running out of her eyes. Real as dirt. Till you were dirt too. They'd discovered America, and what was it but dirt? She looked outside. The dust had blown off and under the blaze of sun the land was cooking into a piece of burnt toast. Maybe she should go out and start digging, see if she could strike oil. Wouldn't that be a humdinger?

Or maybe she should pull herself together and get up and leave like everybody else. She and Dusty had fought and torn at each other, had driven and goaded and disappointed one another nearly as far as human things can go. And now he'd made her taste her own blood, and she was still here. And what if from now on he made a pleasure of beating on her? Or if she stood for it. . . . It made no sense. And if she left . . . what would she do? Go wandering through the world, probably, only by herself, waitressing at some cafe or bar. Trying to cadge drinks and lure men home. Even now there'd be snickers behind her back, not to think of the future.

She got up from the table and gave herself to the task of fixing supper: cut up meat and fried it with sliced onions and put in the tomatoes and chili peppers and set the pot on the stove to cook. What with the mechanic and the vet costing an arm and a leg, it might be the crew's last good meal for a while. Every time you took somebody a car or a body it seemed they wanted you to set them up for life. She'd make a big pot of chili that would either tide them over for a couple of days or feed whoever happened to wander in. Once she'd done that, she washed her face and cleaned herself up a little. She was needing company. She'd see what Billy Bigelow was up to.

She could count on him. He'd been with them forever, first as electrician, carpenter, handyman, what-have-you, and now, after the defection of Carnaby the Great, he was featured as Bigelow the Magician. He could pull cards from out of people's pockets and from behind their ears and discover scarves where they hadn't been before. He had mastered appearance and disappearance and seemed to want to climb to ever higher steps of illusion. Though sometimes he would simply take a pile of long thin balloons and blow them up, twist them into dogs and lions and elephants and kangaroos and send them sailing out into the crowd.

She found him sitting on the couch in his trailer reading a *Time* magazine. Probably months or a year old, since Billy never bought one. But the dates never interested him, it never mattered to him when an event had occurred.

"Dream Girl," he said, "come on in." He was the only person who ever called her that, and it seemed to be the only image he'd ever had of her: up in the air on the high wire. If it were anybody else, she'd be convinced she was being made fun of.

"Been looking at some moon shots they got here. All crust and craters."

"My God, why don't you look out the window? Isn't that desolate enough for you? If you get up and go outside, you could be on part of the moon they haven't discovered yet. The lower part."

"You really think the moon looks like this," he asked.

"If it don't, it's missed a bet." She'd come over to joke a bit, but the direction the conversation was taking her, making her think about where she was, only brought on her irritability. She wished Dusty would come back so she could throw something at him.

"You know what I think?" Billy said, taking off his glasses so he could see her more clearly. "I think they go out and take all those pictures and say it's the moon."

"Why'd they do a thing like that? Besides, you got all those rockets going up and men coming down in capsules and stuff."

"Oh, you could fake that." Billy said, with a snap of the fingers. "No trouble at all. Just take a picture, put it alongside another and say it's the moon."

"What on earth for?"

"Because you got to keep one step ahead of the public. You got to keep them wondering, always in suspense. Otherwise they'd get so bored and dull in their minds they'd turn back into tree frogs. There they'd be, rocking back and forth going mumbledyboo and their eyes would go crossed and their lips would droop and pretty soon they'd be squatting in clusters like fungus, just trying to keep the burner going so life wouldn't go out altogether."

"You got some imagination."

"No, I mean it. That's why you got to have carnivals. Probably they got a secret genius agency somewhere with people that do nothing all day and night but think things up, one leap ahead of the rest of us."

"But all you're talking about is plain lies."

"Of course. What other kind is there? Except some lies are plainer than others. People need them, couldn't get along without them. Think about what people have believed, beginning with the earth being flat. All you have to do is get it into their heads and then they swear it's true."

"But now look," she said. "Nobody really believes you find cards behind their ears."

"They'd like to. And if you could convince them you got some leetle secret, they'd believe that too."

He was always playing these games with himself, and she loved the way he twisted everything around till you didn't know whether you were coming or going. She'd lost all her anger. "Well, if everything can be a lie," she said, "then everything can be true just as well." She hadn't the faintest idea what she meant.

"Because people believe it? Then anything can be the truth, can't it? Like all that stuff about living past lives. That could be true."

"Suppose it is. I can't say it isn't. I can't say people haven't been on the moon."

"The people from the future would be living right now, wouldn't they?"

"And how would you know?"

"Use your head. It's got to follow," he said. "And suppose you could go back to the past and you killed your grandfather, would you be alive now?"

"Of course not," she said offhandedly, even though she knew she was being had.

"But then how could you go back . . . ?"

"Why weren't you born with two heads?" she wanted to know. "Then one of you could live in the past and the other in the future and tell each other all about it.

"Probably fall flat on my face," he said, "and the present would go leaking through."

"Through the hole in your head." She stopped, all used up. "How come you don't leave like the rest?"

"The show must go on," he said.

"Come on," she said. "What show? This flea-bitten, half-assed . . ."

"I love you, Alta—you have such a high opinion of we serious professionals." She couldn't tell if he were teasing her or making fun of himself, or maybe both at once. "I'm a magician."

"And an electrician and a carpenter and—"

"A man of parts," he said.

"Is one of 'em a stomach," she asked. "I've got chili cooking."

"Gotcha."

◆

Back in the trailer she stirred the chili, added some oregano and cumin and then sat down to look at the copy of *Vogue* she'd slipped out of the dentist's office the time she had a toothache in Biloxi.

The sun had really turned on the juice, so she tried to get a little relief by opening the window and turning on the fan. But the flies came in through a tear in the screen and buzzed around her head, and Pansy sat and snapped at them. Now and then she glanced out the window to watch Fred taking care of his horses. He'd taken them out of the trailer one by one and tethered them over by some scrub cedar. He'd brought out hay and water and then had lingered in the heat, grooming them, talking to them, trying to soothe them and make up for a life that offered no explanations, just endless travel, unexpected stops, dust storms, injury and inconvenience—all for the sake of those few triumphant moments in the ring when Ginger, his wife, leapt and danced across their backs.

Every now and then a car or a truck would come whooshing past with a rush of hot air and a slash of light, then go plummeting on into the distance. She had no idea when Dusty would be back. Maybe he'd just taken off like the others. Then a truck—not his— appeared, slowed and finally stopped across the road from the horse trailer. A lean, wiry man got out, took a leather bag from the seat and walked over to where Fred was working with his horses. The vet. As she watched them, a couple of tow trucks pulled up and parked. A burly man, T-shirt sticking to his chest, sunglasses, got out. Then a tall guy, cap on his head, long arms, big hands. Burt, their equipment man, emerged from the rig and came over to talk to them. Then a lot of backing and maneuvering, hauling of chains and attachments. And after a time they were towing the truck away in the direction of what she supposed was a town, though more than likely nothing more than a mirage. She'd believe it when she saw it. But no Dusty.

Then the vet was gone too, and she watched Fred lead the horses back into the trailer. That done, he walked over to the trailer where he lived with Ginger, who leapt from one horse to the other while they raced round the ring, who went up into a handstand or did a flip at the height of their motion, who was beautiful to watch. There was a lightness in her. They deserved better, Alta knew. They were young and, like everybody else who'd been drawn in, had the dream painted in their heads. All full of enthusiasm. Dusty's dream was their dream. She'd seen it happen over and over again. And he wasn't lying when he went on painting the sky in vivid colors. He believed every word of it: it was going to happen. Then, one day, they woke up. He owed them money, like he owed everybody money.

Now she knew they were leaving too. She didn't get up to say goodbye, though she and Ginger had sat in each other's trailers and traded intimacies. And Ginger had showed her bruises on her body in places that didn't show. And sometimes she'd wept: Fred was fonder of his horses than he was of her, treated them better. And to tell the truth, she was sick of the smell of horse. Fred always smelled of horse. Alta didn't go over to say goodbye, because chances were they'd come across each other when they least expected it. In this business you were never surprised.

She felt bad about the money, but there was no help for it. If their paths did cross and Dusty were flush, he'd pay off. That's what he said, and she had no reason to doubt him because so far Dusty hadn't had any money. She watched Ginger climb into the cab of the trailer while Fred went back to drive the one with the horses. Then they were gone. Why wasn't she leaving with them? Was one kind of wandering any worse than another?

For a time she sat there blank and empty, all used up. The anger of the morning seemed as far away as last month. She wasn't even waiting for anything. She turned off the chili, then let the evening move in around her. She sat with her dog in her lap. The deepening sky was a rich blue, a mingling of blues, lighter and dark, with a smoky feeling underneath; it came down into the landscape, softening the edges of the mountains, turning brown slopes to lavender, to indigo, to darker shapes yet that made all of it one vast stillness that reached far beyond her, perhaps to the borders of the world. There were only the little lights of the few trailers left: animal trainer, giant and midget, magician-cum-handyman. That was the carnival now— the scrapings from the pot.

From out of the indigo she saw headlights approach, then heard a truck pull up and stop. She went outside. Dusty was back, but with somebody with him in the front seat. She bent down, leaning on the side of the truck to look in. A girl. She could just about make her out in the gathering dusk. Though she looked to be no more than seventeen-eighteen, she knew everything a woman could know and then some.

"This is Grace," Dusty said, by way of introduction. "Amazing Grace. Wait'll you see what she can do. We'll hit the big time yet."

I know what she can do, Alta thought. Amazing, all right. Probably one of those street kids that had left home at twelve or thirteen, soon as their periods started and they had their union card for womanhood. Then they peddled it on every street of every town in the great U.S. of A. Double A for Amazing. Then she noticed a childish face in the narrow seat behind Dusty. A boy. But so wild he looked like some creature that had been torn away from the land and still carried in its eyes the reflection of the water hole from which it drank, the snug of the nest where it had spent the night still clinging to the fine white hairs on his arms.

"Does he talk," she suddenly asked.

"The words have gone out of him," the girl said, "but the singing has stayed behind. He knows the ballad of Kitty Moreno and Amigo and the Battle of Glorieta Pass and Indian Joe and his fight with a bear and the loves of Pajarito."

These are barely human things, Alta found herself thinking, for she had learned to recognize such and they were not new to her experience. And here was another set in front of her that she might look at and talk to and never understand. She could ask questions till her teeth rotted and it wouldn't make a ghost of a difference. There they were, almost cringing in the seat of the truck. In the back with the boy, she noticed two crates that looked to be the dimensions of their personal property and inside which something stirred and moved with a vaguely animal and somewhat sinister quality. She didn't ask what.

"You want something to eat," she asked, for she could recognize hunger too, though on what level she couldn't always tell. "I've got a pot of chili on the stove."

They stepped out of the truck, the girl rubbing her arms against the evening chill. Alta saw a square of light as the door of Billy Bigelow's trailer opened. He'd be coming too.

She looked off into the distance before she went inside: over in the mountains it looked as though a storm was brewing up. A sudden flash of lightning and the mountains stood out, every slope and draw outlined in angular crossings of brilliance. If it rains, she thought, it will pick up the dust and the sky will fall down in mud. First they'd nearly been swept away, now it was more than likely they'd be mired down. Or else the water could come tearing down the mountains in a flash flood.

"Come on inside," she said, and went to the stove to put the fire on. Dusty was still fiddling outside in the truck while these two stood uncertainly in the doorway. "You can wash up in there," she said. The boy's eyes went roaming around the trailer as if it would take getting used to. Alta went about setting the table.

Here they were, just another pair among the number she had seen in the procession of all the broken, ill-formed, misbegotten things headed out of the world and onto the road, moving from town to town, never calling any place their own. They were her family, if you could call it that—they were her fate.

She closed the front door. It was getting cold now as night took over the desert. She was closing the door against the night, against the rustle of lizards and the spines of cactus, against whatever shapes lay in the darkness and whatever moved in the silence. Then Billy Bigelow and Dusty came in talking about the day. Only the sound of voices and the smell of chili seemed warm and real.

2

This was his last chance. He refused to say it to himself. He kept ducking the words as if they were bats flying at his head—because they might act like a curse and break his luck—but they were there anyway. He rubbed the ivory head on his gold ring, trying to persuade the Lady to set the Wheel of Fortune on its way up and to keep off the dark influences of Saturn, and fingered the objects hanging in the truck cab: a large pair of white plastic dice with black spots, a little silver horseshoe, and a rattle from the snake he'd once run over in the middle of the road. But it was from the ring, he felt, that he'd derive the greatest benefit. *Now or never.* The little ivory head with the mouth shaped as though it were blowing a smoke ring, and whatever had shaped that white ivory head as a tangible effigy of luck; whatever power.

Ordinarily he walked around as though luck were an element of the air he breathed, a current of energy flowing through his mouth and speech, his arms and their labor. He'd had his ups and downs, Dusty had, but luck was always waiting for him over the next rise. He'd put on the next show with the new set of acts and knock 'em dead. The public would be magnetized; so much in demand, he'd be turning away offers by dozens. Only now it was different.

Although he was alone in the truck, Alta driving the trailer with Grace and the kid, he felt her beside him as a cold, disapproving presence. Bad luck for a man. Puts bad feeling in the air, like burn smoke, a woman deciding she no longer believes in you, even if she's going to hang around and take her chances anyway. Takes off a fine little fuzz on the edge of your luck. But he was going to bring it off in spite of her. Old tom-cat that he was, he'd go out for one last fight anytime.

This time Grace was his luck—he was convinced of it. What else had led him to the theater in that one-horse town with the flagpole in the center and a statue of the man who'd killed more bears than anybody else in the territory, when he could've walked into any one of the twenty bars that lined the streets and lost himself in the seductions of the shot glass. In the right mood he was a man for a drink. But it was the theater that caught his eye. A theater with two adult films and Grace in between. He sat back a few moments in one of the ancient moldering plush-covered seats, till Grace made her appearance. He felt all the hairs on the back of his neck stand at attention; then it was all waves of heat in front of his eyes. He could recognize talent when he saw it. *That girl*, he said to himself, *will make my fortune or I'm blind in the eye and destitute of a brain. Living with her, a state of permanent erection. But if any man can stand it, I'm the one.*

While the rest of the audience—a score of ranchers, half a dozen Mexicans and a half-breed Indian—stuck around for *Locker Room Co-eds* and *Sisters and Brothers*, Dusty was out of his seat and around to the back, bent on purpose, trying to organize his spiel. He made his way to the dressing room, where Grace was drinking a cherry coke and reading a hair-style magazine till it was time for her to shimmy on again. He wanted to make a deal, though at the moment his only materials were bluff and nerve held up by thin air.

"Gorgeous," he told her, "you are absolutely number one." She looked at him as if at a breed of strange animal. And when he suggested they might have a future together, she waved him off like a fly —told him he'd better forget it and truck on out of there—and went back to studying her magazine. "We'd be equal partners," he promised. "Look," she said, "I'm busy." In desperation he made one last fling: "I'll do anything." She paused then, looked him in the eye with such a sharp blue gaze he felt he'd even had his skin unzipped and was standing there in shuddering nakedness. She wasn't free, she told him. Her manager took care of everything and wasn't about to turn her loose. If he wanted to talk to him, he was back at the place.

The manager was probably her pimp as well, Dusty figured, and the place, when he finally found it, was a ramshackle adobe with peeling pink stucco. Decor a la trash heap: an old washtub and rusted bed springs sitting in the yard, thistle and sunflowers growing around them. At one side a boy—perhaps eleven or twelve, he looked small for his age—was sitting on the ground, making shapes out of mud or clay. Dusty couldn't tell what they were, if anything, though they resembled thick, badly shaped towers, arranged in circles like the towers of a forgotten city. Maybe that was it. But he was too preoccupied to puzzle out what the boy was doing. Out back it looked like someone was trying to get a little corn growing. They weren't having a whole lot of luck, it looked to him, what with the dry patches where nothing had come up and the rest shriveled with the heat and dust.

He rapped at the screen door. No answer. "I'm looking for Mr. Priam Gilles-pie," he called to the boy, who went on making his strange fetishes. Suddenly gathering up several and leaping to his feet, he began throwing them one after the other. A howl of pain and sudden surprise came from the weed patch behind the bedsprings, and a black and white cat streaked away with its ears down.

Dusty rapped again, then wandered over to the other side of the house. This time he noticed a green rocker under a box elder, the leaves limp with dust, offering the only shade for maybe ten miles, and in the rocker an old man asleep with his chin on his chest. He looked as though he might've been sitting there for days: A stubble of grizzled beard sprouting out of the neglect to shave, a thatch of gray hair that stuck out at the back of his head, and a fusty smell of stale cigarette butts and unwashed underwear. He was wearing a T-shirt for the sake of coolness, but still had his suspenders on, one looped down over his arm. The top button of his faded dungarees was open to allow for the greater expansion of the bulge around his middle.

He came out of his sleep yawning and stretching and muttering once Dusty woke him up—blue eyes cloudy and vague, then turning shrewd as a ferret's as Dusty explained who he was and what he wanted. Gillespie asked for a sum that took his breath away, and they argued and bargained for an hour while Dusty made calculations in his head, bought and sold, borrowed and scraped, invented and rejected a dozen schemes. His strategy was to wear the old man down: coming out boldly, backing and filling, trying to mesmerize, making up his scat as he went along:

"Fifty, fifty, take away five. Best damned offer you'll ever get. You gotta allow: cost of removal and large-scale expense, superfluxations of the overhead and surcharged expectations of the receipts. What d' you say? Forty-five, take away ten: pad the palm of Uncle Sam; hand in your pocket all the time. Best damned offer you'll ever get. Grace in this fleabag—you know what it's like. The crowd's a tease. You know that as well as me. I shit you not. The dying concupiscence of the crowd—the old eye and you're dead. Thirty, twenty, take away ten. Take your money and call it a day. A man's gotta live, keep on his feet, move on the globe. What'll you take? What'll you take? Thirty, twenty, take away five. You all done, you all through? Take it or leave it—put yourself in a showman's shoes. Best damned offer you'll ever get."

But the old man hung on like a bulldog. He seemed to gain strength in the jaw from sheer force of argument, while Dusty's voice grew raspier as his brain swam and his hopes dimmed—till he was ready to weep with vexation. Finally, pushed to the edge of all or nothing, he heaved a sigh and gave in. By God, he was going to have the girl if he had to walk out of there shoeless and in his underwear without a dime in his sock.

"You aiming on going over to the Seven Cities?" Gillespie wanted to know after they'd concluded the bargain. "Always thought I'd make it back there myself. Hear they still pay top dollar in the clubs. But now that I'm getting on, I don't have the wind and the enterprise I used to."

The Seven Cities? Dusty was dumbfounded. He thought he knew every city and town and hamlet and slick spot on the road, but he'd never so much as heard of them.

"You don't know the Seven Cities?" The old man wore a leer of satisfaction at such ignorance. "Fancy that. The fabled Seven Cities of Cibola and he don't even know about 'em."

"Come on," Dusty said testily. Gillespie was really getting his goat. He owed him a sum he was already beginning to resent and he had yet to face Alta, who would be stropping the blade to skin him alive. "I've been in every town big enough to hold a tent. I've crossed this land so often Rand McNally could use my brain for a reference."

"Well, around here it ain't no secret. Everybody pertends they're not there, 'cause they know they got a good thing. Even the goverment, they pertend too—but people are swarming over there all the time. Cheap liquor and gambling and dope and palaces of pleasure." He smacked his lips. "Wish I was younger, I tell you, and I had me a real stake. I'd sure head back. But my Mercury's all beat up and broke down, and it's a hard trip over the mountains even when the weather's good."

"You really been there?" Dusty said, still convinced the old man was trying to sell him a bill of goods.

"Just Ventura City." He shook his head. "Quite a place. And they've made some improvements since my day. Once you've seen it, you don't have to look any farther—makes Las Vegas look like a kindy-garden."

"Funny thing," Dusty said. "Once I heard a guy going on about a town of that name. Only he was wild drunk, breaking up a bar in La Junta, Colorado. So I didn't put any stock in it. How come it's not on any map?"

" 'Cause it's never been settled who owns it. There's this piece of territory between us and Mexico, so hard to get to that for a long time nobody even bothered. Though some of them explorers went looking for it. Then when it got all built up, with all the traffic going back and forth, looked like it was just easier to pertend it wasn't there, since nobody could decide who it belonged to anyway. Uncle Sam, he says, You forget about it and we'll forget about it. And Mexico, she says, we'll forget about it, if you'll forget about it. Well, they argued like that for months and years, and then they both agreed to forget about it.

Now it's like a separate country, only you won't find it on any map. Because then you'd have to pay attention to it, go to war over it, send in terrorists and revolutionaries and missionaries and reformers. And that would be a nuisance since there's a world full of them already —excepting for the ten percent unemployed."

Dusty was on fire. A new act, a new territory to conquer. He ran around the rest of the day and part of the evening making phone calls, trying to talk loans out of the bank and the finance company, ready to put his whole carnival in hock. He would've been able to talk his way into and out of anything. By the end of the day, he had sold his equipment rig to a rancher and had mortgaged the rest of the carnival to the bank. And he came back, cash in hand, to pay off.

"Come on, Grace, get your things packed."

"She don't want to go back," Gillespie whispered, "but she's yours and you can get her to do what you want, even if you have to take a hand to her sometimes. But she'll put out, let me tell you. She'll give it everything she's got." The old man's eyes seemed to mist over as he gazed after her, but more than likely, Dusty thought, he was dazzled by the sight of all that cash. He watched as Gillespie counted the money carefully, took out an ancient wallet and slipped it in: all his worldly wealth—going, going, gone.

"Now I can retire to Arizona," the old man said, "eat a fresh orange from the tree every day." He paused to savor the pleasure in anticipation. Dusty was getting antsy; he wanted to get out of there before he was aswarm with second thoughts.

"Wait—I forgot to tell you," Gillespie said. "You'll have to take the boy too."

And now here he was, headed over the mountains with Grace as his passport to luck. For a time the blacktop burned straight into the distance as though it was just one more flat barren stretch to get through. Ahead was a mirage shimmering, then evaporating when you came up to it. As he drove, Dusty was planning. He'd mount three acts, maybe four, depending on the facilities: The Amazing Grace, the giant-and-midget routine and Bigelow the Magician. He wasn't sure yet what could be done with the elephant and tiger, but that fellow Sam could do anything with animals. If the old lion hadn't died and the mate grieved to death, he'd have had something more impressive to go with. But after they made their wad in Ventura City, maybe he could freshen up the animal act, buy some new talent, put together a whole new outfit. Carnival for the Gods once more.

The road began to climb. He'd play the giant and midget for comedy, as usual, but with new routines, a new emphasis. The midget would be Jack the

Giant Killer and the giant, Tom Thumb. Swaggering midget and terrified giant—that would get them. And Grace for the last. Build up and let her be the climax. So he drove on, scheming and dreaming while the rest of the carnival followed his lead; ready, if unwilling, to take the high road into the mountains.

◆

"If Grace doesn't want to go there, what makes you think the rest of us do?" Alta had raised this question before they set out. And she still thought it was just one more of Dusty's hare-brained schemes. Where were they going and what was he getting them into this time? Billy Bigelow was more philosophical about it, as he was about most things. "Well," he said, "it's just one more place. Think of it that way."

One more place. Well, she was tired of places. Sick of them. But once she recovered her temper, at least she was reconciled. Curran and Donovan were in the middle of one of their interminable wrangles, however, and had set off in a paroxysm of bad feeling.

It started this way. Curran had gone through a period of staring at himself in the mirror, continually measuring various parts of his body, reading in books about dwarfs and midgets. All his life he had been called both dwarf and midget by people who weren't fussy about such distinctions. And though he'd felt a certain niggling dissatisfaction, he wasn't sure the distinction mattered all that much. After all, anybody could be short in the leg, long in the torso, or vice versa. But now he was full of concern about which he actually was.

In his latest bout of discontent, perhaps he was reaching for something secure by way of definition, a sense of himself as circus performer because uniquely qualified by virtue of his size. If his body were, in fact, perfectly proportioned, he was simply a little man in a place where, like anyone else, he could use his talents—a professional.

But now that he was approaching middle age, a certain thickness had gathered around his waist. The tape measure was unkind. He was left standing in a thicket of doubts and ambiguities, wanting definition and certainty. He wanted to find a gold nugget lying in his path.

In that worst of all moments, Donovan had caught him holding a tape measure, staring disconsolately into the mirror, a book open on a picture of P. T. Barnum's most famous midget. "What's this?" Donovan said brusquely.

Mortified, Curran hastily closed the book and ducked away. But Donovan was on to him, prodding and poking, joking and teasing, till having wrung out his partner's admission, he burst into a roar of laughter. "What's the difference?" he said. "You're still a freak." And still roaring with laughter, he left the trailer, the midget hurling after him everything within reach, both words and objects, till he stood breathless with rage and astonishment.

That he should be so entirely revealed, the very live-wires of his sensitivities exposed . . . and by Donovan at that. For though they worked together, were bound together, if grudgingly, by whatever bond of feeling or necessity, there were times when Curran looked down on the giant as a great blundering stupidity. For Curran had had the benefits of a superior education, lovingly supervised by his parents through a series of tutors. And he had been of an inquiring turn of mind.

For himself, Donovan claimed to have broken the top of the I.Q. tests and for a time, to have belonged to Mensa, where only people of superior intelligence gathered to drink Earl Grey tea and espresso coffee while debating intellectual issues and living the life of the mind. But finally he decided there was altogether too much of him to fit even into the life of the mind, and he dropped out. Still he liked to brag to Curran that he was not only bigger than everybody else, he was smarter too. Whatever else, the conviction certainly made him a trial to live with. When he got going, he was happy to argue the midget tongue-tied. His thought shot up and out in great spiraling leaps until it coalesced at some level of understanding that, in effect, left the midget on the ground gaping at a piece of sky-writing. His own mind moved slowly. It must be, he concluded, because his brain was small.

But this time Curran got one up on him. At first it didn't occur to him to think of revenge: he simply retreated into himself and for a whole day sullenly refused to say anything. Which was punishment enough. For Donovan was a talker, a great spinner of words. He liked the sound of his own voice, and whether he admitted it or not, he depended a great deal on his companion, as though he took his reality as a giant from being in the society of a midget. To be met with silence was a goad and a torment. It set him at various bits of nervous activity. He clipped his nails, both toenails and fingernails, cleaned the wax out of his ears, and in an agony of boredom, was ready to begin counting his pubic hairs. Finally, yawning heavily, he fell into his specially constructed bed and took refuge in sleep.

Breakfast came and went in excruciating pantomime. Then suddenly, from the midst of one of his ruminations, Curran said, "Suppose you could just get out of it?" He hadn't really intended to say anything. Once more he had betrayed himself.

Words. Something to go on. Donovan seized on the chance. "Get out of what? The carnival? You're not thinking of leaving—you'd be crazy. Where would you go, what would you do? You're not as young as you used to be." Now that he'd been given an opening, he was afraid to stop lest the silence fill it up again.

Curran continued to stare into space. Then it occurred to him to put Donovan off the track, dance around him, you might say: he was agile enough. "That wasn't what I meant, if you'd like to know. I meant: by reaching for it, and beyond."

"All right," Donovan said, jocularly, ready to go along with anything. "But you'd have to be my height to do that."

"Capturing the jewel," Curran went on, "the nub of God's own watchband."

Donovan forced a laugh. He was nettled. Here was some kind of mystical gobbledygook, and the little creep was pulling his leg. Now he'd have to try to get the better of him, beat him at his own game.

"Why not downhill to the dugs of winter?" he suggested. "Suck the tits of the old mother—the bitch."

"Not down, you idiot—up. If you know what I mean, why do you have to make frogs' eyes?" As though to imitate him, he gave Donovan an exaggerated stare.

The little guy was getting under his skin. "Down is up and up is down," he said breezily.

"Only when you're out of it," Curran said. "Otherwise, if you go too far down, you get bit by a Tasmanian monster. Past down to down under." There was a moment's silence. The words that had come out —as though they had a will of their own and didn't depend in the least on his comprehension—gave Curran a certain thrill. He was so fascinated by the sound of his own nonsense, which seemed to put out a tendril of sense without having anything at the roots that he wanted to go on playing. "Oh, the luff and ketch of an idea in the fell of its beginning," he said joyfully.

Ignoring the look of disgust that met him, Curran was caught up in a sudden splendid vision of himself breaking up sentences and words, taking a hammer to them until they all lay in pieces of pure sound without meaning, and putting them together again in breathtaking patterns until whole edifices of utterance appeared, perhaps illumined with significance. And if he could do that, he would leap out of himself. Then it occurred to him that no one would be able to understand him in the least and, in fact, would look on him as a gibbering idiot.

"You ought to try speaking in tongues," Donovan said. "It doesn't make any sense, but some folks get a thrill out of it."

Curran fell into another of his silences. There were all kinds of tongues: cats' tongues and hyenas' tongues and monkeys' tongues. Cat howls, hyena laughter, monkey chatter. He wanted a sound all his own. And he imagined himself going among such creatures as though they might confer on him the one he wanted. And he knew what it was. He would have liked the long hollow call of the loon. As a child, he'd heard it reach far across the lake and fill up the woods, haunting and mysterious, and another answering. Loony? Crazed by the moon? Crazy with longing?

"Holy Moses," Donovan said, getting up, knocking over a chair in the process. "I think I'll find me some quiet place to beat on the floor and foam at the mouth. Better the D.T.'s than to loaf around this mad-mobile anymore."

Curran looked up. "Half a loafer is better than the shoe on the other foot," he said. The door slammed. He'd driven him out. For the first time Curran could remember, he'd won.

Let him go. He'd be back. Most of the time it was Donovan's rages he had to live with. He had a talent for hurling things. Open the door and out went dishes, cans, shoes, bottles and half the furniture. Usually, it was Curran who had to collect what hadn't been broken or carried off by the dogs. Hard on the environment when Donovan got into one of his moods. Whereas Curran's habit of discontent was brooding.

When Donovan returned, he was armed with the evening newspaper and the latest copy of *Scientific American,* which Dusty had bought for him in town. When he wasn't performing, which he did with both satisfaction and contempt for the crowd, he read newspapers and this, his favorite magazine. He knew everything that was wrong with the world and everything that had been invented or might be to put matters straight. He spent hours reading and making choice remarks on the stupidity of those in charge. "Oh, the shitheads, the fart-brained fools—they know that won't work. And they've been tinkering with engines since the birth of industry. . . . Here they are poisoning the air, polluting the sea, stripping the land. . . ." By the time he'd read the newspaper from one end to the other, he was fortified with enough fact and opinion for a whole week of cynicism. The rest of the time he spent in fantasies of beautiful women making love to him in such elaborate ways—tits down, cunt sideways, ass up —he'd got as far as seventy. If he and Curran were really hard up, they played cribbage, in matches that went on for days and were won with gloating, lost with humiliation. Such were their lives together.

Their relationship always carried a certain amount of banter, from the good-humored sort with a bite under the surface to the kind of sarcasm that showed its teeth and claws. They were both divided and joined by the understanding of what had brought them together. This time, however, Donovan had gone too far.

"We're here only to be laughed at," Curran said, interrupting Donovan as he read his paper. "Isn't that enough for you?"

"Shall I kiss you, sweetheart?" Donovan said, rattling the page. He had been reading about a new rookie basketball player—tall, seven feet, four inches. It made him nervous. What did it mean to be a giant? "Lord of eye sockets," he said grandly, "take away my funny bone and let the wind blow through."

So now they bounced among their discontents into the mountains, along with Alta's skepticism and Billy Bigelow's equanimity, while Dusty planned his next miracle. Then, in a single instant, they forgot what was on their minds and held their breath, attentive only to the road, if you could call it that. It was a strip of indifferent blacktop, curving sharply, dangerously narrow, hugging the sides of the cliffs. It was as though nature had been thoroughly opposed to its being there in the first place, blasted out of those cliffs. And where the edge dropped off, the chasm was at times a thousand feet deep, down to where a dry creek bed marked a strip among the sparse vegetation. Grinding upward in second gear, the little entourage climbed the hills, everyone fearing for the brakes. Dusty hardly had a chance to worry about the animals being bounced around, the curves monopolizing his attention, and it was easier for him in the truck than for the others in the trailers. Whenever a car approached, they had to slow down to a crawl and let it work past, for the road was barely wide enough for two vehicles.

In the very middle of the day, they came to an abrupt halt. A rock slide had deposited a ton of rubble on the road, blocking all passage. Just their luck. Dusty fumed behind the wheel. They waited hours for a bulldozer to appear, then more hours for it to scrape the rocks over the edge of the road. Meanwhile they got out of the cabs, wandered around, watched the rocks tumble below, cracked jokes with those likewise stalled in the cars behind them, ate sandwiches, drank coffee, and became stiff with waiting and boredom. Donovan managed to work up a crap game with a couple of fellows in a land rover—threw boxcars three times on the first three rounds.

It was nearly dark when they were able to go on, now like insects feeling their way along, only their weak lights to help them along the strange road. Just when their eyes were strained beyond all weariness, they came round the last curve and hit the smooth and the straight. The billboards were all there to meet them: the Peacock Palace, Go-Go Inn, the Uni-corner, Ye Olde Black Magic. A topless dancer did a shimmy, neon snaking up her hips and thighs; champagne spilled from a bottle, frothing with bubbles; gold pieces tumbled into a pool surrounded by nymphs, decked only in décolletage formed by necklaces of pearls.

Then came the lights of the city itself, a dizzying splendor, a galaxial dazzle, as if the city were a belt of fiery stars. The whole spectacle hit the nerves in the scalp, the soft place behind the ribs. Tears of anticipation sprang to Dusty's eyes. It was going to happen. He was going to enter as through a doorway and find that his dream had become the real landscape.

3

P erhaps because Ventura City lay in a valley surrounded by mountains and to reach it you had to ascend to a pass of nearly fourteen thousand feet, nearly as high as many of the surrounding peaks, and then make a curving descent on a road that put your heart in your mouth, so that as you broke into a sweat and were tossed between the terror of possible disaster and the wonder of how you'd come out alive, you might be convinced, having made the trip in one piece, that nothing could induce you to do it again. It may have been for this reason that the Chamber of Commerce greeted you with a great neon-lit signboard:

YOU'RE HERE NOW
IN
THE CITY OF FOREVER AND A DAY
AIN'T YOU GLAD YOU MADE IT?

More than likely the C of C had something more in mind than the harrowing ride down the mountain: to make you forget your brush with death as quickly as possible in one of the places of dissipation and amusement along "Los Labios," as they were called. For the city had been given its shape by a rather unique geological circumstance, a deep gorge that divided it in half—the two parts having been connected with a series of bridges. The gorge was formed in prehistoric times by a river snaking down from the mountains, creating a great widening maw in the earth. Then the river had disappeared; you had to dig for water now, to a depth of over a hundred feet, and then more than likely you'd be cheated of your labor when your well went out a few weeks or months later. And when you were lucky enough to find water, owing to the presence of so many minerals, it had the taste of a mouthful of copper pennies. In years of scant rainfall, water had to be rationed.

The other geological feature was a mound south of the city in the foothills with an outcropping of giant cones that resembled a barrage of rockets about to take off into space. The major luxury hotel built there offered its guests excursions by burro through "the Steeples," as they were called, ending with a barbecue of buffalo steaks from a private herd, served on flat rock shaped like an inverted altar.

Nearly all the other hotels, fancy restaurants, night clubs, strip joints, gambling casinos, massage parlors, sex shops, theaters and bars were lined up on either side of the gorge for more than a mile, their neon lights flashing one another promises and invitations across the gap. These were the prize locations, though more than once a car had broken through the railing or a drunk wandered over the edge, falling to the rocks below. These casualties were usually taken with a shrug. On these wide streets so brilliantly flooded with light, fluorescent and neon, if anyone came to grief, it wasn't because he couldn't see where he was going.

The rest of the city fell away from where luxury bloomed in the center. First the back streets with the cheaper night clubs and strip joints, the topless bars, the quick sheet hotels, the all-night porno flicks and the twenty-four-hour fast-food counters. Mixed among these were grocery chains, clothing outlets and the adobe houses and apartments where most of the city dwelt—the hotel clerks and cashiers, the bartenders and taxi drivers and musicians and waitresses, all those who made their industry of other people's play. From there the sidewalks soon gave out, the streets grew darker and dustier, the city less coherent: gas stations and warehouses and used-car lots took over; machinery rusted among broken bottles and cans in the weeds of vacant lots. Then, after a series of rutted dirt streets where only the poorest lived—Mexicans and Indians, for the most part, and the very old, the very sick—the un-stuccoed adobe huts, the grudging gift of mud to human habitation, ended and the city met the desert, miles of barren landscape studded with cacti and inhabited by lizards and jackrabbits.

Somewhat to the north, just before the hills began, was a little oasis called Enterprise, and there the hotel and night club owners, the restauranteurs, the highly-paid entertainers, the operators of the casinos lived, their gates guarded, their landscapes gardened. As opposed to the city, it was a quiet place, where the women could lounge by their swimming pools and listen to the ice clink in their gin and tonics.

Now that the little troupe had arrived, Dusty rushed around in his usual fashion, getting himself known, making contacts with agents and club owners, trying to show his stuff and get something going. Meanwhile, the rest of the carnival, when there were no appointments with booking agents, wandered the streets, bedazzled, gawking like tourists. Except for Grace, who'd been there before and seen it all, they went out separately or in pairs, then came together late at night or late the next morning to compare notes and, if possible, outdo one another's feats of description. This was difficult to do, for the city seemed to have come into existence out of a sense of hyperbole. Most of the exchanges were of the breathless sort: "Did you see the—?" "Yes, but did you see the other—? It's really something."

Alta was taken by the facades, which not only appealed to her passion for color and variety but absolutely dizzied her by their genius for invention: a Moorish castle all in pink; a great Swiss chalet; a rainbow-colored, tower-ornamented "fairyland" with ballooning plastic clouds and faces peeking out among the drifts; a mountain grotto with an aviary of tropical birds and waterfalls played on by colored lights, each day a different bird call featured with flute accompaniment; a great red plastic dome, in front of which a giant mechanical kaleidoscope continually shifted pieces of glass illuminated by changing lights. Inside, the guests could watch the change of patterns under a barrage of strobe lights, while they listened and danced to Super-Rock. For hours afterward, Alta saw spots of color dance before her eyes, and it seemed she was looking at life in a continual fever of sensation, flaring up like a skin condition, but more complex and interesting than the measles.

Perhaps because he was close to the ground, Curran particularly noticed the sidewalks, some of which consisted of hard, colored plastic—red, blue and green—and some studded with pieces of vermiculite or flecked with mica so they glittered. In front of one of the casinos, the sidewalk was a solid mat of silver dollars. With some amusement, Curran watched a drunk try to pick some of these out with his fingernails. He'd crawled around on his hands and knees for half an hour before the cops finally hauled him away.

In some ways Billy Bigelow was the oddest sightseer of them all. Alta couldn't fathom him. He never wanted to go with the others, and for a magician he showed a peculiar disregard for the spectacular. Taking his obscure route, he went around collecting bits of occurrence like a scrap collector. For some reason, the boy always trailed along beside him, Billy keeping up a perpetual monologue that required no response, the boy making none. They rose and went out early while the rest of the carnival slept.

"See that old lady over there . . .?" He picked up whatever the morning had to offer. This time an old woman, bent and hobbling on little skinny legs, moving so slowly out onto the roof of the apartment below that it could have taken the rest of her life to get there. She was carrying a pan of scraps. "Lookee— there's a big old yellow tomcat over there. He's waiting for her." They watched.

"Going to take her the rest of the day to work her way back inside. Arthritis must've got her. And the rest of the city can't make it out of bed at all. Fast asleep —all bleary-eyed and stuck to the mattress. Nothing around but the trash bags: cans and garbage, like everybody cut their lives open and let all the junk come spilling out and now it's got to be hauled away. Bet the dump is some interesting place. And now you've got the cats and dogs out sniffing around, seeing if there's something in it for them, even if it's only worth peeing on. You see," he said to the boy, "not even a kid out playing in the street. Just you and me. The rest of them are asleep, all in the fumes of pleasure. Breathe it in all night, soak in it all morning." A blue figure approached: sandy-haired chap with freckled skin. Came toward them, walking briskly. "There's the mailman," Billy said, "making a little shiny trail through it all, the way a slug does on an early morning romp through the garden—and that's the only thing right now connecting it all together."

So he went on observing and commenting, the two of them wandering around as the food stands began to open and the laborers went off to work, some stopping for their first drink of the day. Hungry by now, he and the boy stopped for coffee and doughnuts, Billy chatting with the woman in the newspaper kiosk. Then they set off again.

As it worked around to afternoon, the city was beginning to gather its forces. By that time Billy and the boy had walked for miles. They were tired. For a time they sat on one of the park benches along the gorge and watched the streets begin filling with people. They fed the pigeons. They bought hamburgers and watched the sun set. Deepening sky and early stars. Then, as if by a signal, the real crowd materialized, and they watched the surge of people and the play of lights. The streets were jammed, the traffic thick. The city had come to life, ready for a blast. Presto! It had been transformed.

"Time to go home," Billy said, "and get out of the way before they run us into the gulch." And heading back to the trailer, they left the city to go on without them.

◆

At first Gus Donovan and Eddie "Weebit" Curran made the rounds of the city together, rather enjoying the comment they aroused. But after the novelty wore off, they seemed hobbled together like a kangaroo with an inchworm; for the midget had trouble keeping up with his partner, who not only had long legs but a restless disposition. There were places he wanted to go—on his own.

"Look here," Donovan said on the third afternoon following their arrival, a wave of boredom having already overtaken him. "I got business. How about you go your way and I go mine."

Curran's lip trembled. He merely shrugged and looked aggrieved. But Donovan was in no mood to think about his feelings, much less humor him. "See you later," he said, and thus ditched him.

He had seen signs for various massage parlors during his peregrinations around the city, each one lighting up a pleasant fantasy. He'd heard about massage parlors, and he wanted the full treatment. Why not? He was free and had the afternoon to kill. They were to gather that evening at Ye Olde Black Magic, where Dusty had managed to book Grace for an act. He sauntered along agreeably, taking his time. First he primed himself with a couple of whiskeys that set up a pleasant warmth in his innards. Then he went around like a careful shopper: one place looked too much like a beauty shop, another impressed him as a dump. Then he looked into a window featuring a great sea shell that embraced him in an iridescent pink glow, the silver letters of the word "Massage" trembling deliciously above. He went in, and found a redhead under whose hand he'd have been glad to breathe his last breath. My God, he thought, making his request. Oh, my God.

Undressed, he became suddenly shy in his nakedness, but the girl, chatting away to put him at ease, made him feel like melting butter. "Well, you sure are a big guy, aren't you? Haven't had anybody as big as you. Gonna take a lot out of me, working you over. You're gonna be a real challenge."

Her laughter rippled down his spine as she led him over to the table, directing him to lie down on his stomach. His buttocks exposed, his legs hanging over the edge—he had to move forward and let his chin rest on his hands—he felt somehow foolish and terribly vulnerable, yet eager and excited. "What's your name," he asked her. "Sandy," she said, taking off her green cotton smock. She stood in front of him topless, her slender hips holding up the bottom of a pink bikini with metallic threads running through it. Her flesh shone as if polished, and her breasts were two honey drops he'd have been glad to catch in his hands. *Sandy,* he said to himself, glad to have a name for what was standing so enticingly in front of him.

As she went around behind him her scent went to work on him, and the moment she touched him a thrill went up his spine like an arpeggio. Rubbing oil on his body, she began to knead his shoulders. He felt her breath on the back of his neck, warming a little spot of his nape. She worked along his back, her palms moving rhythmically along his spine while she murmured, "You're so big, oh, you're so big."

How intimate a pair of hands could be! Like a caress, convincing him that he existed only for her, that she cared only for him and that if he but asked her, she would love him forever. And while her voice caressed him too, he closed his eyes and let go of his mind. *Go on,* he said to it. *Go off and play by yourself for a while.* He wasn't sure he wanted it back as, drawn into her perfume, her touch, his great frame seemed to rise from the table and float a few inches above it. Oh, sensation—how much better than thought! He didn't say a word; somehow it would have broken the spell, in which every nerve leaned forward in anticipation of what she might do next. She had stopped talking, seeming to concentrate on his muscles and the contours of his body. In that silence, the two of them met on the pinpoint of their mutual concentration, ready to venture forth into yet another region of sensation. Her hands were on his buttocks, the suggestions combining so richly with those teasing about his groin. More than once her breast touched his back. He seemed to hear her voice murmuring warmly in his ear to the rhythm of her movement, "You're so big, oh, you're so big."

And something big was building within him. Every spot she touched had been roused, so that it continued to hum with feeling even after she left it. He sighed deeply as she worked along his thighs and the backs of his legs, kneading away the tension while he breathed out the collected troubles of his life and let the other something take over. By the time she had him turn over, he was roused and waiting, each touch an exquisite agony. Every pore and atom had come to life, every fiber and tendon, muscle and ganglion stood at attention. The tangle of her red hair brushed his face, and the warm curve of her breast touched his body as she worked around the pectorals. "Tight up here, aren't you?" she said. "Well, we'll have you so relaxed . . ." Relaxed? When it was all building, all the parts of his body tributaries flowing to the main stream? Midriff, belly, the insides of the thighs, with the pleasant buzz of alcohol in his brain, in his guts, it was all building . . .

"You're so big," she murmured as she bent over him, stroking the lovely stalk that had risen straight up just for her. *Ah,* as she stroked him. *Oh,* as she bent over and opened her lips. Still building, the great streams coming together, coming—then the mighty jet, the explosion in the brain. My God! It was out of this world!

◆

On the street again, Donovan felt restless and dissatisfied. Abruptly his hour had ended, as though punctured. She told him to hurry up and get dressed, she had another customer. And before he had a chance to take her hand and ask her about a little drink after closing time, she shoved him out. Not only did she charge him extra, but double, because he was so big and had, after all, taken a lot out of her.

To overcome his letdown, he went on a binge of nervous eating: chow mein and pizza and Kentucky fried chicken. He filled himself as if he were a great gaping maw. Then it all lay on his stomach like lead. He wished he could get rid of his body, throw it away, and yes, pitch the mind along with it.

Wandering aimlessly along a street, belching unhappily, he stopped, his eye arrested by a sign: SUPERMAN UNLIMITED. What in the hell was that? He found himself looking at a man so much larger than life that he almost filled the whole showroom window. Looking, even he could have been lifted up and devoured by the gleaming smile, radiating good will, the perfectly even teeth ready to give a sparkle to the meanest commonplace. Oh, the charm of the man! He could run for Congress and win by a landslide; he could manage a company and bulldoze the directors, bedazzle the stockholders. Women would bend over for him, children run up to give him their ice cream cones, puppies wriggle and wet the floor. Open and clean and straight from- the-shoulder. A man you could count on. The hands beckoned while the words promised: *You can do it too. Get the personality you need to LIFENHANCE your job.*

Donovan had to stare at the word before he could determine whether it was a piece of foreign language, which always made him suspicious. He read on: *Give your personality a Face-lift and Face the World. Re-program Your Life!*

He was beginning to think he was in some contest of mystification with Curran when the door opened and a young man blundered into the street. He would have been well-built had he been aggressively athletic. But it wasn't in him. His bones were well-padded and he stood there, a large soft man. Even had he made it to the football field, by dint of long work-outs and practice, the opposition would have run him over, nailed him to the ground and left his brains for scrambled eggs. The eyes—well-intentioned, intelligent, and unsure—and the rather full, soft mouth gave it all away.

"You're interested, are you?" he said to Donovan in a friendly manner. "I'm going in for my final treatment later this week. Henry Snyder here," he said, extending a large, gentle hand that, even so, was lost in the giant's paw.

"This stuff do you any good," Donovan asked. "Or is it just some kind of come-on?"

"Oh no," the young man assured him. "Quite the contrary. They've had a very good performance record. I've talked to some of the others who've been through the program. Big men now," he said admiringly. "Buckley Wilson, the bright new light of Outward Transit; Copenbender of Modular Techtonics; and Corby Locker of Projectile II. They've all been through it—and they're different men." Clearly, he'd been sold on it. "Like being reborn."

Donovan was intrigued, if skeptical. Could you, he wondered, make an eagle out of a dodo? They were standing in the middle of the sidewalk, Donovan a large obstacle to the passers-by. He moved aside to make room for a woman with an armload of groceries and nearly flattened an elderly man into the side of the building. He looked down, halfway apologetic, while the old man shook his fist, not exactly in Donovan's face, because he couldn't reach that far, but in the general direction. He turned back to Henry Snyder, as the old man went down the street muttering curses. "Reborn?" he said. "How's that?"

"If you think about it, it's an effort to set nature straight."

"Really?" As far as he was concerned, it would take some doing to put the old broad on the right track. What could you make out of a giant?

"I was just going to have a little afternoon pick-me-up," Henry Snyder said, in his somewhat formal way. He struck Donovan as young and not-young, as though he'd approached youth, decided it was all folly and moonshine and was veering off in the direction of middle age. "Would you care to join me?"

Just what he needed: a pick-me-up. Several, in fact, considering the state of his inner life at the moment. If he drank enough, the afternoon might slide away, ease him into evening. "Lead the way," he said, eager to move into the embrace of the Happy Hour.

As they turned the comer, Henry pulled a balled up handkerchief from his pocket and mopped his brow. "Grueling, those sessions. You can't imagine . . ." He looked at the handkerchief, stuffed it back into his pocket. "Stephanie would have a fit if she saw me," he confessed.

So. Being remade—or whatever it was—was not exactly a snap.

"In here," Henry said, opening the door into a warm darkness filled with bibulous laughter and noise.

They moved among anonymous backs at crowded tables, through an obstacle course of chairs. "Excuse me. Excuse me," Henry said, holding close to himself, stepping gingerly. "Sorry," he said, jogging an elbow. "So sorry," he said, stepping on a foot—all mere shadows in the dark interior. He bumped against a chair back, and part of a woman's drink sloshed over onto her skirt. "Terribly sorry," he said. "Clumsy oaf," she snapped, leaping up, daubing at the wet. He hung over her contritely. "Listen, I'd be glad to ..." "Get lost," she told him.

Donovan followed along behind. No doubt he'd squashed a few feet, jiggled an elbow or two in the process, but he was used to that.

The way he figured it, you see a tank coming, you give yourself the benefit of getting out of the way.

"Come on. It was an accident," Henry said, as though he were trying to assure himself. He steered Donovan over to a comer, to a round table that seemed as small as a child's footstool.

"Don't they believe in lights in this joint?" Donovan said, sitting down heavily. "Or are they expecting a raid?"

"Allow me," Henry said when the bar girl approached. He ordered a double Scotch. Donovan considered a beer but decided there'd be too much foam in his stomach on top of the food; he was in the mood to get drunk. "Scotch," he said. "A double." He turned to his host. "Okay, now tell me how I get to be a superman. I could do with setting nature straight. Give me the scoop."

"Well," Henry Snyder said, "you know the way things go—how nothing ever seems to get matched up right. Suppose you have a family of round-shouldered thinking types, all books and conversations on deep subjects. What kind of kids do they get? A bunch of sports-lovers—outdoor types that want to play football and ride horses and go hang-gliding."

"Yeah," Donovan said. "Or put two athletic types together that can barely grunt the alphabet and they turn out a genius like me." Henry deferred to his example. "I had a cousin who grew up in a family of doctors, and his dream was to become a ventriloquist." "It figures."

"He turned out all right, actually. Became a doctor like the family wanted. Miserable, of course. Till he invented a voice box for cancer patients who'd lost their larynxes. Made a fortune."

"My cousins all wanted to be millionaires."

"Oh. What did they end up as?"

"Bastards."

"Yes, well. . . ."

They seemed to be getting off the subject. "But this outfit you're fooling around with—"

"That's the incredible part," he said enthusiastically. "They fix the square peg to fit the round hole. My case, for instance. Ever since the cradle, I've been groomed to take over the family business: Law school, management positions. But I've never been what you'd call a go-getter."

Donovan looked him over again. The bone structure was there, and the trimmings: Square face, thick curly hair. It was the eyes, all right —something missing in the voltage.

"In fact—" he lowered his voice—"there was a period when I'd sit in the law school library, books open all around me, and I'd be staring out the window. I was fascinated with birds."

"Tweet, tweet," Donovan said, absently, making wings out of his hands. Definitely not the eagle type.

Henry looked at him quizzically, let it pass. When the Scotch came, he took it eagerly, tipped the girl. "It took a long time to cure me," he said. "And the sessions . . . They say I've been very tough. Strong traces in the psychic paths. Energy drain."

"It figures," Donovan said. "So then what?"

"You've got to change all that," he said. "A matter of psychic surgery."

"You mean they cut on you, like those nuts whose brains—" "Not exactly. You see, most people have these energy drains. Nature again—the kinks you've got to straighten. You know how it is with kids growing up, how long it takes them to get into the right slot. They want to be actors or foreign correspondents or songwriters or engineers. Then they discover that's not the right thing at all." "Yeah," Donovan said. "You wake up at forty and think you should have gone to law school or forgotten about the trumpet or hung around and carried out the empty bottles."

"It would save a lot of strain and confusion if people knew what they were doing, put their eggs in the right basket."

"You're telling me." He felt that nature owed him a few explanations. "And this outfit takes up the slack, works out the kinks and puts you where you belong?" It sounded too good to be true. He wondered how he'd do as president of a company, a big outfit.

"Wherever you are, it makes you fit."

"Suppose you want to be something else? Make yourself into what you've dreamed about?"

"Riskier," he said, "but they do take candidates. There *are* positions. Of course there's a waiting list."

"Hell, I've been waiting all my life. Sounds just like what I've been waiting for. Opportunity," he said, kissing his fingertips, "you sweetheart, you." That is, if they had any room for him on the list. He'd always taken up a lot of room.

"You can come with me, if you like, when I get the final treatment," Henry offered. "In fact, I'd look upon it as a favor. I don't want the Old Man along," he said. "It would just make me nervous." "Be glad to," Donovan said. Maybe he'd get something out of it. A chance to improve on the disaster he'd always been: (A) Breaking chairs, knocking over lamps, shattering family heirlooms. And when he was in a temper, more of the same. In temper or out of it, nothing that wasn't bound in brass or made of brick was safe around him. (B) Eating everything in sight: ham, ram, cheaper mutton, bully beef or bear. (C) Being led by the nose by women. For when he wasn't hankering after them in the flesh, they haunted and fidgeted in his brain. (D) Wallowing in the throes of a violent boredom.

His name was the middle syllable of disgusting.

But if he could get a trade-in, even a quicker body for a slower mind, it would be worth the experiment.

◆

Left in the lurch. Abandoned, that's what. Ditched like a little kid when the big boys want to go off to play. That's how Curran saw it. He watched Donovan's big back disappear around a corner, was almost tempted to follow him, spy on him, tease him later. He felt ornery. So that when a little mangy, mud-colored street dog came up to offer its commiseration, he spurned it with his foot. "Get off," he said, and watched it sidle way, its eye out for another kick. Ashamed, Curran glanced about to see who had seen him: perhaps a holy man in disguise, pointing a finger at him, saying "You are a shit."

He stood moping just to the side of a peep show, where a circle of bulbs, specked with dead insects, burned hotly, ineffectually in the afternoon sun. A couple of prospective patrons approached the box office window, scrutinized his dark expression, apparently took his presence as an ill omen and, reorganizing their intentions, took off.

Curran paid no attention, absorbed as he was in the bitter reflections of the moment: that not only did his whole future lie threatening, uncertain before him, but even this very afternoon. True, they were all to meet later that evening to catch Grace's act at Ye Olde Black Magic, but that was, in fact, a galling reminder. For two whole days he'd had to expose himself to the smirk of booking agents and, after he'd put out his best, watch the smug bastards stub out their cigarettes and shake their heads. Sorry. Not what they were looking for just now —maybe some other time. The usual crap. He knew all about it.

While Dusty brayed and swaggered: He'd done it, hadn't he? There they were, broke, fighting to stay alive, hanging by a thread, and he'd got a booking for Grace. Pulled them out once again: "Just leave it to old Dusty." Proud of himself, the big blowhard, even though he'd burned up a lot of shoe leather and worn his voice down to a hacked-off squawk. For he had made the rounds, talking and glad-handing and trying his brand of salesmanship till he looked like he'd been on a three-week bender. The most he could get was this one spot for Grace in a second-rate joint, not even on Los Labios, but two blocks away, surrounded by porno flicks and adult bookstores. But it was for three nights a week plus the weekends, and the money was good. Grace was their meal ticket.

And that's what bothered him. He was a performer, after all, part of the show, had always paid his way. Now he was in a strange place with nothing in sight, not even the promise of future opportunity. "Temporary," Dusty had assured him. "Purely a passing inconvenience. Get ourselves back on our feet and you'll be back in the limelight, what d' you say? Don't get down on your chump." Hand on your shoulder and the hot wind of optimism. Count on Dusty every time.

And if that wasn't bad enough, he was alone now and had the afternoon to get through. Unprotected. Every other place he'd been he was part of the carnival. He felt safe. And he'd taken a lot off Donovan just so they could be together. In his company he could put up with all the guff, even take a certain satisfaction in his uniqueness. But he didn't like going into places alone. He'd never gotten used to people staring at him, whispering. They never allowed him to forget himself.

He spent a couple of hours sitting on a bench next to the gorge, eating peanuts and throwing some to the pigeons. Stupid birds, making their dumb noise. Billy Bigelow and the boy had come along, but he hadn't gone off with them. The boy gave him the willies, somehow. Even more than most kids. Curran didn't take to children, though they were a big part of the crowd he played to. Didn't want any part of them. They were in two different worlds: let them keep theirs, thank you very much, don't let anybody think they had anything in common. When they looked at him wonderingly and said "Isn't he funny?" he almost hated them. He loathed the cruelty of children, all the more because it was innocent. And Donovan really got to him whenever he condescended to him, treated him like a child.

He was tired of sitting—his backside felt like pins and needles. It was too much like waiting, sitting there waiting for your life to be over. He walked across the street, looked briefly at photographs of the celebrities who were performing that evening at the Grotto and wandered on down one street, then another. He hadn't noticed where he was going and by the time he looked around, he'd lost all sense of direction. He walked the streets for an hour, each time convinced he had turned back toward the gorge. He asked directions from a tourist in dark glasses and Hawaiian flowered shirt; from a gangling teenager and his girlfriend; from a hard-faced matron with silver-tinted hair, all to no avail. He walked in the directions they pointed. Nothing looked familiar, and he was convinced they were all in a plot to confuse him. The day was waning, the clouds of evening beginning to form overhead. He felt a surge of panic.

He passed by a yellow-brick high school where some boys were shooting baskets on the playground. "Hey," he yelled to them in his rather flat voice. "Can you tell me how to get back to the gorge?" First one, then another, paused in his play. In a moment they stood around him, almost in a circle.

"What's the matter, Shorty? Lost your way?"

"Yeah," Curran said, roused almost to belligerence. "I'm new here."

"Think of it," one said. "Poor little boy has lost his way."

They laughed. "Well, little boy. You can come and be our friend and play basketball with us."

"He can be our basketball—we'll throw him."

"Yeah, how about it?" They all laughed.

"Don't touch me," the midget warned. Tall and menacing, they surrounded him.

"Little boy thinks we'll hurt him."

"Little boy better be nice . . ." They were closing in.

Suddenly Curran did a flip, then another, catching them off guard. Then, butting his head into the groin of one who blocked his path, Curran drove through the space and ran for his life. He didn't   look back, though he heard yells and hoots and thought he heard feet running behind him. He ducked down an alley and into a garbage can tipped on its side. Footfalls thundered past on the pavement.

He lay there in the stench for what seemed hours, trembling with the rage born of terror. The darkness and silence closed around him. Then he crawled out, brushed himself off and straightened his clothes as best he could. The town was alight now, and the concentration of colors gave him his bearings. He found Ye Olde Black Magic on his own. Entering quickly, he spent almost half an hour in the men's room, sponging at a dark spot on the knee of his trousers. He was a meticulous, even sharp, dresser having spent a small fortune on tailors. He liked a good tweed jacket when it was cold enough; otherwise a light linen. Once in a while he took to something quite sporty. Fortunately, the day being hot, he'd left his jacket back in the trailer. But the trousers were a ruin.

When he emerged, he was still so angry with Donovan and filled with such malevolence toward Dusty that he wouldn't go near either of them, but sat down by Billy Bigelow and ordered a beer in a tone of voice that made the bargirl write him off immediately as a nasty little creep.

♦

Dusty was tight, he couldn't help it. He'd cracked a few jokes to put himself at ease, but he was whistling in the dark. And he couldn't get a rise out of anybody. Alta sat and played with the olive in her martini, Donovan was leaning back with his eyes closed, and the midget gave him such a fierce look he'd almost forgotten the punch line. Only Billy Bigelow had anything to give him, good old Billy.

It wasn't much of a place, he had to admit. Had the air of continually changing ownership, as though no sooner had somebody bought the place, slapped on a new layer of flocked wallpaper and thrown up another set of chandeliers than he gave it up as a bad job and got out from under. Why was it, he wondered, some places were like that. Now it was all hung with scarlet silk doodads, and Tiffany lampshades reflected all around the fruits and flowers of light. But it was no good. Couldn't get rid of the smell of the past. Couldn't bring in the right clientele.

A few tables away, the present owner was sitting with his cronies. Bald head stuck between his shoulder blades, folds of fat at the neck. Face like a ham hock. No class, couldn't appreciate it if he recognized it, couldn't recognize it anyway. Dusty had put on a performance for him, a real show, tried to hand him his future on a silver platter. Nothing. Sat there chewing on his cigar like he was watching paint dry. A mere flicker of an eyelash for Grace, faint lift of a smile at the corner of the mouth. The only life coming from the gold tooth in the uppers. Okay, he'd put her on, see how it went. Doing him a big favor. Who was he trying to kid? Dusty caught himself drumming his fingers, sat back, tried to look casual, ordered another drink.

"Calm down," Alta said. "I feel like I'm sitting next to an ant hill." He shot her a look she knew: *Okay, you've found me out, you don't have to broadcast it.* She knew him too well, knew how he was all over hives when a show was coming off. A wonder he didn't have ulcers. Well, it had better be a good one—for the sake of she didn't know what.

It was starting. There was Grace. Standing on a round dais that came moving forward till it was right at the center of the dance floor. Pretty fancy for a joint like this, Alta had to admit. Standing there with her arms raised, expression on her face like she knew a secret the audience wanted to know.

She was splendid in a strapless gown with a bodice of silver scales and a bouffant skirt like a white cloud sprinkled with silver dust. She looked good, Alta conceded. When Dusty had come back with the news, full of himself as usual, Alta had hunted through the costumes to see if there was something the girl could wear. "Listen," Dusty said, "none of that trash. We got to do things right." And he'd taken Grace off to the city to buy her an outfit. Alta spent the rest of the day sorting through the old frills and furbelows from her days of triumph, trying things on, lamenting the refusals of zippers and split seams and faded crescents at the armpits. Old stuff, and depressing. Why had she hung onto it so long? And there was Grace looking like a million. Alta could look at her without envy: she'd had all that once. And everyone deserved to have it, at least once, that brief glory. Even if you spent the rest of your life, arms open for it, waiting, hoping it might come to you again.

For a moment Grace stood undulating with the music, looking at the audience as though she were asking them to appreciate only this: a lovely girl in graceful movement. Then, as the band launched into the second round of "That Old Back Magic," she whipped off her skirt and stood there in a body suit of silver scales, thighs thrust forward, arms stretched out. Coiled about her thighs were two copper-colored snakes. There was a slight gasp from the crowd.

As though at a signal, the snakes began to move up from her thighs and across her belly in opposite directions until they girdled her waist. She danced then, undulating her hips and torso, faster and faster, the snakes coiled around her waist. And as she leaned back, arms akimbo, they moved across her forearms and circled her arms up to the shoulder. She danced with them as bracelets and arm rings. They moved across her shoulders and she wore them around her neck. The music slowed, as though it had grown tired, the horns wanting to slip into something quieter. She brought her hand up the inside of her thigh, over her crotch, while a horn yearned. Slowly she twisted her body and raised her arms, snakes on her shoulders. The beat quickened. Putting her hands to her chest as though to give her heart away, she gave the zipper a quick pull and the bodysuit fell away, and she was standing in a bra and g-string. She wiggled her torso, swung out her hips. The snakes crawled down across her breasts and circled her waist once more. Donovan moaned.

The patrons took a while to get used to the snakes. They looked on, fascinated and repelled. Whispers and muffled, nearly embarrassed comments.

But the girl handled the snakes as though she had always worn them on her arms, around her waist, as though she lived with them and knew them and they couldn't harm her. The audience grew easier, safe and glad of whatever separated her from them. For the way she danced was something almost terrifying, as though it was the snakes she danced for, or some power she had to appease. Grace seemed almost in a trance as they moved over her body: eyes nearly closed as she moved to the music, sometimes whirling like a dust devil, sometimes undulating slowly, moving her hips and shoulders, just floating along with the music.

Billy Bigelow felt as though he'd been taken out of himself and set down in a strange place. She was beautiful. And beautiful in the way she moved and the way the snakes twined around her arms and waist and moved over her figure, all sinuous curves. The snakes brought him to a feeling that went all the way down past fear to something he couldn't describe. And he knew that a powerful magic lay inside a person who could handle them, suffer to wear them on her very flesh —a magic quite beyond his own paltry brand, he was the first to admit. None of your tricks here, sleight of hand. There were powers here that required, he was sure, total surrender. You couldn't be afraid. The creatures would know that first thing, and treat you with contempt. No, you had to get past that, and once you crossed that threshold, well, he didn't know . . . maybe something else opened up.

He looked around at the crowd. The murmuring and dumb fascination were gone. They were exclaiming their admiration, excited, clapping, not holding back. The music, the dance, had worked on them. Little explosions of applause. She was an artist, all right. He watched the expressions on the rapt faces. Maybe, Billy thought, we all want to be artists. We just sublimate it with sex.

A little tattoo of drums and Grace pulled away the right half of her bra, exposing her breast. A boom from the kettle drum. She pulled the bra free, then with both hands lifted her breasts, held them out, an offering with rosy, erect nipples. The music swelled as she thrust out her pelvis and the snakes moved down over her breasts, coiling around her waist, their heads swaying out. A prolonged burst of applause, and the excitement in the room had come to a pitch.

Dusty leaned over to Billy Bigelow. "I think we got 'em beat. The best show in town. Heard they were packing them in at The Farmer's Daughter. Girl dancing with a mechanical dildo chasing her all over the joint."

"No shit," Billy said with interest. When Eve dropped the apple, it bounced off the head of Sir Isaac Newton. "We live in a mechanical age," he said.

Then suddenly there was a roar, a great pulsing wave of sound. For as one of the snakes was crawling up between her breasts, Grace had taken it into her hands. Then she opened her mouth and took its head inside.

"My God," Donovan moaned. "Oh, my God."

Curran's face went white. He felt sick to his stomach. The girl was crazy—out of her mind.

Someone threw a handful of coins in the direction of the platform.

"Christ!" Alta exclaimed. "What a way to earn a living."

"Didn't I tell you she was amazing?" Dusty said.

Now the patrons were throwing coins on the floor, trying to hit the dais. Fifty-cent pieces and silver dollars clunked and rolled while Grace, unmindful, swayed to the music and let the snake slide away. Somebody wadded up and threw a bill, but it wouldn't carry. A man stood up, pulled the credit cards out of his wallet, and threw the wallet. In a storm of applause, the money was coming in like a hard rain. "Better than a collection plate," Dusty said. "We'll be rich— fucking rich!"

He was on his feet before he knew it, yelling and clapping while the dais retreated and the curtain closed and Grace was left to quiet her snakes. One of the waiters came out to sweep up the cash. A round of drinks appeared suddenly at their table, and Alta looked up to see the wave of a hand from a few tables away. Then a man got up and moved through the tables and chairs to where they were sitting. Short man. Dressed to the teeth. Gave off an expensive sheen. Rings on his fingers. Glitter of diamonds. Bought them hot, Alta decided when he came up. Fallen off the back of a truck into his fat palm. She disliked him immediately. Presence that hit you like a bad smell. Hair like a dandelion going to seed, little black mustache above the lip. Eyes that had lifted the skirt of every woman they'd lit on and seen the works. She saw how he'd started out: at the back of some little store as narrow as a shoe horn, girlie magazines in front and illegal betting in the rear. Everything shady, cheap and vulgar. Or else a loan shark, small time at first, then betraying his partner to the syndicate. Then, somewhere along the line, he'd hit onto something big.

Dusty, flushed with success, didn't even notice the stranger who was standing right next to him, holding out his hand, ready to introduce himself.

Alta gave him a nudge. "Company."

Dusty leapt up out of the chair and took the proffered hand while the owner nodded at Alta, flashing her a row of capped teeth for good will. Even his smile is crooked, she thought. She caught the name, A. P. Valdomar. When Dusty invited him to sit down, there was a shifting of chairs to make room. The music started up around them and couples were standing up to dance. Alta sipped her drink and let the sound wash over her. She couldn't really hear what they were saying as Valdomar leaned forward confidentially to talk into Dusty's ear. Only occasional little snatches: "Great little girl . . . a real star . . ." Dusty eager and interested—led by the nose, she thought.

She wanted to leave, wanted Dusty to take her back to the trailer. She wasn't tired, but was full of disgust. Now that the novelty had worn off, she really didn't like the city, wanted the days back when they were a carnival coming into the little towns in the spring with a sense of expectancy in the blood, to help people forget their worries and troubles, forgetting her own in the process. Or making the rounds of the state fairs late in the summer when people were fat and prosperous and full of good humor. Not an easy life but, looking back, she missed it.

Dusty got up. "See you back at the place," he said to Alta. "Me and A. P. here have a little business to discuss. Billy'll give you and Grace a ride back."

Yeah, she thought. Sure thing.

The others left not long after. But she didn't go with them. She was feeling low. The more she had to drink, the more the liquor made her feel rotten—till she was down to the tops of her socks, then to the soles of her boots. "Sure you don't want to go back?" Billy said, trying to persuade her. "No, I'll get me a taxi when I'm ready," Alta answered, thinking she might not even make it back that night. Maybe just curl up somewhere in an alley behind the garbage cans and let the cats keep her warm. And knowing better than to meddle, they left her alone.

Maybe the only way, she thought, is to go so far down you hit bottom, then maybe you can come back up again. She was watching a young couple, a girl sitting on her fellow's lap. He had on some kind of uniform—sailor maybe, she couldn't tell. The girl had her arms round his neck, smooching him. It made Alta wish she had someone. Then the girl pulled off her wig and waved it around, yelling *"Toujours gai, toujours gai."* A man, just part of the act. She, a pro, had been taken in.

She ordered another drink, a margarita this time, and watched the dancers. Suddenly she wanted to dance herself. She tapped her fingers on the table in time with the rhythm, swinging her leg. She'd put on a red crepe de chine dress with rows of fringe on the skirt, a dress that went back to the Twenties but was back in fashion again. She was looking good, if she did say so herself. She'd spent a lot of time with her hair and her make-up, and she was still a woman worth looking at, damn it. She took out a cigarette. She didn't smoke much, but tonight she was on the town and feeling down and she intended to indulge all her vices. She leaned back, letting herself go with the music, all mean and horny and sad.

But someone had come up and was bending toward her: Would she care to dance? She looked up into a dark face. Handsome. Black hair descending into sideburns. Mustache. Black eyes that held a gleam of humor or pleasure. Smooth, she thought, but not slick. She liked the way he moved and talked. A gentleman. A man who knew how to treat a woman. She got up to dance, stubbed out her cigarette, and let him lead her to the dance floor.

They moved well together on the floor. He stepped into the rhythm as though it had been in his feet all the time, just waiting for the music to begin. But he had an eye for her, for what she was doing, responded to that, took her past it now and then with just a touch, a gesture to guide, nothing heavy-handed. She was impressed. She knew about movement. It hadn't been all that long ago—in her mind, it was like yesterday: there were some things you couldn't forget. She was beginning to enjoy herself, and added a few fancy steps. Her partner broke into a grin as he responded. Like a streak of bright sunlight. She was taken into the warmth of that smile, into the heat of the dance, sweating away liquor and misery. He was all right. He liked what she was doing. People had begun to watch them. The next number began, and they put themselves into it. When it ended, they were so whipped out that they burst into laughter and staggered to her table.

His name was Pedro. He sat her down and ordered drinks, then took out a little pouch and some papers and rolled a joint. He lit it, inhaled once and offered it to her; he'd had practice, she could tell. It had been a long time since she'd had any grass. Couldn't do it when she was younger because it affected her timing and couldn't afford it now unless somebody offered it to her. She was beginning to feel mellow. Dancing had taken her out of the dumps. And she was enjoying this man's attention. Dusty had deserted her.

"Now, that's *a lot* better," Pedro said. "I was looking at you a while ago and I said to myself, Now here's somebody that needs a little cheering up."

"You did?" she said, surprised and flattered. "Well, you read me right."

"Then when I saw all your friends get up and leave, I said, Now there's a woman who doesn't deserve to be left alone."

"Business," she said, after she'd inhaled deeply, let out the smoke. "Money," she said. "And trouble too, I suspect. You got to live, but it's a strain."

Her companion sat back, took a deep drag from the cigarette, held it a moment and took another. "Keep it as long as you like," he said, handing it back to her. "There's more where that came from. Put yourself in the state you want to be in."

She looked at him. "I'd say on the other side of where I've been lately."

He smiled. "Why not?" he said. "That's what it's for."

His voice touched her like the pressure of kindness on a hand. "You know all about it," she said.

"I grow it, I sell it, I live and breathe the stuff." He gave a little soft laugh. "There are lots of different states you can get into. I smoke it when I'm eating or making love or listening to music or taking a walk or reading a book. And it's always a different thing. Whatever I'm doing, it takes it to another place—where it's not just something you're doing, but something you *are* doing."

She'd heard it all before, but somehow, listening now, she was fascinated. The only state she'd like to return to was flying though the air on a trapeze. To that state of excitement. And a few times—the last time was so long ago she could barely remember—when she'd made love. And she knew what she'd been missing for the past weeks and months. The feeling she was alive. Everything had passed through and nothing had stuck. Now it hit. *Now.*

And Dusty. *Dusty striking her and the blood flowing from her lip. Dusty hitting her and the life flowing out, leaving her. Ghost-faced, white. Toads' bellies. Milk spit. The blood flowing and something fleeing. Catch it before it gets away . . . before it's too late.*

"—all the things you do in a day," Pedro was saying, his voice, soft as a velvet glove, drawing her back. "Everybody's trying to get into a state," he said. "All the things you do in a day. They come and they go—"

Going, flowing. Catch it before . . .

"—even the act of love. But with this—"

She looked down and saw the cigarette between her fingers. She put it to her lips.

"—you open a doorway and go to the other side. You eat a piece of bread and it's only that. Or a glass of wine. The essence. Like perfume. Nothing in the way. Nothing. And music . . ." He leaned back, as though sinking into it.

She'd left him. A horn had picked her up and was taking her down a long passageway. Going along, going along that thread of sound. Drawing her, that horn, into the thread of melody, unraveling her, spinning her around. Round and round to the end of sound and down she was going, oh down into the dark warm mouth. The melody, melting and floating. Boom, now, boom—she was beats of the drum. The horn had left, the drum moved in.

And then his voice came back, droning, making words: "Now down where I come from, people, poor folks, shopkeepers and all get drunk on mescal. Fall down in the street and yell and scream. They see things . . ."

Melting, his voice melting. Spaces between the words. Slow, so slow she couldn't get to the next word. Leaning over, she was leaning over so far she might fall into the space. She looked up at him, into his eyes. They were drawing her, might take her. What if—she wanted to pull back. Away from his eyes. What if she couldn't get out? She tore herself away, threw her gaze to the dancers. Black back, pink rump, an arm shaking, a leg making a big to-do. Whirling around: the sound and the beat. The wild hair of a dancing man . . . Wanting to take off in all directions. She started to giggle, couldn't stop. Funny. It filled her. Hilarious. Inflated her, lifted her like a bubble.

And Pedro's voice came in: "I got some coke in my room," he was saying. "You want to try some?"

He was offering her something. Whatever it was, it was okay. He was going to take her somewhere, if only she could stand up. She looked at him again, looked down at her red dress, the fringe making waves of red. Red as blood. Life. She wanted to try some. She wanted to lose herself in the blood of life. She wanted him. Let him caress her slow and easy, till every nerve of her skin vibrated. Let him enter while the music built and quickened: the thrum of the electric bass. Blood beating, yes, let it beat. Drums and horns and guitars. Drums quickening with a deep beat-beat. Horns awakening her blood till the pulse throbbed in her head. She'd ride the music, rise, pumping faster, till she and it shot up with one great blast of sound from all the instruments, flaring and melting together. The blending and the surge. Release, forgetfulness . . . out of this world.

◆

"Grace is going to make a film."

"Wonderful." Alta was still trying to climb back into her eyes, into sight and hearing, trying to climb back into her skull from wherever the night had left her, from wherever drink and drugs had carried her, on what wave, carried her while a man moved inside her. Not that she wanted to come back at all. But now, having slept away the whole day, she found Dusty in one of his fits of enthusiasm. She was awake enough, though, to feel wary, to have a care for Grace.

"What kind of film?" she said.

"Love story. Sort of—"

"Go on."

"Well, lots of sex. She's on an island, see, a tropical island, with tigers and elephants—there's money in it for Sam too."

"Wonderful. And how would they get on an island, these animals? Swim there?"

"Hell, I don't know. Maybe it's just a tropical paradise."

"Around here?"

"For crying out loud, I didn't write the script. Maybe it's a desert paradise. You think the audience is going to care? I mean, right in the middle of a good screw they're going to say, Where'd that tiger come from?"

"I think that'd be the first question to pop into my head. I mean if one came nosing up while I—"

"Look, they aren't going to care if elephants grow from daisies or eels from spaghetti. Anyway, she comes on the island from a wrecked ship, see, and there are these four guys there—"

"Four sex-starved guys ready to jump on one defenseless girl. What kind of percentage is that?"

"Look, it's just a film—right?"

"Yeah, it sure sounds high-minded. Have you asked Grace?" "Why should I? She's done it all before."

"I don't want her getting hurt."

"Listen, you act like she's a piece of your property. Hell, I paid enough for her. She's an investment."

"Paid enough—that's what you care about. You're already going to get plenty off her, just for what she's doing right now."

"Listen, it's her career. She's got a great future. By the time we pull this one off, we can put together a show the likes of which you've never seen, believe me. I can go to the banks—My God, they'll throw open their arms when they see me coming."

"Sure. Maybe we can let Grace be torn apart by tigers and trampled by elephants. Think how the audience would go for it. I don't like it," she said. "That guy last night—if he's the one—he'd rape his grandmother in the garden if he could get a nickel out of it, and a plugged nickel at that."

"He's a businessman, goddamn it," Dusty said. "You don't have to love him."

He left her then, and she was free to drink a cup of Sanka, go back to bed, read a magazine, bang pots together, curse the stars or forget the whole thing. Her head still throbbed and right now coffee promised no comfort. She foraged until she found the bottle Dusty had bought to celebrate Grace's debut and poured herself a drink. Forget the whole thing. It was the one thing she couldn't do. For it was starting all over again, maybe worse this time. It was not only that the dream had him in thrall, but now she sensed that a kind of recklessness had crept in, or desperation. He was going to get there; he didn't care how. He wasn't that dumb about people. If he knew what he was doing— and that was the corker—maybe he didn't care anymore. What was Grace to him? What was any woman, for that matter? Herself least of all. When he'd drawn her into his plans for the future, she thought it was love. A golden cloud had surrounded her, or so it seemed. But it was the glow of possibility he was in love with, she told herself bitterly. And since then, there had been a succession of young girls. Svengali always looking for his Trilby, the woman he is going to make famous. Meanwhile he reaches for the desirable part between the legs: the pouch for his poker, the ding for his dong, the harbor for his ship to come in. That was the trouble when your parts were on the exterior. Since you didn't have a place to put them, you were always looking for one. And the lucky little chit of the moment got to think she was riding the crest of the wave into the future. Provided she didn't have the embarrassment of getting herself pregnant. There'd been at least one hasty abortion along the way. And even though he wasn't young any more, the old tomcat could still get his way. Even Ginger, before they'd had the sense to pull out. And now Grace, if she didn't watch herself. Only this was worse: She virtually belonged to him, and he could do anything.

This time, though, she was going to put up some kind of fight, though she didn't know how just yet. It wasn't jealousy and it wasn't spite. She'd been that route. Oh yes, it had been a blow to her pride when she found out that Dusty couldn't leave be any woman he thought might be a piece of his future. Once when she'd come back to the trailer unexpectedly and found him in bed, this time with the rising young queen of a balancing act, she'd yanked her up by the hair and thrown her out bodily, heaving her purse after her so that it fell open in its flight through the air, sending change, lipstick, comb, among other items scattering in all directions. She was sorry about it afterwards. The girl was quite young, rather a pretty little thing, and didn't really deserve to be slapped and yanked about... when it was Dusty she should've worked over. But she was angry, and when she blew up there was generally a little sweet period afterwards when he tried to mollify her and assure her it was only a passing fancy. He'd trot back with flowers and candy, and once even pearl earrings. But these days he told her she was an old woman.

Well, there was life in the old girl yet. Dream Girl—that was her name, wasn't it? Maybe she could have her dreams too. Maybe that was even what her name meant—the girl who dreams. Why not? And she had a sudden inkling of why Dusty couldn't give it up, the dreaming. For didn't it hold something of that feeling she got when she'd been up there on the trapeze, giddy with the thrill of danger and freedom, as though she were floating on the aura of the world? But what was her dream, and how could she get hold of it? Maybe she could dream a future for Grace. God knows, she didn't have any other doorway to the future. And here was Grace come to her, at the right age to have been her daughter. The people of the future are living right now, Billy Bigelow had said. Sure they were. And Grace was one of them.

It had occurred to her one afternoon when they were talking about Grace's birthday coming and Alta had thought of baking her a cake. Hadn't done it in years. And something cracked open and she found herself talking about her own youth, her growing up. She'd been born late when nobody wanted her. By that time, her father, who'd been ground into the dirt by the Depression and spent most of his time out of work and dead drunk, had wandered off God-knows-where and her mother had gone on the road, so to speak, peregrinating from Omaha to Detroit to St. Louis to Mishawaka, seeking out one piece of family or another to squat with as long as they'd put up with her. Which varied from less than a week to a couple of months. For her mother was a woman of wide-ranging tastes and uncertain habits, rather like a cat that rubs against your leg one moment and is off on her own the next. She liked men of all shapes, sizes, proportions and dispositions. When life was good, it included a man to keep her, and when it wasn't, she landed down among the relatives: pillar to post.

And it was that, Alta said, that gave her an early impression that you couldn't hold onto anything for very long. Seemed like her whole life she'd been leaving a trail of things behind her, like some broken truck rattling down the highway. She herself had run off and thrown herself on the world when she was hardly more than a girl.

"Imagine," she said, "going off with a circus. Can you think of anything more stupid? Just what a crazy kid would come up with, having no better sense. And nobody cared enough to take the trouble to come after me." She took a drag of the cigarette she was smoking and let out a puff. "Just as well. I came by wandering and dreaming naturally," she told the girl. "If you don't belong anywhere, it's all you got."

Grace had looked at her and in the space between them there came a little flare of recognition. They had seen each other stripped of time and circumstance. Why, any way you look at it, Alta thought, she could be my child, child of my spirit as well as my flesh. And then she told her how she came to be on the trapeze.

So here was the difference. Alta saw her not as one more in the string of girls that populated Dusty's past, but as one she wanted to hand the future to, if she could only figure out what it was. And maybe she *was* jealous this time, but in a different way—jealous of her own, of something precious she didn't want to let go of or see ground into the mud. And she'd make a start by keeping an eye on Dusty. Things were still too rocky between them for her to flat out set herself against him. But she'd certainly keep an eye cocked, lest any harm come to the girl. Probably wouldn't do her any harm to be in a skin flick— might even enjoy it—but she still didn't like the whole business. She couldn't warm up to any type that walked up to you smelling like a dead cat. It didn't take much thought to sniff out his past. She'd have preferred Grace's snakes for company.

◆

The girl was a trooper all right, Dusty thought, with an admiration that went beyond the satisfaction of a fat wallet. She *was* something. At first hanging back like a shrinking violet, showing about as much life as a wet soda cracker. Considering how she was a girl that could move her body like a diagram of the atom, all the time with a pair of snakes circling her belly, it sure looked like she was going to be a downright disappointment. Wouldn't say a word, wouldn't even shake hands with the man that was going to make her fortune.

But when she was on the set with the actors, that was a different story. In fact, she'd amazed him once again. They way she started joking with them, flirting and playing and smiling and teasing. And *they* sure thought she was something.

Yes, she was his girl all right—holding her own up there with the actors. Good-looking fellows. He had sat there admiring their bodies —well-built, rippling with muscles. Quite a contrast to the first skin flick he'd seen, years ago in a Mexican whorehouse. Black-and-white, surface grainy. A man like an orangutan and a hard case that looked like she could have wrestled you to the floor. Then after mounting her, the hairy bastard had turned and ejaculated at the camera. The whole thing was enough to put you off sex for a week. But these guys knew what they were doing—they had class. Even Alta could have looked on with an appreciative eye.

Getting the stuff set up took a while, the cameras and lights and all, and explaining the different positions and where they came in the sequence. One scene was a smasher. He was thinking about it, Grace beside him in the truck, as they drove back to the trailer. She was pretty worn out now, poor kid, leaning back with her eyes closed, half asleep. He could sympathize: show biz took a lot out of you. He wanted to reach over and pat her knee and say, *You were gorgeous, kid, out of this world.* But it would've broken the silence.

And he rather liked driving along, letting his mind roam over that scene in the grass—how she'd found her way to the island with hardly a stitch on her. And there's the handsome lover waiting for her. And she's all ready for him, thinks he's the only one on the island. And she's kneeling there in the grass, letting him take her from behind. But then here comes the second one, wanting some too. So she takes him into her mouth, while the other one's busy in the back.

But then here come the other two. She satisfies them too, she's got two hands, hasn't she? So they're all getting it at once. My God, what a lot of movement! Front and back and either side. Impeccable sense of timing. Good thing there's only four of them. But what really got him was that when they came, the two on the sides, it was like a fountain falling down her cheeks while different colored lights, all the colors of the rainbow, played over it. It was something to remember, the semen running down her cheeks. At the same time he was thinking what a beautiful girl she was, high-toned, whatever her experience had been. Dress her up and you'd think she was money and class. Not the least bit cheap or vulgar. And yet there she was. It excited him to think about it, because she seemed to be enjoying herself too. As though she were in the middle of a celebration surrounded by four willing servants. Pleasure from all directions, giving and getting.

Still there was a niggling dissatisfaction in his mind, and he kept searching around trying to locate the reason for it. She excited him and yet—he wanted her and he didn't. He wanted her before she'd ever had a man. But if he'd been the first to do it, she wouldn't be the same. He wanted her both in her purity and in her lavishness of enjoying men, reveling in their bodies and taking her own pleasure. That was the kind of woman he'd always dreamed about—who could be that with a man and yet give you the impression she was doing it with you for the first time, or else that she hadn't really known what it was all about till you came along.

He'd never really had quite such a woman. She was always there, beckoning, promising, as he went from one to another, a bee among blossoms. He liked them young, he liked them with some of the shine taken off, provided they stood in awe of him because he'd had many women and could take them to where they hadn't been before. A wife could never see that. Marriage bred the expectable, and from there it was downhill all the way. Not that he could blame Alta. She'd taken her knocks. And still he had to hand it to her—she was a real woman. Every now and then he couldn't help looking in her direction. But now she was getting on his nerves.

"You want something to eat, honey," he asked Grace, as she sat up sleepily. "We can stop and get a steak."

She shook her head.

He hadn't touched this one, hadn't been able to work up his confidence. She made him uneasy with himself. Just turned herself off when she didn't want you coming near her fences. Picked up her marbles and went on home. She could give you a look that killed any notions that might be lingering in your brain. He was too smart to force himself on any woman who looked at a man like that. He wanted her to want him. So far she hadn't, though she'd done everything he asked of her, without a quibble. And there was something tender, almost deferential in the way he had come to speak to her. Though it didn't seem to cut any ice. You want money, she seemed to be telling him, you'll get it—but you won't get me.

◆

When Donovan arrived at the offices of Superman Unlimited, Henry Snyder was already there, terribly eager to see him. He hadn't been able to sleep, he was so excited and keyed up. He wanted to get the ordeal over and done with so he could get a start on his future that very afternoon. The young woman assistant, her dark hair perfect in a French roll, was trying to soothe her client with a glass of papaya juice. She looked up at Donovan through a pair of pink, butterfly-shaped spectacles that put her in such an advanced state of fashion he was momentarily taken aback.

"So glad you came," Henry said, leaping up and shaking hands with him with a vigor that might've been born of nervousness, but was certainly in keeping with the personality his frame was supposed to support. "They're setting things up now. The treatment will begin in half an hour."

Donovan felt the young woman's gaze measure him, perhaps with the momentary wonder at what might be done with this prodigy. The eyes behind the tinted lenses were difficult to read, the expression having very little to do with the smile she was offering—a free bonus whether he was a client or not. "The support factor is a definite plus." He felt he'd been given some kind of clearance.

"What's going to happen?" Donovan said.

"Bring the charts," Henry suggested. He smiled, opened his arms. "My life is an open book."

Her heels clicking smartly on the imitation marble tile, she went off to get them. Nice shape from behind, Donovan acknowledged. Cute little bounce. Good disappearing act. He toyed with her potential till Henry's agitation at his elbow interrupted him. "I forgot to introduce you," he said, smacking his forehead with his palm. "It's one of the first Super commands."

By the time she returned, he had got hold of himself. "I want you to meet Miss Stephanie Magid," he said, with such casualness that Donovan had to hand it to him.

She gave Henry an approving look: the slow learner who finally catches on. "First, you see, we do an impulse chart," she explained, opening the folder. "You can follow it here—we plot the graph from various life situations to reach an aggression quotient. Positive determinancies reduced by incidences of hesitancy, indecision and unrest, fluxed by an outside variable. We measure adrenalin as well as muscle response and blinking frequency—"

"What's that?"

"Distortion factor."

"Meaning?"

"Tics," she explained. "There are, of course, many kinds of tests. That's the fatigue readjustment scale... Then we feed all the information into a computer in order to determine the necessary psychic agents to establish the personality." She showed him a final set of blue graphs. "This is Henry's profile," she said. "A bit low on the scale." But then, looking brightly at Henry, she said, "It just means we have to try harder."

"Then what," Donovan asked.

"First we drain the blood from the body—in stages, of course—and introduce a substitute with a higher energy density. This is to feed the brain and increase the efficiency quotient of the heart. Actually—" she paused—"the heart is a much more archaic instrument than the brain. Really unsuited to the present evolutionary stage." The pink butterflies passed in front of his vision. The full lips. Her words, like snowflakes on a warm ground, seemed to melt away as soon as they hit his ear. She was standing very close to him and occasionally brushed the hairs on his arm, an agreeable tingle. Lovely. He caught the warm scent of her hair and was escorted on another wave of distraction: tits up ...

"Then we introduce electric impulses into the brain, eliminate old habits of thought and program new ones, really re-pattern the circuits—to fit the life situation."

"Does it work?" Donovan said, bending forward with interest, as though to nuzzle the back of her neck. Was it one of those thin, gauzy bras she was wearing, he wondered, or was she actually braless?

"Certainly," she said, with an upward glance, a cutting emphasis. "You've noticed our picture display. That's Line Winchester," she said, the throb of admiration enough to make any man jealous. "An absolutely amazing fellow. He'll be running for the U.S. Senate again this fall."

Donovan looked over at Henry to see if he might be suffering by comparison, but apparently he, too, was heartened by the successful example.

"At least three social functions a day. A brunch for the League of Women Voters in the morning, a rally with the Young Republicans in the afternoon, and a full-dress $100-a-plate banquet in the evening. Gets about three or four hours of sleep per night. Tireless on the job. Says our program changed his life. Even improved his digestion. He can go from cake doughnuts to a hog roast to a cocktail party with liver pate and caviar, with no ill effects to the stomach."

"Must be a helluvan interesting life," Donovan commented, impressed as much as anything by the food angle.

"He's a man of iron," Miss Magid said, with a lift of the pupils from which she might have launched into a pleasant fantasy. But only for a split second. "And our sensory detectors in the skin are a feature item. A great help in sales conferences, closings: you know your client's reactions before he does himself." She laughed softly, as did Henry.

Sensory detectors. Hoptoads of the nerves. He could tell her a few things himself. "But suppose you start a career and move onward or upward to something else?"

"Three updates come as part of the original package," she said. "Are you interested in being programmed for a new position?" "Well, yes." He knew seventy of them and one more wouldn't hurt. He wondered how many she knew. "Something challenging," he said. "Lots of stimulation. Mental highjinks, of course."

She looked at him suspiciously.

"Suppose I wanted to be president of a corporation."

She smiled. "We do have prerequisites . . ." She was about to explain these when the attendant summoned Henry Snyder into the operating room for the preliminary relaxation exercises. He seemed considerably more at ease than when Donovan arrived, and Donovan felt envious: to be put at rights with the world by an act of instant transformation . . .

"You see," Miss Magid went on after Henry left, "we have to be very selective, for only certain clients present the right potentials. We're a young company, still developing, and our research is by no means complete. Actually," she said, in a confidential tone, "Henry is one of our risk cases." She bit her lip. "Strong pressure from the family. They'd tried everything—were about to give up on him. But they were willing to make the investment. It's so expensive," she explained; "it's like floating a stock issue for a person's future. The investment will pay off in the long run—"

"Unless you're hit by a truck or a falling meteor."

She did not appear amused.

"Well, I hope he turns out great," Donovan said, trying to win back a place in her good graces.

"So do I. He has a strong tendency to distraction. Stubborn sensitivity circuits. A lot of weakness in the chest area. But if he can do it," she said, "anybody can. It offers a lot of hope."

On the wall above her desk, a panel of lights flashed on. "They're going to begin now," she said. "Would you care to go into the amphitheater and watch?"

She led him down a hallway and they climbed the carpeted stairs to a doorway, which opened to a darkened amphitheater. All Donovan could see was Henry stretched out on the table, eyes open, various electrodes attached to his head, surrounded on all sides by machines and attendants. They were monitoring the heart, and Donovan could hear its steady beat through the amplifier.

"Even the heartbeat will change," Miss Magid said. "It'll purr like a new Mercedes. They'll do the blood first."

There was very little to see, only the prostrate figure on the table and the little colony of psycho-surgeons and assistants adjusting dials. "The whole operation—does it take long," Donovan asked.

"In this case, yes," she said. "Almost a complete reconstruction of the personality." Her voice sounded tense.

After a period Donovan was beginning to find boring, there came a sudden flurry of activity on the floor. They were sponging Henry's forehead and his face looked quite gray.

"What's wrong?" Donovan said. But Miss Magid was already on her feet, hurrying out the doorway.

The activity on the floor was increasing. After a moment Donovan too got up and left. He wasn't going to wait for the outcome. But Miss Magid waylaid him in the vestibule, her face streaming and triumphant, lights flashing behind the pink butterflies.

"They've cleaned out the sensitivity circuits," she exclaimed. "It's going to be all right." She sank into a chair. "It was a close one." "Glad to hear old Henry's going to make it," Donovan said, relieved.

"But wait'll you see the new Henry—he'll be dynamite!"

"I take it you have more than a friendly interest."

"Well," she said, bristling a little, "it's true that Henry will need a wife someday, one to further his interests and . . ."

"Yes, well, uh, we never talked about the, I mean, you get all that energy and, if there's a difference, that is, if you've been having trouble . . ."

She caught his drift. "Why, of course—that'll be better too. He'll be able to do it every time."

♦

The eye Alta was keeping out was deepening in its suspicions. Damned if she'd trust that greasy piece of left-over breakfast to do anything that wasn't mean and lowdown and ornery—for a profit. If Dusty got his money out of him, he'd be lucky, even though, she had to admit, he'd advanced a nice piece of change. But she'd keep an eye out anyway. It wasn't Dusty she was worried about. He could damn well take care of himself, and right now whatever he did, wherever he landed, it didn't much matter. But Grace was different. She might know a thing or two, but that didn't mean a girl could protect herself in the world.

Alta hadn't liked the idea from the beginning, but right now she was in a frazzle, a good arm-twisting, hair-pulling mood. Imagine— a whole film sequence out there at the Steeples, out in the middle of nowhere. These shots couldn't be done indoors, so they claimed. They had something up their sleeve, though she didn't know what. There'd be a bunch of them out there. But all the same, it smelled fishy. Why else had they gotten Dusty out of the way? Giving him names and addresses. Luring him off somewhere else to try to put together a new deal. Led by the ear. Ready to throw more of the green into the wind. She could see currency flying up over the desert, whirling up like a flock of birds and being blown into the four corners. Dusty never knowing what was going on. Leave it to Dusty. She was sending Billy to check out this film business— that was her little secret.

They were to do the shots of the animals in the morning, Grace in the afternoon. Grace being discovered on her desert island—as if they couldn't concoct a little scenery in a decent place. She figured that Billy could take her out there in the afternoon and hang around with the kid; they had nothing else to do anyway.

She was interrupted in these plans by a rapping on the trailer door. And here came Mister Flotsam himself, Mr. Queer-Eye-Stop-You- Dead. What did he mean coming round before anybody was decent? He wanted Grace now. There'd been a change in the schedule and they were going to shoot both sequences in the morning.

Alta was ready to put up a fight—the girl didn't even have time for a decent breakfast. "They won't let her starve," Dusty said, "don't you worry."

She was left to speak her discontent through her plates and pots and pans. She threw the knives and forks down on the table. She had never cared too much for the domestic, but at least it had this use. She was nearly in a passion by the time Dusty left, in a taxi this time. She insisted he leave the truck, she needed to go into town. But he'd already planned on the cab: he was making contacts, had to look good.

An hour after Dusty had gone, she roused Billy and he and the boy took Dusty's truck and headed out toward the Steeples. Not much of a road, in fact only a narrow, rutted blacktop with stretches of dirt here and there. The hotel flew its guests in by helicopter, a measure of its exclusiveness and their privacy, for it was a world complete in itself, the total holiday for a price: swimming pool, restaurant, bar, gambling rooms, night club, beauties on call. The road was used only by a couple of ranchers who grazed their herds in the area, one cow per square mile, and clattered over the road in trucks, whipping up the dust behind them.

Except to get a better view of the rocks, assuming you wanted one, there wasn't much point coming this way, Billy thought. It was like moving back into the Pleistocene era, not offering much by way of diversion or companionship unless you fancied the rocks and maybe the vulture sitting there with wings that looked like pieces of leather umbrella. The rocks, the Steeples, looked as if they'd been there from the beginning of the world, like something an ancient god hadn't been able to use but couldn't bring himself to throw away. They evoked a certain awe, these rising cylindrical rocks, from their sheer magnitude, but they were as pitted and dead-looking as the skeletons of giant cacti.

The boy had come along: the boy who now lived with him, ate with him, slept with him, who belonged to him as much as his shadow— though he had yet to hear a word out of him. Made him prickle all over just to think about it. Ever since he and Grace had joined them, the kid had started hanging around him, at the same time pretending he wasn't. He just happened to be there, not really paying any attention. But he was joined to Billy by the corner of an eye. Let Billy start to move out of his field of vision, and suddenly he was underfoot. He seemed to have another set of eyes. Then, one day when Billy came inside his trailer, the kid was waiting for him. He'd brought his blanket and a bundle of his few small possessions. He'd stepped inside his life, joined it in a simple wordless transaction. He'd come to stay.

"Well, I don't know what they'll be doing out here," Billy was saying, "but they sure could have improved on the territory." Now that the kid was around, Billy found himself talking aloud a great deal, although he'd always found pleasure in a kind of ongoing dialogue with himself. Even though the kid never made any response, he found more support for his theories, opinions and conjectures now that he had an audience. Billy didn't try to weave any sort of magic: he wasn't out to convince, trick or cajole. He never knew whether the boy listened to anything he said: maybe it flowed into his ears like so much empty wind, resonating slightly as it moved through his brain.

The paved road had given out entirely as they headed in the direction of the rocks. He could see a van off in the distance, though he lost it again as they wove through a rock formation. When he stopped the truck and got out with the boy, he was completely disoriented. He looked around, trying to figure out where to go, where they might be doing business. Then he heard a cry that came to his ears like the sound of a bird. Then he heard it again. He wasn't sure, but it sounded human.

"Come on," he said to the kid, starting off in what he hoped was the right direction. He stumbled on what could have been an attempt at a path, something animal hooves had worn, and followed it among the broken rocks, over mounds, among the towers of stone. They climbed a small hill and saw ahead of them a sheet of rock about waist high from the ground. On it was Grace, held down by three of the men, while a fourth knelt and was trying to force into her crotch what looked like a small rocket.

The scream Billy heard as he and the boy approached grew into another, while someone yelled, "That's right—give it everything you got."

This ain't no acting, it flashed through Billy's mind, the cry spontaneous with terror. But the boy was ahead of him, already in action. He had bent down, scooped up a handful of rocks, and running up, began pitching them. His aim was deadly accurate. On the back, on the head. In the moment of stunned surprise that caught the men who held her, Grace kicked and pushed her way off the rock. One of the men tried to grab her. But she was free.

The boy continued to pitch the rocks, assisted with less skill by Billy, until Grace had reached them. "Kill them, Kill them," the boy gasped. It was the first words Billy had heard him say.

◆

"My God, what's happened?" Alta cried the moment she saw the girl's face— pale and frozen, the eyes like somebody had snapped the light off inside. "What happened, Billy?" she demanded, looking at Grace, all over welts and bruises, seeing Billy dust-covered and grim, trying to read something even from the boy, who stood like a stone.

"Take it easy, Dream Girl. She'll be okay."

"How come she's hurt? she demanded, touching her gently. "Come on, honey. We'll take care of you. You come over here and let me fix things up." And she fussed over her and tried to make her comfortable. Then, turning back to Billy and the boy, she set out a plate of crackers and cheese to tide them over till supper. "Now tell me what happened," she said.

And Billy told her how they'd found Grace, and just in the nick of time.

"I knew it, I just knew," Alta burst out. "Just wait'll I get my hands on him." She was so furious Billy could hardly get out the rest, but somehow—despite her frequent interruptions, questions, swear words and the like—he managed to tell her the story.

After Grace had come floundering up to them like a broken-winged bird, they'd been cut off from the truck. Somebody'd had sense enough to think of that immediately. So the only place they could go was up toward the low cliff beyond. Grace was dizzy, reeling—he had to half-carry her up. The kid kept up the action at the rear, throwing down rocks every which way till the men thought better of trying to follow them. It was a struggle to the top of the hill. Pretty uninviting, but at least it wasn't sheer rock. It was hot, though, and hard going. But when they'd clambered over the edge, they found they'd had a stroke of luck. Just down the slope was the city dump, and past the piles of tires and worn-out stoves and refrigerators and mattress springs and rusted iron, past the smoke of the garbage pit, was a little unpainted shack, a truck parked beside it. And a man shoveling refuse into a pit of burning trash. Slowly, careful of the girl, they worked their way down the hill and approached him—their promise of rescue.

The keeper of the dump was an old man with a face so darkened by sun and creased by weather that he seemed aged beyond any human calculation. His features were as primitive as the landscape. This was, you might have said, the first rough-hewn idea of a nose when smelling was first being invented. Or maybe it grew that way from what it had to smell. Same with the mouth: looked like it was only for opening and closing on something to eat, and nothing fancy at that. Limited use for speech. When Billy came up, he could hear a kind of tuneless whistling, almost buried under the voice, a sort of accompaniment for the work.

He didn't hear them come up. They had to shout. Then he rubbed his hand across his eyes as though he'd been disturbed from the only vision he had—of what could be burned and what could be buried, of what must be pitched and what might be saved—and having been disturbed was suddenly forced into something alien and questionable.

"Yasaythegirsbennurt," he said, squinting into her face. It was a mumbling speech that caused one word to lean over and fall into the next, the meaning pulled out from under like the rug from under a card house.

"Hurt bad. Be much obliged if you could drive us back into town."

The old man stood there as though waiting for the stir of volition and its first sluggish movements.

"Please," Billy begged. "It's a matter of life and death."

"Gottagitmakeys," the old man said, turning himself around to walk toward the shack.

Billy carried Grace to the truck. "You be okay in back?" he said to the boy.

With her leaning against him, eyes closed, he waited for the old man in an agony of suspense. Then for a moment his eye was taken up with what he had been seeing all along. On the fence around the dump-keeper's shack were heads of cupids and various saints, each impaled on a spike, heads decapitated from church statues, and maidens and martyrs from public buildings that had been torn down. Interspersed among these were plastic Christmas wreaths and funeral wreaths the old man had saved from burning.

"This is where all things gain the rubbish heap," Billy murmured to himself. "All things equal in loss. Where the dead gods are buried." And there they sat back of the rising smoke and the smell of garbage. Would they come to life again? he wondered, struck by a feeling he'd never had before, rather dizzying. Who were the gods anyway, the ones this carnival was set to play to?

Then he told Alta how they'd come back to town, straight to the hospital and had to wait forever, it seemed, before somebody would look at Grace. Which was why they were so late. And all the while, as Alta was listening, busying herself around the kitchen, putting something together for supper, she muttered things like "Goddamn" and "I knew it was bad news from the beginning." Grace she left undisturbed, hoping she'd sleep. "Damn that Dusty. Where is the skunk anyhow?"

But he didn't return in time for supper, and they sat down and ate without him. And he didn't return that evening.

"Listen," Alta said, "I say we get out of this place before something else happens. He can stay here and work all the deals he wants." "Better let me go back and look for him," Billy said. "God knows what's happened to the truck. I left the keys in the ignition."

"Well, you'd better come back," Alta said, "because I'm all for getting out of here—the sooner, the better."

When they finally crawled out of town a week later—on a day when the clouds hung in gray smoky cobwebs in the distance, presaging rain in the mountains—they left behind not only the truck but Sam, the animal trainer, whose tiger had escaped during the shooting and, having scattered the buffalo herd that grazed the land behind the hotel, was last seen disappearing into the hills. Dusty they had found in an alley, beaten up so badly he could scarcely move. Good suit torn to shreds, elbows out at the sleeves, he lay bleeding and unconscious, skull fractured, two ribs broken. And though she ministered to him during his recovery, it was all that Alta could do even to look at him. He had sold the girl, that's what he had done. And that was, she felt fiercely, passionately, just one more betrayal of her.

4

"Now you see it, now you don't. You think you're going one way— past the buried city, through the tunnel, beyond the mountains, maybe to the Promised Land. And here you are—stuck right in the middle of nowhere. Can't see the hand in front of your face, let alone the way to somewhere." Billy looked out the window of the trailer. Fog thicker than fleece. Thicker than midnight, for it was dark too. "Might as well be floating through space," he said, turning to the boy, then back to the window. "Yep. Nothing to hold onto. Not a name for a thing or a thing for a name. Everything set afloat. You and me and the lamp post and the dog peeing on it. Nothing tied down. Don't know why I'm standing here looking at it," he said, turning away again.

He walked restlessly to the end of the trailer, turned around and searched his pockets for a coin. He'd gotten started on something that seemed good for a few minutes' entertainment. Why not, if the muse gave you a tickle? Better than staring into the fog. He held a nickel in the palm of his hand for the boy to see; closed his palm, opened it. "Now you see it, now you don't."

"Appearance and disappearance. A trick of the eye. And that's the way with everything under the sun. There's a gnat in front of your eye and flick! It's gone. Even a star. Takes such a long time appearing that meantime Methuselah's grandson is halfway to the moon. And by the time he gets there that star has gone out of the universe for good. Think of that. Nothing but a black hole with the light of olden days living in your eye." He thought about it. "How's that for illusion? And everything that's ever happened: here one minute, gone the next. Some things take so long saying goodbye—a lifetime, four generations, six eons—but it's all the same disappearing act...All those statues and ancient cities and old civilizations ..."

For out there somewhere lost in the fog, half-buried, was the site of an ancient city, so they'd heard, belonging to a people who'd come and gone and left only broken stones behind. Columns of temples dedicated to unknown deities for arcane purposes. People came out to wander over the ruins, carve their initials on weathered stone, set out picnics on fallen gate markers and pediments toppled and scattered by some violent upheaval and left to the lizards to crawl over.

And before that, so it had come to Billy's attention, a sea had covered these mountains. Older stones and fossil shells lying around to hint of that lost life. Opposite to the stars, whose light was so long in coming, were those creatures both animal and human who were so long in going that their goodbyes still lingered to meet you in the sun and air. Ah, Billy thought, the art of appearance and disappearance had thus reached such extremes that he and the rest of the carnival, the creatures of a moment caught here in the midst of the brief span of their lives, could pick up the fossilized shells and look at the ruins and starlight and weave all the fantasies they wanted about where things came from and where they'd gone, about all the realms lost in distance and time, while they lay lost in the fog, the future not yet happened and the past already congealed behind them.

"And where's the nickel? In my pocket, in my sleeve? It's all a trick —to deceive the eye. The whole secret of illusion. And the whole universe is in on the act. Every deed that was ever done and everything you've ever seen. And here we are, one little flash between *remember this* and *hold onto that.*"

Now Ventura City—that was immediacy for you. Nothing so insistent as a human being with money in his pocket, craving a good time. The whole city ran to you, offered to fill up your hunger and thirst and boredom and the empty spaces in your conversation and the black holes in your head. And then you got to go sleep it off. And wake once more. Watch the stirrings and motions of the city coming back to life: the sweeping and mopping of the floors of the bars, the going-ups of the awnings of the shops, the taking-downs of the chairs from the tables. Watch the food stands and the newsstands raising up their shutters, while the stores with the furs and leather goods and silver and gold jewelry kept theirs closed like late sleepers, waiting for the tourists to come. Hear the scrape and the bang, the bump and the clatter being joined to one another with a whoosh, the city revving up, the cars and motorcycles, the trucks and the buses taking over, honking and roaring, beating off before the air could touch their hurry, disappearing into their watch-my-dust.

He reached into the boy's shirt pocket and held out the nickel. "There," he said, "you see the only thing I'm good for. I can play the game with coins and scarves and cards and rabbits in a hat. But there's no magic to it.

"Now magic," he said, pausing to think on it, "that's a different kettle of fish. That would be throwing things up in the air without having them come down. Up like an eagle. An up without a down. Imagine that." The idea tickled him. He saw himself throwing hammers and feathers and stones and flowers and starfish into the air. "I could be a master," he said. "Billy Bigelow, the Master of Up. Can't you see it? All outside the laws of gravity." He looked at the boy, inviting him to enter the landscape of up. "Get rid of all the clutter that way—clear out the whole joint," he said. "Or, if you could pull the up things down, change sea into sky and sky into sea. Fish swimming in the air, birds flying under your feet. Turn the whole place upside down. What do you think of that?" He whisked it all away. "Nope," he said. "None of my doing. I'm a now-you-see-it, now-you-don't man: coins and cards and scarves."

Magic was something else again. He'd once got hold of some books about it. One time or another he'd gotten a book on just about any subject you could imagine: *How to Understand Your Dreams. How to Find Water in Places You Didn't Believe It Existed. How to Predict the Future. How to Make the Most of Your Life.* And some of these books he'd read. But his dreams were still a mystery; he'd never learned how to find water or predict the future. And his life had been pretty much what it had always been, a combination of ups and downs, things here one minute and gone the next. And he'd read about people who cut wands from hazel trees with the single stroke of a dagger at precisely the point of sunrise and tried to gain the power to change reality and themselves. He'd read about magic but was stuck with illusion.

But he had guessed something about the boy that had troubled him. The kid wanted the real thing. And Billy sensed that the boy had come to him thinking he had something to offer along that line. A couple of days before they'd left Ventura City for good, Billy had wandered out in the scrub looking for the kid, who hadn't been around all that afternoon. He came across him out of sight behind a hill a short distance from the trailer. Billy kept quiet till he could see what he was doing, coming in as close as he could to spy him out. The kid was standing inside a circle drawn in the sand, eyes closed, chanting strange words. Then he stopped and picked up a coke bottle full of water and sent some flying the direction of the four winds. Interesting, Billy thought. Wonder what he has in mind. Then the kid held up a bird feather and let it go sailing in the wind.

But this was not play—it was all deadly serious. He could tell from his expression, from the tone behind the strange words that seemed to lift off from something uncanny in the boy himself. Billy was reminded of the episode of a few days before.

"You sure got a good throwing arm and a good eye," he'd said to the boy once things had calmed down. And for some reason he said, "You know, once

I read about a magician so powerful he squashed his enemies by having a brick wall fall down on them."

"Is that true?" the boy demanded to Billy's surprise, breaking out of his silence once again. "Is that really true?"

Maybe it's true, Billy thought now. It was true that you could hate somebody bad enough to kill him. That was a power in itself. And maybe you could change reality with it. The trouble was, he figured, the boy had the dangerous desire to do it. He was not one to be content with mere illusion. And what was he going to do with this kid, Billy wondered, who had suddenly and without warning stepped into his life? That was the trouble. You never knew where you were anyway, what ground you stood on with any other human being. Everything was up in the air.

◆

Places. She'd been in all kinds of places and this was no place at all. It was the hole you fell through, the space where the bottom had dropped out. Alta looked into the fog, which had a strange yellowish cast. Old fog, she thought. Probably'd been in too many places and picked up more than it could hold of the dust and fumes off people's living: smoke of their hurry, the breath of their rheums and disasters, the scum of their miseries and defeats and the hot blasts of their angers and frustrations. So now it was no longer the fresh opaque moisture from the hills but something thick as a human cough that lay over them and kept them from moving. Couldn't see a thing, couldn't move an inch. Just barely got through the tunnel through the mountains, put Ventura City behind them, thank God—thought she'd never get out of that place alive—when there they were, right in the heart of the fog, clouds of it boiling up around them. The only thing was to sit by the side of the road and wait for it to lift, wait for morning.

But it wasn't such a bad time. She was tired of driving, tired of listening to Dusty pissing and moaning. Now it was quiet, peaceful —Dusty asleep and Grace keeping her company over a cup of Sanka. She was glad for her company, even when she sat there not saying a word. The boy was too much for her. Too wild and unfathomable. She was just as glad Billy had taken him over, or he'd taken over Billy, for it was hard to tell who'd done what; she didn't envy Billy the task. But Grace ... she couldn't have said what Grace was to her. The daughter she'd never had—that was easy. But more than that. The friend she'd always wanted. That too. Maybe even more. Looking into her eyes, she seemed to catch something of her own reflection, to see something of herself in Grace's experience in the world, even if she didn't know what-all it had been. Anyway, she found herself talking about the places she'd been, the places that she'd thought forever buried, forgotten, covered over in the drifts of years and time, everything now rolled up into the thickness of one moment lost in fog. But breaking into it were the things she remembered.

"Did I tell you about the time I was in Seattle?" she found herself saying. "It was when I took off on my own, right before I joined up with the circus. I bounced around plenty, let me tell you. I'd just decided to quit school for good and was on my way to look for a ride out of town. Passed by a restaurant and I look up and see it's The Lucky Inn. And I thought, I'll be needing some of that. So I went inside. But it was one of those fancy joints where the waiters roll out with the smiles and bend sideways to keep your water glass filled to the brim and clinking with ice and talk at you like they got all their breeding at a Polite academy ... Anyway, I took a look at the menu —fancy meals for fancy prices—and I knew it wasn't the place for me. So I got up and walked out. Only when I got to the street, here comes a man calling to me, wanting to know what was wrong. And when I told him he said, 'Come on back in, I'll give you a meal. No strings attached. Maybe you'll bring me luck.' So he sat me down at a table and brought me a piece of meat that melted like butter in your mouth and a big fancy potato with sour cream and chives, and I ate it all right up. And then he wished me good luck and goodbye and shook my hand and let me go. Imagine that."

Grace smiled.

The man hadn't wanted anything from her. Only luck—what a joke. Hard to imagine a time in her life when she'd been that innocent and untried. She hoped Grace could remember such a moment. She wanted to give her one, give her a moment when all of life seems to lie before you, a shining path. Was there anything you could give to somebody out of the past, out of all that was used up and wasted and gone wrong? She looked at Grace, who was getting sleepy. "You go on ahead," Alta told her. "I think I'll sit up awhile. We sure ain't going anywhere in all this."

"I don't know," she said, while Grace was rinsing her cup under the faucet, "ever since the days I was up on the trapeze and didn't have a care in my head, I've been looking for a place to live." She lit a cigarette, noticing that the polish was chipping off her thumbnail— a silvery pink polish she was trying out. She wondered if she should go back to red.

"Every time I've landed in a place and seen the streets looking all fresh and interesting and leading I-don't-know-where, and people looking at me and smiling and saying hello, and little kids playing on their tractors on the sidewalk, I've thought, well, maybe this is the place. Maybe I could settle down here and get some kind of a job and stay in one spot. And then I'd think, pretty soon I'd get to know the way to the grocery and the things on the street would start to look like the same old stuff and I'd put all the names to all the faces behind the counters and pretty soon we'd get to harping on the weather and Miz Minnie's bad back and her alcoholic stepson and her no-account, half-witted brother and what a saint she's been in all the trials of flesh and spirit, and I'd be sick of it in a week and every nerve in my body would be itching to get out." Red nail polish, she decided, a definite improvement.

Grace touched her on the shoulder. "Goodnight," she said. "Sleep well."

"Good night, honey. Sweet dreams." Maybe once it got in your blood, Alta thought, it was like a virus and you couldn't get shut of it. And when it broke out, you had to pick up and go. The wandering bug. Once you got bit . . . She sat playing with her cigarette. Billy could blow smoke rings inside smoke rings, but she'd never developed the knack.

Maybe there was only one place, she thought. Inside your skull. And you couldn't trust that. Get a little high or a little senile and you'd go wandering, maybe forever, cut loose from your moorings. Then where would you be?

She watched Grace brushing her hair in front of the mirror. Just like any other girl. Only she wasn't any other girl. This one who danced with snakes and had a raven for a pet. Pet, hell. Part of her act. Taught it words too. Grace had told her a story. It was such a wily bird, so full of tricks, that in the beginning when the first man had no woman, the gods took the raven and made him into a woman.

"There," they said. "She'll always be a torment to man. That's what she's for."

"Why's that?" Alta said.

"So he wouldn't get too pleased with himself," Grace told her.

That was a thought. Alta finished her cigarette, started to take out another, then thought better of it. She had the place all to herself now, but even so, she couldn't settle into the quiet. Ever since Grace had come, a powerful desire had seized her, an inexpressible emotion that kept welling up. She wanted some dream of the future that included her—to give her something. The effort frustrated her. At least Dusty knew what he wanted, and perhaps at some point you could have said it was a good dream. Before he tried to tear a piece out of everybody's life to get it for himself.

But Grace was already of the world, knew too much. You could never go back on that, deny what was already your experience. She couldn't treat her like a kid. But even so, in expectation of Grace's birthday, she'd bought a two-pound bag of flour. And though she hadn't baked a cake in years, she could at least read the recipe on the back of the package. She put away her cigarettes, dumped out the ashtray and lit the oven. She was wide awake, not an ounce of sleep in her. She was going to bake a birthday cake.

◆

The fog lay heavy and amorphous, at the same time breaking and shifting so that a space opened up for a few seconds, allowing you the illusion that you could see something, then closed up before you could tell what it was, or that there'd been anything in the first place. He was in a foul humor, Curran was, stuck there, unable to sleep, trying to while away the hours by laying out games of solitaire that he never won and by squinting into the fog, mesmerized and frustrated and angry with himself on top of it all. Why was it you had to keep looking at what was blocking your view, knowing that your looking wasn't going to make it go away? And he was angry with Donovan for being peacefully out of it.

The giant, a great rumbling heap sleeping behind him, a volcano endlessly threatening to erupt. Donovan could easily have taken the title of World's Greatest Snorer. Why not, bag of hot air that he was? Prided himself on his brains when it was his gut that had all the talent. Ate enough for an army. Then had to snore it off. And he, Curran, had to live with it all: watch him tuck away a meal that would have raised the standard of living in an undeveloped country. Disgusting to watch. And then listen to him sleep. Curse him. Curran got up, went back to the bunk and gave the giant's shoulder a shake. Donovan mumbled something, shifted his bulk, and after a moment's silence regained the rhythm of his snoring.

As though daring himself to get drunk, the midget poured himself a whis-key and stood looking out into the fog. Now there was a moon, a slender crescent that ruled a clear stretch of sky. And to one side he thought he could see the ruin of a broken column gleaming faintly in the moonlight. On the ground as well there seemed a faint shimmer of light, like the glistening of water. Here the earth seemed to have only one idea endlessly repeated: the idea of rock. His eye, he thought, must be playing him tricks, or else the whiskey. But, feeling more wide awake than ever, he had a sudden inspiration. He rummaged around till he found a flashlight in the tool kit, put on a jacket against the night chill and went outside. The fog seemed to be lifting somewhat, though great patches of it still clung to the floor of the valley below. And it was indeed a broken column that he had seen, one of several that might have supported a temple.

He was curious to see more. He walked along the edge of the road for several hundred yards until he saw what looked like a stone step below the level of the narrow shoulder. He lowered himself down, not pausing to worry about how he'd get back up. The steps led downward into a path that took him round behind a hill, where he came to broken columns that rose from the stone floors and scattered ruins of statuary and carved pediments, faintly and partially illumined by a bit of moon and his flashlight.

So here was the ancient city they had spoken of, his alone in the quiet and the fog, while all the rest were asleep, not knowing what he'd found. But he knew what he'd do. He'd spend the night wandering through it peacefully, away from everything, and watch the dawn come up over it. For a few hours he would be free.

At the moment he'd have been glad to forget the others altogether, all the ill-fated lives around him, all caught up in emotions that did them no good. He was filled with contempt. Dusty had been mismanaging the show for years now, his head filled with grandiose schemes. Full of himself. Oh, he was going to make it this time—just watch my dust. Hah. Now he had a fractured skull to show for it. Beaten to a pulp. The hot wind knocked out of him. And Alta. Curran had only slightly more sympathy for her. She should have given Dusty the boot a long time ago, taken her good looks and her talents and done something for herself. As for the rest, Billy was a simple-minded fool, harmless enough. He couldn't say a whole lot against him, another who could've gotten out and made it in the world on his own. Probably too much of a coward. And Donovan was simply the longstanding curse of his existence. He didn't know what he would do or be without him.

He wondered if the world outside the carnival was any worse than the prison he lived in. His world, the one he was condemned to, was the only one where he had a place, if you could call it that. No way out.

He didn't know what to make of Grace, now that she had come. She appalled and fascinated him. To the extent he could feel any sympathy for anybody, he could feel it for her. She was young, there was nothing wrong with her body; yet here she was with the rest of them. In fact, she was beautiful and full of life. Fiery when her temper broke out, a match for any of them the one time it had happened. And at times quiet and lovely; nice to you. Asked you how you were, gave you a cup of coffee. Yet she was no better off than he was, which gave him a little prickle of satisfaction: you didn't have to be a midget to be humiliated.

He wondered what had brought her down to their level. She never spoke about her past. But then who did? In his time he'd been around a few hoods whose pasts must have been like rotten logs: turn them over and watch the creepy stuff crawl out. Grace hardly spoke to him at all. Donovan had told him there was a butterfly tattooed on her shoulder. But everyone had seen the other, the word *Amazing* just under her navel. That was merely self-advertisement. In a carnival everything made the claim of being amazing. But none of it was. Only tricks and freaks.

As for the butterfly . . . He wondered what color it was, but didn't ask Donovan, who would have made some joke at his expense and probably wouldn't have told him the truth anyway. He pictured first a yellow swallowtail, then an orange monarch, these being the only butterflies he could identify. Suppose it was black, he suddenly thought, horrified quite without reason. He tried to picture her bending towards him, her face close to his. Suddenly she was kissing him on the lips, and heat flowed through him. How awful! What woman would kiss him without making fun of him?

He wanted to get rid of her, even the suggestion of her, but it was as if, in summoning her, he'd been momentarily possessed by her. He wanted to be free of her too, along with the others. He didn't even dare to think about the boy.

He found himself standing in front of the statue of a woman, the figure for whom the temple was built. She stood behind her altar, larger than life, with great elongated breasts like eggs and a belly to suggest the mindless fecundity of the womb. Indeed, her robes were decorated with various animals and insects. A large fly paraded behind the lion and the dog, and fruits and vegetables bordered her skirts. The midget flashed his light all along the parade. What about creatures like him? Did she claim him too? Then he played his flashlight about her features to see what she thought about the whole business. But she wasn't looking at him or anywhere else in particular. She didn't appear to be thinking at all. She reminded him of something, of the expression on Grace's face when he saw her dance in the nightclub—totally self-absorbed.

When she danced and the snakes slid around her arms and twined around her waist and moved upward toward her throat, and the lights played over her body and the sequins glittered like stars, she seemed to be in a world that had nothing to do with the eyes that ogled her. She wasn't aware of them. He didn't know if she was happy or sad, then, or just out of it. She seemed to be living behind her eyes, in a place she was led back into when she danced. While the snakes and her movements kept everybody rapt in fascination, she was gone. They were caught and held, but they couldn't get where she was. At least he couldn't. And he envied her. He watched her at other times and she was like everybody else. But she had been elsewhere, and for him there were only two worlds—the world inside the carnival and the world outside. Two cages where he could live in solitary confinement.

And here was the lady they had to thank for it all; or so somebody had once thought, taking the trouble to set up her statue. She wasn't looking at you either, nor at the fly or the dog or anything else she had hatched. She remained above it, while the rest of the lot went on generating and dying. Curran bowed with great ceremony. "Thanks a lot," he told her. "But I'd just as soon have been a spectator."

Behind and above her altar was a frieze carved for a doorway, from which he could see what looked in the dimness to be a garden full of sculptures. He shone his light on the frieze, saw a lion attacking a bull. The bull had gone under with an expression of agony so powerful he could almost hear it bellowing, sobbing out its death, whereas the lion, having sunk in its great claws, seized the neck in its teeth, ready to tear flesh from bone. Triumph gleamed in his eye as the bull sank to its knees. The victor. Carved in stone, they were paired together for eternity, killer and victim, so that the lion was bound as much as the bull and carried the same memory of broken flesh, bore the same knowledge of the other's death, becoming part of what he took into him, as though in the course of the sacrifice the victim exerted his power, and blood and memory flowed back and forth along the bond. Devourer and devoured. Sometimes, Curran thought, it was not all that clear which was which. For if you took another into you … As he looked at them, their flowing emotions evoked a horror that brought what was even worse, a terrible pity. He hated it. I've seen it all before, he realized, and I'll see it all again. Where had the idea come from, and the sense of *déjà vu*? They were bound like lovers, it struck him. Brought together through the need to torment and to be tormented, to devour and be devoured. Horrifying. Was this the ghastly punishment for being alive? Deliver us, he found himself saying. Deliver us from this death—and turned away.

To get into the garden, it was necessary to walk beneath this portal. He had no desire to do so. A wild and knotted growth lay beyond. Cacti of various shapes and bushes and spiny plants. And figures in the blurred darkness. Yet now that he was here, he was curious about what was out there. They were strange figures, he saw once he was in their midst, human figures and drag-on-like creatures and dogs and birds and jackals, some with wings, some with human heads. Each set of statues held sway over some spot of its own, some in little grottoes, with seats on which to recline, as though to view the figures in their various sports. A stone promenade connected them.

He stepped quickly past a group of monkeys cavorting with humans, some in intimate embrace. Obscene, this gross embodiment of lust with no distinction. He hurried on as a surge of self-disgust came over him. Now he stood in front of two lovers, the woman gazing over the shoulder of the man, smiling not so much at him as at the dark-winged creature that opened its claws, spread its wings behind him, while the man, unconcerned, perhaps ignorant of that presence, reached for her hand. As soon as he stood near enough, the midget felt a dark, uneasy attraction, though he didn't know what it was that tainted the air around the lovers. And so it was with each group of figures: if he didn't turn away immediately, a fascination began working on him, a kind of perverse pleasure he couldn't tear himself away from.

And when he reached a group of youths in chariots chasing a bevy of maidens, scattering them in all directions, he was overcome with eagerness. He climbed the steps to look out at the women, who ran frantically. One was about to be struck by the wheels of a chariot. The hair stood up on the back of Curran's neck. How exciting to see the women fleeing, to experience their terror, catch the hot breath of the chase and the laughing heedlessness of the youths flinging themselves forward in the chariots. And he saw himself under the hot lights of the tent where he played clown to the roars of the crowd, suddenly charging into those laughing at his antics, riding through their midst, routing them left and right. How he would have liked to see their faces.

But farther on, the blood still pounding in his head, he found what appeared to be the same youths. Their faces were the same, but their bodies were those of dogs, and the women were astride them. One of the creatures was looking up, fatuous, into his mistress' eyes, licking her hand, while she exchanged knowing glances with one of her companions. Disgusting: Curran remembered how Carnaby the Great had been led by the nose. For some reason, he'd become infatuated with a woman neither young nor pretty, a married woman at that. Curran remembered bad teeth and a coarse laugh. A woman who'd lain in wait for him, who came round every night after his act was over. She'd worked her magic till she'd overpowered his and he quit the carnival for good. And all the while Carnaby's wife—she was there too, watching her rival with her devoted dog. Carnaby's wife resembled the statue farther on, of a woman whose hair flew in all directions, whose eyes were fiery jets, who looked as though she'd scratch another's eyes out. It was all there. And he recalled how Donovan had followed Grace around during her first week. The center of attention. Curran had watched them, had stood and watched.

He was standing at the foot of the garden, where a path led off to the right to another spot self-contained in its own walls. At first he couldn't see anything, then he picked out one little figure over in a corner. He followed the path, flashing his light, and made his way to it. It was a small stone figure, the size of a child. The pose was utterly rigid, seemingly frozen for eternity, its face completely void. Only the eyes seemed to hold anything human, but as Curran looked into them he trembled all over. The eyes expressed such cold indifference they could have killed. Everything within was stone. There was nothing personal in the hatred that came from those eyes, yet it was hard to resist such an impression.

Quite against his will, Curran remembered an incident years earlier, one that Donovan had teased him about for a long time because it always got him riled up: Elise's child running from him in terror when he had come to visit. He was glad when at last time had let up on him, Donovan had wearied himself with his own repetitions, and Curran had finally been allowed to forget about it. But it had put him shy of children ever since. Looking at the figure, he saw fixed in stone a grudge against innocence, a cold heart of envy. And something else too. He thought he saw as well the capacity to live and die within oneself, if that were possible. To give nothing to the future; if he were mortal, only his bones to a dark place. And maybe that would be a good thing, Curran thought: nothing to carry you forward, nothing of all your sins, or the unresolved effects of all your actions visited upon the world—even your name unremembered. And yet that was terrible, too. Nothingness. Unbearable. He couldn't look at it anymore, and rushed back the way he had come.

He was brutally weary. He wanted to get back to the trailer and close his eyes. But as he looked around, he couldn't tell where he was. The paths led in various directions from the little enclosure. He started off on one but after coming back through several groups of familiar figures, he was again at the little stone figure. He started off through another series of serpentine loops and a different set of sculptures. A man and a woman twined in an embrace so that their bodies could not be pulled away from each another, both looking as if they were being suffocated. But Curran was no longer interested in these gestures. It was dark and he wanted to get out. Not just dark, but foul. Everything touched some secret vulnerability, threatened him with contagion. Who had worshipped here? He tried to follow the broken columns of the temple to the way back, but the path was deceptive. It took him round a hill and lost him, then led him back to the same spot. It turned around on itself or went off into nowhere. He was ready to weep, he had so exhausted himself with fruitless wandering in this deadly place. The light was slow in coming. There was no use. He sank down on a stone, weary to death and buried his head in his hands.

◆

Meanwhile Donovan was having a terrible dream. He dreamt he was too big to be human. The various organs and limbs of his body were so far apart and his brain so feeble that they could no longer keep in touch. The network of nerves was breaking down, owing to various excesses and long abuse: the overseers had gone on long junkets to other parts of the body, indulged themselves in extravagant meals and long drinking bouts and neglected the job back home. Messages went astray along the nerve endings and never reached the vital centers, sometimes not even when they were made out in triplicate. Little groups of upstarts were trying to work things out on their own. A great deal of confusion. Conflicting impulses.

All of a sudden he looked down to see blood trickling from his leg. He must've cut an artery. But he felt no pain. The brain was under new management. He was being run by a large committee, of which no one was clearly in charge. A message was sent out—What's happening down there?—but it seemed as if a signal would never arrive. There was no pain. Messages petered out along the nerve endings, too weak to leap the synapses. And when one finally arrived, nothing came of it. The committee members couldn't agree on a course of action. One impulse suggested that clotting agents and antibiotics be sent immediately. But a great inertia absorbed the governing body. They contemplated setting up an ad hoc committee to deal with the problem. There was still no pain. Donovan seized his leg in horror. *I am watching myself bleed to death,* he groaned. There was still no pain.

◆

He had fallen into a pit, into such a depth and darkness that the thought of trying to find his way back to daylight was unimaginable. For a week Dusty had lain in the hospital unable to move. Beaten bloody, bones broken, skull fractured: he lay in a stupor of pain and forgetfulness. Then, when the world came back and the pain localized in his head, chest and legs, something remained numbed beyond pain, shattered. Now his ribs were taped, his arm in a cast, but his mind still lay below the surface of his injuries, unable to move. When he tried to think, whatever he caught hold of fell into fragments. The show was over . . . his luck was shot. What was left? Nothing.

Over and over he came back to torturing himself with what might have been. For there was a time when things were as different as the day is from night, the elephant from the flea—a time when the world was fresh and his luck brand-spanking new. A time when the thrill was in his blood sharp as pins and needles, when his confidence ran high and people believed in him. Old Man Booker had been alive then. "I like your style," he was always saying. "You could turn corn into gold nuggets. You've got a way." That much was true. And in those days, it was people who could recognize a real flair who made all the difference.

He'd gone to Booker. "Look, Dream Girl and I have got it made. Can travel all over Europe if we want. I've got people begging us to come. And it's money in the bank. But I want my own show."

And Old Booker had said, "You got the nerve and the guts, boy. I like your style." The old man had staked him, staked him good. He'd auditioned every act himself. Chosen every costume. Everything— down to a gnat's eyebrow. And the show was terrific. A smash.

If he could've had three years, he'd have had it cinched. But it took time to build a reputation. Too many people wanted their money. Couldn't blame them, of course. You had to eat. But things had started slipping away from him. That summer in Chicago. Race riots, worse luck. People scared. Receipts down. A tent caught fire, God knows how. He'd relied too heavily on two big acts. Had to trim down the show.

By the time they reached San Francisco, he felt things slip a little more. Nothing bad, not then. A few little chinks in the armor of his luck. When his two big acts moved over to the competition at the end of the season, he didn't care—the season was over. He'd have time to gather his forces. Confidence was the main thing. Nations and currencies rode and fell on it. And circuses. And when you figured a buck wasn't worth more than a plugged nickel, that's what you had. So half his energy was spent trying to convince people they belonged to the winning side. Oh, he talked things up big, much bigger than they were. Every new act he wanted, he had to do a sell job. Make them think they'd take in twice as much money as what was offered. Till he believed it all himself. If he could convince them, luck would step in and do the rest, make it all happen. Old Booker had staked him to the next round, and he'd been able to convince the banks.

The third round was the closest. He'd nearly done it that time. Down in Texas he'd struck oil: a millionaire who loved the circus. And he'd back Dusty all the way. It was then that he wanted to tie-in circus and carnival and try to make their appearance the occasion of a week-long celebration that would take in the whole town.

"Look," Alta had said. "For the first time we're in the black. We've got good acts. What do you want to ruin it for? You're like all those fools with a going business who try to make it into a chain. Kill themselves with work if they don't go broke."

"This ain't no grocery chain," he yelled. "Sure, you can get along just fine if you always think small."

"What do you *want?*"

"You think I've been burning myself out just to run some flea-bitten circus? You think that's what I quit the big time for when I was making a pile? Listen, I want the best and the biggest. Stop dreaming and you might as well be dead."

Now the dream was shattered forever, and he himself was more dead than alive.

◆

Billy Bigelow sat up in bed. Something had awakened him, but whether in his sleep or from outside he couldn't tell. He sat listening. Outside it was a splendid morning. The fog had cleared away and the mountains in the distance stood under a glowing pink light like the inside of a shell. A tower of cloud was piled above. Again he heard it—a faint cry. He thought of Grace. He got up, put on his clothes that were lying across the end of the bed and went outside. Down below he saw the broken columns and beyond that a piece of cloth waving. Again, the faint cry. He leapt down the embankment, down the stone steps, gained a path that took him toward the waving patch of blue. Now he could recognize Curran's voice: What was he doing down there?

"Don't come any farther," the midget called. "Stay where you are and I'll come to you."

Billy remained where he was, in an enclosure of broken walls, various paths. To his surprise, he saw a little spring, the clear water flowing over rocks and into a small inlet that fed a pond ringed with stones. Here in this god-forsaken place. He went over to look. The pond was quite deep, he could see, the water was surprisingly clear and full of light. Great orange and speckled carp swam lazily by, disappearing under pink water lilies. He knelt at the edge and, as he looked into the water, seemed to look all the way to the bottom. From below the surface came flashes of green and gold and black. Then all the fragments came together. He could see trees and the towers of buildings. As he continued to watch, the planes of light broke into doorways and streets.

"Where are you?" Curran called, not far away now.

"Over here. Come quick. I want to show you something." He continued to kneel, watching the colored lights that shifted and beckoned in various directions.

The midget hesitated. The experiences of the previous night held him in uneasy thrall. Towards morning an owl had flown above him with a mouse in its claws, and he was terrified. If he didn't look at whatever this was, he would be spared one thing at least. He could take Billy's word for it, even if Billy was a fool. If he looked himself, no telling what he might see. He'd had enough visions for one night.

"Come on," Billy urged. "I've never seen anything like it." But the moment he said it, it was gone. Billy knelt for a moment longer, hoping it would reappear. But now all he could see were carp and water lilies, pretty enough. He wondered if he'd really seen anything. Optical illusion, probably. Light playing and shifting. It was pretty far-fetched, he had to admit. A buried city at the bottom of a fish pond. So inviting that it made you want to leap right in, dive down below the fish and lilies and see for yourself. He must have imagined it. He got up, shook himself as though shaking off a dream and started toward the midget to lead the way back. Now you see it, he thought; now you don't.

5

This was a haven she had come to. After all their wandering, all the uncertainties of the last few years, together with this latest disaster, it was, if not paradise, a place of pause and rest, a place in which to gather herself together, sort out the pieces, discover what life there was still left. As yet she had no space in which to dream—a luxury she still could not afford. But she could peel an orange and drink her coffee on the patio in the morning while the sun shone on clusters of day lilies and geraniums and pots of red and white amaryllis around the stone wall outside and watch Rina making her slow way around the garden with her watering can.

Rina was in no hurry as she tended her garden of herbs—medicinal herbs, herbs for cooking and for teas. And Alta could take in her slowness as she bent down under the soft dome of her still plentiful white hair to examine her plants, cutting blooms here, taking leaves there, pulling some up by the roots for whatever brew she was making, till the basket on her arm was overflowing with plants. Every once in a while she stood up and you saw a strong face, freckled and wrinkled, but projecting its strength in a powerful nose and intelligent eyes. It did Alta good just to look at her. Her mouth was kind. She smiled at Alta, took off one of her gloves to brush back a strand of hair and, having acknowledged her presence, went back to work. Alta loved her. Sometimes she thought that if she could enjoy anything it might be digging in the dirt, finding out what different plants held inside them. She liked the way their names rolled over the tongue: Aloe Vera, agrimony, wild lettuce, valerian, damiana, passion flower, chamomile.

Rina was an old woman, on her way to being a hundred; not even her son and daughter-in-law knew her exact age. But she was never idle. The plants having been tended, her basket full, she was now on her way to the kitchen to cut string-beans or clean fish from the lake to cook for lunch for the family and assorted others that took their meals at the hotel.

"Life is full of surprises," Alta was always saying to herself, though she had learned never to be surprised by anything. Not even by a family of Greeks running a little hotel out in the bush, three generations of them still speaking Greek to one another, welcoming travelers who found their way to Old Town. Except for the family, there was no one in the hotel except a retired army officer known as Captain Valor, who had lived there for years. Now the straggling remains of the carnival had descended on them, Dusty no longer able to travel and Alta herself quite worn out. The hotel stood at the center of what a hundred years ago had been a boom town, a thriving city. A great quantity of silver had been discovered; before that, gold the Indians had worked and made into ornaments. But once the gold and silver were mined out, most of the inhabitants, including the Indians, had left. In recent years a number of those having some quarrel with the twentieth century—painters and poets and vegetarians and pacifists, various kinds of loners and loonies—had begun to move into and restore the abandoned houses and boarded-up buildings. Some more or less camped on the premises, living without plumbing or electricity. Others dug wells, brought in generators, sewed curtains and repaired rotted timbers. By now it was a thriving community, almost like an extended family, absorbed in one another's lives, with fierce loyalties springing up, fierce quarrels breaking out, the chief activity being to sit over coffee and gossip while the kids played hide-and-seek in the alleys and vacant houses.

Across the bridge, over a river which ran when it rained and narrowed to a trickle when it didn't, was New Town, where the efforts at living were more avowedly experimental and communal. Here there were groups and cults— recently inspired religions, economic and sexual experiments. A new group had recently established itself under the spiritual leadership of the Reverend Ronnie Earl Hoskins, a former truck driver who'd founded his own church, was starting a school, intended a hospital and was gathering funds for a powerful television station to broadcast his message into the hearts and minds of those awaiting his word across the continent.

Alta had no interest in any of this. Just to get from one day to the next took all her energy. When she was sitting on her balcony or on the patio, it seemed enough to be doing only that, drinking her cup of coffee and looking out into the day. Even if she *was* supposed to be thinking things out. Like Dusty with his schemes and his columns of figures. But she had no head for it. The best she had been able to do at any point in her life was to figure out how many there might be around the table for supper, or how to listen when somebody was in trouble. She never went in for the long haul. But now she was in charge, running the show. What a laugh! As if she could. The slot was open, though; the king having abdicated, thrown in the sponge. And there they were: nowhere to go, nobody to tell them what to do—not even the wrong thing. They were missing the mainspring, old charlatan that he was.

Fortunately there was money. At least she'd taken care of that. Got hold of most of the loot before Dusty had the chance to throw it away. Had filched a good whack of it right out of his wallet before he had taken off for town back in Ventura City. Once in the bank it would have been out of her hands. And that's where it had been headed. The rest lay in a little safe in the trailer, money for a good long while.

It was one less thing she had to worry about. Otherwise she might have been living in the desert, waiting for the ravens to pluck out her eyes. She didn't have to worry, of course. Nobody asked her to. Certainly not the girl. But she did anyway, wondering what was going to happen to her. She couldn't spend her life polishing her nails, reading and rereading all the old magazines in the trailer or in the hotel lobby. The rest of the time, apparently, Grace wandered the streets, especially in the evening around dusk. There were children who latched onto her, when she was in the mood, and took her places: to the old Indian burial ground, the so-called Hill of Holies where the mad hermit lived; out to the Dulsweet Silver mine; places like that. But she didn't seem to have any particular friends, though she smiled and was pleasant. She seemed glad to be alone. Alta noticed that the eyes of the old army officer sometimes lingered on Grace as she passed, but you couldn't fault a man for looking at a woman.

And Grace wasn't a child anymore. Yet what was she supposed to do in the world: marry some guy who repaired TV's or sold insurance, or ran a mortuary or a MacDonald's? Not some carny, God forbid, wasting her life like she had! Alta had tried to tell her a thing or two, being so crammed full of information that she could spare a little, God knows. But it seemed like she just kept rummaging and rummaging, coming up with scraps that had nothing to do with the future. You couldn't live and feed on somebody else's rubbish. So much for Grace.

When she'd thought her way to the end of that cul-de-sac, all she had to do was turn around to land in another. She could think about Dusty, who wandered around in his own brand of gloom—a new feature, a new performance. She had no idea what to do about him either. At least she could talk to Billy Bigelow.

She was glad to see him now, coming out to join her on the patio, book in hand, reading glasses in his pocket. He pulled out a chair and sat at the table opposite her.

"Billy," she said, "I'm caught 'twixt a rock and a hard place."

"How's that, Dream Girl?"

"Well, there's Dusty for one. Every day it's the same. I thought that now that he was starting to heal up, he'd be back to his old self. But he doesn't care about anything."

"Yeah," Billy said, "I been noticing."

"Can't even ask him a question. Just waves his hand like he's brushing off a fly. Then he says, 'Do what you damn please.' "

Billy nodded. "Well, he's been hurt where it hurts the most."

"You mean a broken head wasn't enough?" Alta said with a snort.

"You know what I mean."

"He deserved it," she said fiercely. "They'd have killed her. For what? He sold us out but good. And you're worried about his pride."

"I'm not defending him," Billy said. "Terrible thing all the way around. Doing what he did. And to have nothing but your pride to protect. No, I'm not condoning anything," Billy said softly, "just looking at the pieces."

"I don't know why I bother with him. Somebody should've thrown his carcass to the crows a long time ago."

"I don't imagine you have to tell him."

"Yeah," Alta said, lighting up a cigarette despite her vows to quit smoking. "It doesn't require special delivery to get the message." She could have danced up and down on him had she wanted to, but she wouldn't have derived any pleasure from it. Nor could she feel any pity either. Only a space without any feeling at all was left, a space like old Jello. Yet somehow she couldn't abandon him. Their years together had got to be a habit, she decided, and now all she had was the habit.

"It was crazy," Billy said. "He was like a bulldog hanging on by his teeth with his eyes closed. It was the desperation in him made him do it."

"But when he was already raking in the cash," Alta said, raising her voice. "He got greedy, that's what. Yeah, I know, he's so all-fired fixed on one thing, he can't look anywhere else. And that moment it looked close." She let out a little gust of exasperation. "But if anything had happened to her," Alta said, "I'd have killed him. I would've."

"I don't doubt it, Dream Girl," Billy said. Nor did he for one moment. She'd have sent him to eternity on a shotgun blast, his initials carved in capitals on his gut. Nothing subtle, only lethal.

"And I'm worried about Grace too," Alta went on. "Her future. She's just a kid, really. Only she's never had a chance. When do you suppose she was ever just a kid. All the wrong kind of experience. The kind that leaves a mark."

Was there any other, he wondered. He didn't admit that the boy had him stumped as well. At times when he looked at him, he saw an old man, gray and dwarfed like those children who age and die scarcely before they've begun the journey through life. The white hair, the long face. But his body had been left lean and muscled by what sort of savagery he had no idea. And he wondered if the human would take or be rejected as alien, like some skin grafts.

He and Alta remained silent for a moment, staring off into their separate spaces. And this book he was looking into, to tell him what, for the sake of whom—himself or the boy? "Now this is what you need," he said. "Master the techniques and you can change the nature of reality itself. All it takes is the will and the imagination."

"It's a little late for me," Alta said, "to start improving my mind." Though she had from time to time browsed among the books in Billy's trailer, reading bits and pieces: *Is there Life in Outer Space?*, *Dowsing for Inspiration*, *You can Improve your Memory*. It occurred to her that she'd never found any books about getting rich. But then, she couldn't imagine Billy rich. "How come you're into that now?"

"Thought I might branch out, see if I could take on the real thing. I've been playing tricks long enough."

She couldn't tell if he was leading her on or not, but had a feeling he was up to something.

"When I was young," she said, "I thought dreaming was a powerful magic. Dream it and it would come true. You sure have to get kicked around a lot before that feeling goes away—if it ever does. Dies hard. Funny, you know," she said, "just after Grace came along, I had a dream about her. All in color. Never told anybody. But when I woke up it stayed with me."

"What was it? I read a book about dreams once."

"I dreamt that there was a carnival—not the broken down piece of scrap we've got going, but a real one. People in the streets dancing, singing, drinking wine. And Grace dancing with her snakes coiled around her, the light playing on her face. And something wonderful in the air, like when the sun comes out after a rain. Everybody was celebrating, having a wonderful time." She paused, able to see it again in her mind. "How is it," she wanted to know, "that when you're dreaming it seems more real sometimes than when you're wide awake?"

"Strange thing," Billy agreed. "And why is it you can't see a dream from the backside?"

"What do you mean?"

"Because it comes walking up to you and gives you the come-hither, and you can never see where it came from. Just out of nothing, out of the dark. Maybe if you could see the stem you could figure out the root. If you could see it from the top and bottom and all sides, you'd be—" he paused—"Pablo Picasso or—" he considered again— "one of God's eyes."

"Well, it's too much for me," Alta said. "I can't even see around the next minute." She stubbed out her cigarette, yawned expansively. "I think I'll go have a shower." The idea pleased her. "When the hot water's pouring over me, I don't have to do anything but stand there and pretend I'm shedding my skin and I'll step out a new person, ten years younger and twenty pounds lighter."

"Now you *are* dreaming," he teased.

"Listen. There're still a few guys that look up and watch when I walk down the street."

"Count me in," he said.

◆

The Acropolis Hotel was a large, three-story structure whose boards over the years had weathered to a fine silver color. A Mediterranean influence had given to each room a small wrought-iron balcony with louvered doors. It was a comfortable, spotlessly clean old hotel with ancient wallpaper and creaking floors, wide carpeted staircases with rounded newel posts and long dark hallways. In the rooms were antique bureaus and beds with sagging mattresses.

Elena Triandophylos kept it all in order, rising every morning at five, collecting the keys of the lodgers after breakfast and spending the mornings mopping, sweeping, making beds and, as a final touch, putting a vase with a few zinnias or roses or marigolds on top of each of the bureaus. There were always a few people in the hotel, traveling through the territory. In recent years, various visitors had come there specifically to learn all about the lore of herbs from Rina and to collect seeds and plants from her garden. Then Elena was busier than ever.

Meanwhile her husband, Alexos, went about hammering and painting and shoring things up, for he could never keep ahead of repairs. In the evenings he sat in an armchair in the lounge reading Homer or Heroditus or Thucydides, for he was a scholar and believed in keeping the past alive. Their son, Leftheris, was everywhere— behind the desk to sign in the guests, in and out of the dining room serving breakfast and lunch, behind the bar in the evening. Even so, he was so untiringly gregarious that he found a good deal of time to stand outside exchanging pleasantries with the passers-by.

"This hotel has been in our family for four generations," Elena Triandophylos was fond of saying, and for confirmation glancing up at the portrait of her grandfather, who had come to Old Town when silver was discovered in the Eighties. The fever that scattered prospectors all over the territory had never touched him personally. Being of a practical turn of mind, he figured out that miners and prospectors needed picks and shovels, boots and rope, flour and salt pork. These he brought in by mule, selling them at a premium while money was plentiful and supplies were scarce. By the time the first wave of prospectors had struck it rich or had given up in disgust, he was prosperous. And when the first inhabitants—miners and cowboys and prostitutes and assorted ruffians—settled down to make a town, he had the money to build a hotel, saloon and dance hall. This part of the hotel had been closed off for many years, though for the last few it had been opened up for a great party that included all of Old Town and some of the people from across the bridge, a great Christmas feast with piñatas full of nuts and candy for the children and plates of meat from a whole side of beef, roasted over a pit and served round to the guests.

The chief relics from the past were a portrait of Elena's grandfather, a serious man with dark eyes and a heavily waxed mustache, next to his equally serious-looking wife, her luxuriant hair parted in the center and brought back in two raven wings and coiled into a bun at the back—both of them gazing out from a walnut frame next to the wooden cubbyholes that held the keys to rooms and letters for guests; a gold nugget the size of a walnut, encased in a glass well in the desk; a yellowed newspaper celebrating the opening of the hotel on August 14, 1887; several Wanted posters; advertisements for elixirs and ointments, stove oil and boot polish; and a painting of a woman dressed in a pink silk gown and a black lace shawl, her fair white skin highlighted by two round spots of color on her cheeks, as she stood holding a fan in long, delicate fingers like the paw of a lemur and looking out at the viewer with demure eyes under fringed lids. A little terrier wagged its tail in the corner of the picture.

Billy Bigelow had spent considerable time admiring this memorabilia, but he was even more impressed by a collection of paintings hung around the walls of the dining room and lounge. These were the work, Elena explained, of a famous artist, an outcast who had lived in the hotel because he had nowhere else to go. He had fled from one place to another, persecuted wherever he went because of his views on free love and his general condemnation of society, his "immoral" paintings having been confiscated and burned by the authorities at one point.

The paintings had titles like *The Island of Bal off the North Coast of China* and *Musical Landscape*. When you looked, it seemed to Billy, you couldn't see anything that resembled a place. Hints of a geography appeared in the undulating islands of color, but they teased the eye, suggesting a world beyond the waves or in some other dimension. One landscape seemed to emerge from crescendos of sound forming hills and valleys, melodies bringing out the flora and fauna, in strange and fanciful shapes, produced almost playfully. Nothing was anything you knew, but was suggestive of maybe a plant or an animal or a place where they flowed into one another and became something else. But when you left the picture, you felt you'd been somewhere, had a notion of what it might be like to live there, but without being able to say a word about it.

Billy was interested because he'd once made a stab at painting himself. This had started the summers he was in high school when Charlie Palmer, a sign painter, took him on as a helper. Most meticulous man he'd ever come upon. The first summer he wouldn't let Billy touch a sign till he himself had outlined all the letters and design. Then Billy could paint the insides, being careful not to get even one little snick of paint over the edge. The second summer it was the same, even though Billy had taken a course in lettering by correspondence and could do block letters and Gothic and Old English with the best of them.

He loved the work. He liked the bright colors and the smell of fresh paint. He liked dipping in his brush and laying on a clean stripe of color and then standing back and seeing all the stripes and colors grow into intelligibility. He liked small signs the best, and signs that featured a pair of glasses or a mortar and pestle or a bird like an owl or an eagle or an animal like a rabbit or a horse. But most of all, he admired the pictures that went on the windows of bars and cafes, and even certain stores, or on the sides of buildings and barns. His own first venture in that direction, his "Chew Mail Pouch Tobacco" on the side of Roscoe Stonecipher's barn was the triumph of his junior year.

By then Charlie's business had fallen off considerably, due to the combination of the growing popularity of neon and Charlie's unfortunate penchant for drinking during working hours. Billy's big moment came his senior year when Charlie fell off a ladder and broke his collarbone and wrist. There was an entire wall of a building to be painted: a soft drink advertisement with a mountain stream and trees under a brilliant sun and two happy people, a boy and girl, of course, looking at each other with the smile of discovery of what a soft drink can lead to. He had to paint all that. The thought alone was like a punch in the stomach. But Billy got hold of a book that told you how to lay things out in squares and he worked for a week on that building, fear on his tongue like acid.

When he was finished, the stream looked inviting and the landscape sparkled so convincingly under the sun that you could practically hear the birds twittering; and the young couple who'd discovered a world in a can of soda pop had their anatomies intact—proper hands and arms and legs and thighs that escaped any comparison to the wings and drumsticks of chickens. In one of his sober moments Charlie declared it a masterpiece. And folks around town said, "You're an artist, Billy. You got a real gift."

That fall he went to art school. Perhaps if he'd stuck to landscapes, which he liked, and painted pictures for his friends to hang on their living room walls, he might've done all right. But he wasn't in class for half an hour before he realized that his teacher and the rest of the students had a very different idea of Art. Though he spent a whole year trying, Art was something he couldn't quite get hold of, and eluded and led him on like a will-o'-the-wisp into a swamp.

For a time he thought you could get Art from the thoughtful application of a palette knife. Van Gogh had done all right and Rouault was no slouch. So he laid globs of color onto the canvas with the same kind of satisfaction as a mason laying on mortar. After which his teacher, with an arm around Billy's shoulder, would shake his head and say "Nice try, son," in a way that sent his heart down to his shoelaces.

Towards the end of the year, when to pass the course he had to exhibit five of his paintings, Billy was in a panic. For weeks he hadn't been able to do anything. Finally, applying Charlie Palmer's method, he got drunk and painted a picture over the weekend. That gave him four. It struck him as not bad, actually, maybe even one of his better efforts. But he had no time left to paint another and in desperation he went to his friend Sallie Briese, who was prolific and talented and who actually had among her canvases one that their instructor had not yet seen, done with the palette-knife technique. On the day of his presentation, Billy displayed this one as his latest piece of work. And his teacher, examining first one and then the next with his critical eye, worked his way to the final painting. "Well, Billy," he said, turning to him, "I see I've been wrong about you all along. This last one is really fine. And now that I see it with the rest, I understand the line of your development."

It was then that Billy turned to electricity, which was just as mysterious as anything that might be called Art, but at least you could deal with it in terms of wires and plugs. For a while he even fooled around with neon signs, devising ways of making the letters go on and off and dissolve into figures and scenes. But after a while he settled down to wiring, with a little carpentry thrown in. He was by then a married man, and had to earn a living. His philosophy took a more practical attitude towards life: if you can't screw it or plant flowers in it, you can always make it into a lamp.

Elena Triandophylos took great pride in the hotel's paintings and in the fact that the artist had lived there. In gratitude to the family for their hospitality, he had given them the paintings. In turn the family revered his memory, and kept intact his room on the third floor with all his possessions—his paints and chalks and easels and brushes, his books and clothes and letters. Nothing had been disturbed. Even when the hotel was full, nothing could have induced them to violate his room. Because Elena liked Billy and he showed great interest in the paintings, she took him and the boy up to the third floor, unlocked room 32 and let them walk around inside. Though it smelled like places usually do when they have long been closed up, there was still a hint of linseed oil and turpentine in the air, along with the suggestion that someone, having just stepped out, might come back to work on the half-finished canvas on the easel. The boy gazed at the tubes of paint lying on the table, looking as if he'd pick them up and handle them if nobody were around.

He had also, Billy noticed, taken quite a fancy to the paintings. Sometimes he stared at them, oblivious to what was going on around him, living for a moment on the Island of Bal and not in any hurry to come back. His favorite seemed to be one in which a group of unusual figures whirled about in the air, as though in the midst of some fantastic dance, while below them a young man in breeches and white shirt with ruffled collar was stoking a furnace with a shovel. Red hot coals glowed within. The painting was called *Look at the Angels!* And there they were, whirling around in the hot air, though they weren't like any angels Billy had ever seen.

He was curious about what was going on in the boy's head, but saved himself the trouble of asking. There was no harm in it. And Billy himself still had no idea what Art was, though he suspected this might be the genuine object. Maybe Art was made by damming up the stream you could never step in twice so you could stand in it all the time. It was the best he could come up with.

◆

The Reverend Ronnie Earl Hoskins had a vision of building a great city in the desert—building it out of the very mud of the earth itself. And all those who came to him, from south of the border as well as north, were set to work immediately making adobe bricks, which they shaped and dried in the sun. Their first task was to build a wall extending from the river to the old Indian burial ground, all around the Hill of Holies, going south and west in a half circle, taking in the old Dulsweet Silver Mine, where some thought there might be another vein of silver, and back to the river again. This activity had begun to make some people nervous; a few said it was illegal. But no one knew who was entitled to claim the property, the location of records being uncertain, the territorial authorities so bound with red tape it would take years and possibly generations for the legal machinery to move half an inch. Meanwhile, work on the wall continued. Rumor had it that the Reverend intended to make it a complete circle, taking in Old Town as well. Some of the residents suggested banding together to tear down at night what was built during the day, but others feared an opening of hostilities. The town sat waiting.

The Reverend himself seemed to be everywhere. He'd already been to the hotel once to shake hands with everybody in the carnival and say he hoped they'd see fit to visit him across the river the following Sunday. He didn't seem offended when Alta told him they weren't denominational folks, if that was all right with him. He claimed he wasn't either—that his message was for everybody, same as Jesus, and that he was not only broadcasting his message on a powerful beam into the U.S., but also translating it into Spanish for our friends and neighbors to the south. Each Sunday he proclaimed it in an old garage that served him as a church, which suited him, he said, and after all was no better than the facilities enjoyed by the One he served.

On the Friday after the carnival had arrived, a group of men appeared in the square in front of the hotel and began erecting a platform. On Saturday morning, a crowd began to gather, mostly from across the river, though some from Old Town came to satisfy their curiosity.

Then the Reverend himself appeared, rather like a rancher come to town—a tall, rangy, horse-faced man with a rough, weathered hide, looking as though he'd spent a good deal of time leaning into the wind. He was wearing Levis and a fancy tan-and-brown shirt with pearl buttons and a lamb embroidered on the back, and tooled lizard boots. Alta and Billy, out on the balcony, watched him move through the crowd shaking hands, clapping folks on the back, laughing and joking on his way up to the platform. Strong, Alta thought, wiry but strong. Could wrestle a calf to the ground without a hitch. She liked lean men, as a rule, and she could have admired the Reverend's energy if it hadn't been hooked up to a message. She noticed some young girls in the crowd who reached out to put a hand on his arm as he went past and turned for a direct shot of his smile. A little of the juice of joy. The gushing of the spirit. If I were younger, she thought, I might try my own brand of persuasion just for the hell of it. Just to see if he was proof against it. But the idea didn't enthuse her much. I've had enough trouble with men, she allowed, to last me the rest of my life. She wondered where he'd come from, when the spirit had moved him up this particular highway.

By the time he got worked up to give his spiel, Alta decided she'd had enough and went down to sit on the patio and look at the flowers. Billy retreated into his magic book. Donovan, who'd been making himself scarce, going off he wouldn't say where, had disappeared after breakfast. Only Curran lingered behind, having nothing better to do. He had gone outside to sit on a bench in the town square, interested to see that the boy was standing there in the crowd, wearing a t-shirt and ragged shorts, barefoot, his feet covered with dust, like any ragamuffin. He seemed absorbed in making lines in the dirt with his big toe. Curran wondered what he was doing. Probably listening, though. He had a way of listening as though he weren't, of observing when you weren't noticing him. Sneaky, Curran figured, not to be trusted.

Peculiar. Even so, he felt a growing fascination. Not only for the kid. Something else was struggling in his mind that he had not yet gotten hold of: the way certain people were bent on purpose, growing off in a certain direction like a tree branch. Maybe it showed up early, though not necessarily. For a time they might go on like everybody else, then suddenly they shot off into another space. Like Dusty. Like Rina and her garden. Maybe this fellow too. He was curious to know what had brought him to this platform, and what he had in mind.

First the Reverend told of the marvelous work that was being done, how many bricks had been made and how fast the walls were going up. He had a list of names and statistics. And one he kept referring to over and over—Little Josephine and how she'd made more bricks than anybody else. Now he wanted her to come up on the platform where everybody could see how frail a body held such great spirit. The crowd looked around in itself like a dog in search of a flea, and suddenly discovered in its midst a wizened little black woman, bent and worn by a life of labor, who shuffled up to the platform and was helped up the steps by eager hands. Then the Reverend held up to the crowd one of Little Josephine's hands, so they could see how gnarled it was, how swollen the knuckles were from arthritis. And then the Reverend asked her to tell how much she suffered from the pain and how stiff her fingers were every morning and how she couldn't even bend them until she'd soaked them in warm water. The old woman ducked her head and mumbled something Curran couldn't hear. Then she turned to the Reverend to see if she'd said what he wanted, was given a nod and a smile and then handed down the steps and lost in the crowd.

Now it was his turn: "Now maybe you folks are wondering what I'm doing here. And maybe you think here's somebody too big for his britches standing up here talking like he knows what's what. Because I know you're all good folks and are tired of the goings-on in this world of ours. And you're sick of high taxes and welfare cheaters and wild youths and muggers and unfaithful husbands and wives and hoodlums and big business and unions and warmongers and big government. That's why you're here. Because you've grown up knowing what's right and you want to live, and you want a little peace of mind, and you want to walk the streets without fear, and look in your pocketbook and find a little change left after you've put in your labor and paid all your bills. And that's what I want too."

A loud "Amen" came from the little wizened woman.

Then he went on to tell how he'd come to this place. He was a trucker, traveling the highways from New Jersey to Texas, Arkansas to California. And during the long nights when he was driving across plain and mountain, across hinterland and flat land of your land and mine, there were only the voices on the radio to keep him company, and there was only One there in the cab with him to keep up his spirits.

"And during the day," he went on, "there was nothing to break up the long stretches of road but gas stations and truck stops." And so he had gone from one truck stop to the next, putting diesel in his tank and food in his stomach, joking with the waitresses, bragging about his latest escape from the cops or moaning over bad luck on the highway. Till one day when he was trucking a load of chickens down to Ventura City, he stopped right here in New Town at a restaurant called the Loaves and Fishes, run by a commune, where the food was good and cheap and the people were friendly. And right then it struck him what he ought to be doing with his life: make a place big enough for all the folks who wanted to stop on the road and instead of filling up with just gas and hamburgers, fill up with spirit—park their rigs or station wagons long enough to pray and set their lives straight. And instead of toys and gimcracks on the counters, instead of potato chips and Snickers bars, there'd be cassettes of the Bible and pictures of Jesus debating the Pharisees, and manuals on improving your marriage and keeping your kids from sex and dope and alcohol.

Curran noticed that the boy had dropped down to his hands and knees and was working his way through the crowd like a dog, popping up here and there and staring up into the face of whoever he was next to. No one appeared to pay any attention to him, their eyes were all glued to the figure on the platform, taken up with the great truck-stop being built in their minds.

"Think of it, folks," the Reverend Hoskins went on, "when Jesus and the Disciples went out and gathered everybody together, just like you and me they all had to eat. Just regular folks camping out there, eating and sleeping and answering the call of nature. You got to eat —everybody knows that. So here we are, making a place where folks can come and put up for the night. And find friends on the road. And get away from the troublemakers and find peace. And build the Kingdom of Heaven."

The Reverend had opened the throttle all the way, shooting forward in high enthusiasm. But now there was a shift and a change. The boy stood up and was riveted to the spot. This was the one spot in the desert that was going to be safe, the Reverend was telling them, for the day of doom is upon us.

". . . h a i l . . . fire mingled with blood. Trees burnt up and the green grass. And that's what comes of setting off atomic bombs. 'And the sea became blood, and the creatures and the ships destroyed . . .' And that's what comes of throwing atomic waste in the ocean and polluting the waters. 'And there fell a great star from heaven burning as if it were a lamp . . .' And that's from our enemies getting control of outer space. 'And the bottomless pit shall open.' And that means the St. Andreas Fault is going to split apart and all the iniquity of Hollywood will fall in. 'And men killed by fire and smoke and brimstone.' And that means Mt. St. Helens is going off too. And earthquake and ruin . . ."

Curran had a sudden vision of dark fleeing hordes bumper-to- bumper across the highways, trying to reach the safe spot on the road. Maybe the Reverend and Dusty should get together. Then everybody would be happy. Curran looked around for the boy. But he had disappeared.

♦

Gall and misery and the taste of acid in the mouth: his whole soul the size of a walnut. Now that his body had begun to heal and the apathy in which he had lain for so long had lifted, laying bare his raw nerve, this was what he was reduced to.

Now that the acid was flowing through his veins and he was being eaten alive by his own thoughts, he wanted to cry out. Swear and curse; allow the furious winds to blast his obscenities to the four corners of the earth. For he was a man wronged, utterly wronged from the very beginning. No one would believe the injustice of it all. Consider his sacrifices, the way he had never spared himself, worked his butt off. All this time just trying to fulfill a public service. You had to entertain people or else they'd go bananas, that's what it amounted to.

Considering that they had to spend their whole lives in a cage, just trying to keep cans on the shelves and the dust off the furniture and the bill collectors from carting off the front porch. And after the show was over, they had to go back and look at the paint peeling off the walls and listen to grandpa's cough hacking through their dreams and the littlest kid whining to go pee-pee. But for that one little bit of time when they'd been taken out of all that, when they could pretend that the world was one great big beautiful splash of color, with girls swinging across the top of the tent and daring young men to meet them in mid-air, defying fear and laughing at the pull of gravity, thumbing their noses at death and time. Splendid creatures dancing on the backs of galloping horses, leaping with such grace as to snatch your breath away. Comical dwarfs and giants who could lift up a corner of the world. They were allowed to pretend that nothing else existed but this one great carnival: the miracle of being alive, truly alive for one moment in a gray and dreary swath of life. A moment of salvation.

So what if they were deceived—if after the show was over the giant and the midget pelted each other with insults that could have killed, and the girl who danced on the horses' backs had a husband who beat her? So what? That's what Dusty wanted to know as he started on his third whiskey of the evening, leaning against the wall in a corner of the hotel bar, watching the wash of reflection in the mirror, bottles of colored liquid blending into one another. So what if it was one great deception, one of Billy's sleights of hand? That's what they were asking for, wasn't it? They needed the lie. You betcha. Everybody did, let them say what they would. The truth was what killed you. Besides, the way he figured it, you needed the lie to do what you wanted to do anyway, but just didn't have the guts to admit to. Why else did people kill and conquer, violate and destroy? Always for excellent reasons. Always from the best possible motives. Always because it was the right thing to do. For the sake of the homeland. For the honor of wives and sweethearts. For the greater glory of the Grand Monkey-Monk. And once you'd got that all stashed in your brain, it was okay to go chasing around the world, fix your sights on some creature in the bush with a bone through his nose and either cure him or kill him for his own good. And then you could come back home busting your buttons, all swelled out with manly pride and a sense of duty done and figure on a ticker-tape parade with the folks lining the streets to give you the big hoorah. Probably buy you ten rounds of drinks and set you up in the insurance business—big-man exec, head of the whole shooting match—at the swish of a swizzle stick.

Now here they were doing the old thumbs down on him. The Almighty Himself, most likely. Dusty, my boy, you have done it— have you ever. Probably looking down at him out of the clouds, MISERABLE SINNER written across in skywriting.

But the truth was, he'd always had the public benefit at heart. Considering that the old John Q had to have the lie, considering some of the things done in the name of truth, weren't they better off for having somebody to distract them for a few hours? Get them to sit down inside a tent and keep them out of mischief. And if he, Dusty, had been trying to put together the biggest, most mind-boggling, eye-dazzling, skin-prickling, spine-tingling performances in the greatest carnival in the world, wasn't it because if you could throw yourself into one hell of a celebration, you might cross a threshold? He wasn't sure what sort, exactly, but you might take a leap like the astronauts on the moon and find yourself on the other side of who knows where?

And now look at him. Washed up. Not only a failure but a son-of- a-bitch in everybody's eyes. Alta's, Billy's. Their eyes telling him he'd sold out: the girl would have been a sacrifice to the perverted lust of thousands of viewers, secret viewers screening it all in the privacy of their sick, carpeted minds. Well, he hadn't been in on it. He hadn't understood . . . well, wouldn't believe it was to be a dirty deal from start to finish. When the guy had slipped him another ten grand and said, with a wink, "This is the flick to end all flicks. Here's your vacation money, friend," he still hadn't caught on. The money had temporarily cancelled out his power of understanding. They wouldn't do her any harm, he was convinced of that. Simulate a little rough stuff—no harm in that, provided it stayed in the realm of imagination. Didn't mean they were going to go off and do it. He hadn't let his own imagination roam any farther in that direction. No, it had already taken off with the loot and was on the way to his next extravaganza.

He looked up from his drink to where Leftheris was working behind the bar, leaning over in deep conversation with a couple of locals. Their faces wavered before his eyes. He tried to bring them into focus. See who was on hand to watch him rusting there. *Okay, look, you bastards,* he wanted to announce, interrupting their laughter. *Get your jollies over here. See the broken man. See the failure. Look—one more freak. Feed him some peanuts. See who's been made a monkey of—THE WORLD'S GREATEST MONKEY. Come on, folks, step right up.*

His eyes, making a slow sweep across what the evening offered, moving through the confused blur of faces, suddenly encountered another pair of eyes. They belonged to a tall man who wore a dark blue beret and whose bristling white sideburns and large untidy mustache, together with his fierce red-rimmed blue eyes, gave him an appearance of being both arrogant and distinguished. He had given Dusty a mere nod in passing. Dusty knew who he was, though as far as he was concerned he might as well have been a speck on the ceiling. Captain Valor, he was called, though whether or not he'd ever been in the army had never been subjected to the test of evidence. He claimed to be living on his pension. But his only real activity was drinking mescal, which he imported from Mexico in sufficient quantities to keep him somewhere in the territory between mellow and smashed. The only liquor, he declared, that was fit to drink.

The Captain took his first drink after breakfast, drank with his friends till lunch, paused for the comforts of the afternoon siesta, then took a drink before dinner to prime himself for the culminating encounter with the evening. He had taken on mescal like a champion wrestler, and stood in the midst of the struggle with a powerful endurance. Fought it to a draw. He didn't throw himself on the floor or in the street declaring that he was being attacked by demons, or fling out ropes of words, crazy and incomprehensible. He could claim a modest victory. He could hold his mescal. Which he was doing right now, entering into the final round. He had proved himself. But when their eyes met, the Captain had risen from his stool, come over to Dusty and said, "How about a drink—a man's drink?"

This was a challenge no man could refuse. And when Dusty had felt the hard burn on the inside of his mouth and what seemed like the effects of turpentine in the pit of his stomach, he sighed deeply and gave his benefactor a nod of gratitude.

"It is the only place left for a man," the Captain said, though Dusty wasn't quite clear what he meant. "A man of honor and courage," he went on. "Everything else is kaput," he said, with a downward jerk of the thumb.

Dusty nodded.

"Even war," he said. "Killing is a game with toys: atom bombs, nerve gas. But think of when you came up man to man—your sword, your lance, even your arquebus, your arrow ... Those were the days of giants, of lions and bulls. They've even taken all the glory out of war." He drank off his glass. "They've left us behind, wrecked and torn ... All we've got," he said, pouring both himself and Dusty another round, "are the old songs." And very softly he began to sing:

Old Soldiers never die,
They just fade away.

Dusty spent the night listening to war stories. The next day he and the Captain drank mescal. And the day after.

And they were men together.

♦

They had been at the Acropolis Hotel for more than two weeks before they discovered the letter. Every day they left their keys at the desk and went into the dining room for breakfast; every day they stopped at the desk at various times and picked up their keys and went to their rooms. And whenever they passed the desk, there was a letter leaning to one side in one of the cubbyholes. Finally, one morning Elena came hurrying into the dining room where they were still sitting over breakfast, the letter in her hand.

"For you," she said. "All this time and I didn't even think. My head is like a sieve. Forgive me."

She handed the letter to Dusty, who looked at it, then set it on the left-hand corner of the table without bothering to open it.

"Well, who's it from?" Alta cried, burning with curiosity as she watched him scan the postmark and the handwriting without a glimmer of interest. To think of a letter lying there waiting for them, when they hadn't themselves known where they'd be—it was quite incredible.

And how should such a letter be described? Suppose that someone could step forward and make the brag of having a full knowledge of its history, of knowing the various accidents affecting it through time, the marks imprinted by the circumstances acting upon it, could give such testimony as only the object itself could make, were it given voice. Or perhaps one who could read its history as one reads a man's face —one who for instance could pick up a string of amber beads and see the face of the digger of stones on the Bosporus and know the haunted, the hunted, self-seeking, pleasure-hungry, generous succession of wearers and bearers eager for ornament or possession; one who, upon fingering the beads, admiring their beauty, could see in the glow struck by the light the colors and emotions of the lives they had passed through. One who could know about this letter.

From the outside it was easy enough to describe—a long envelope with a yellowed end from having sat too long where time and sunlight could age the paper. An old envelope such as one would turn up after a haphazard search on the rare occasion of writing a letter. The address scrawled in a hand afflicted with a tremor, and addressed to Dusty the Manager, c/o Carnival for the Gods,

Ventura City, Seven Cities Territory. There is a certain ingenuousness in the hope that such a letter will reach its destination. It came to Ventura City after the carnival itself had limped away, sent without so much as a return address or a "Please Forward" written on it. The postman who took it out for delivery also brought it back.

There was on the part of the Post Office no further obligation than to mark it Undeliverable and send it on to the Dead Letter Office. But the postman in this case, a lanky young man who knew everyone on his route and such circumstantial aspects of their lives as the location of their relatives, their divorces and financial business, their jobs, their friends, their psychiatrists and chiropodists, and even in some cases, their palm readers and astrologers, and who was, as he handed them the mail, delighted to tell them who their letters were from and to read them the contents of any postcards as he stood there on the stoop— "Your Aunt Helen is having a wonderful time in Hawaii," he'd say —this young man was afflicted with more imagination than his profession required. Beyond that, he had an almost religious awe for the unknown contents of an envelope—simply because they were unknown, therefore mysterious, open to speculation, the sense of possibility. The arrival of a letter was an act of fate: it could change your life.

What's more, the young man was an avid reader of mysteries, and fancied himself as something of a detective. He enjoyed looking at a letter and divining its contents, then the next day, as he stood on the porch with the recipient, try through a set of oblique and carefully framed questions to corroborate his guess. He liked tracking people down when they'd moved without leaving a forwarding address. Whatever he didn't know he readily took the pains to find out. Knowledge, he was fond of saying, is putting a letter in the right hands. He hadn't known anything of Dusty or the carnival, but something rang a bell when he saw a poster advertising a reward for an escaped tiger. And he was able to track down Sam, who told him to go to hell, cursing Dusty and the rest of the carnival with such an exquisite choice of foul language that it sounded like the recital of pure poetry, and for final emphasis throwing an empty beer can to encourage his retreat. Still undaunted, the postman discovered a fellow at a filling station who'd seen a giant get out of a trailer to buy a candy bar while a midget filled the tank with gas. Such a pair did not cross his path every day; they had to belong to a carnival. And where could they be going but in the direction of Old Town? And since the only place to send a letter in Old Town was the Post Office, which was the Acropolis Hotel, the postman sent it there.

It arrived on a rainy day, and by the time the postman handed it to Elena, two drops of water had fallen on the edge of the address, smearing the ink, so that the *D* of Dusty looked as though it were being blown by the wind. Now the letter awaited them, carrying the intention of the sender mated with the purposes and decisions of those whose hands it had passed through, who unconsciously contribute to or thwart the original intention, which can break into existence like a match struck, flaming gratuitously. Thus such a letter seems affected with memory, freighted with destiny. As perhaps all things are.

At any rate, it was Alta finally who tore it open, after her curiosity, and Dusty's apathy, had become a form of mental torture. The first thing she noticed was that the lines leaned down the page somewhat drunkenly and the words were difficult to make out.

"My friend," she read,

I am full up to here with orange juice in the state of Arizona. Busted the front end of my late model Cadillac trying to get past a milk truck. Am experiencing a shortage of cash. Knowing you have struck it rich with the greatest little gold mine this end of the continent, you will remember your old friend who has made you the best deal to his own disadvantage you could ever find.

A downright swindle, some would say, letting go of a valuable piece of property what could have made him a powerful fortune on which to retire for life. So thinking of your old friend while lying in the lap of luxury, which you will want him likewise to enjoy with a suitable cut of the profits, please send thereof, c/o General Delivery, Phoenix, Arizona within thirty days upon receipt. Appropriate action will otherwise be taken.

Yours truly,
Priam Gillespie

She read the letter twice, slowly, trying to make her way past the abominable scrawl, the slanting lines, the twisted syntax, to clear an understanding through innuendo, accusation and downright fantasy to some underlying element of reality.

"Who's this Priam Gillespie?" she demanded.

"What do you mean?" Dusty said.

"It's from him, you idiot. Why else would I ask?"

"What does he want? Not that I give a damn."

She read the letter aloud.

"He's drunk or crazy," Dusty said. "Probably both. He was Grace's manager when she was doing her act up at the theater back in that little one-horse town where we broke down."

"I figured as much," Alta said. "Some manager." So a lot of loot had changed hands. And now he wanted some more. The old buzzard. The old greedy-guts. She could see him, guzzling booze, reeling around in his Cadillac, money spilling out of his pockets while the girls clustered around him picking up the loose change, waiting for him to buy them a good time, if that's what you could call having one.

"Well, if he wants something," Alta said, "let him come and get it. He'll have me to deal with." And she tore the letter in two and threw it into a waste basket behind the desk, completing its history.

◆

From where he was standing, on a chair beside the window in his room on the ground floor, Curran could see the two of them out in the garden, the old woman in the long, flowing wrapper she always wore in the morning and, but for the fact he was moving, a fellow you might mistake for a scarecrow. He was not only tall and scrawny, with big hands and huge knuckles, and not only had scraggly red hair, an untidy mustache and a crooked chin, but also looked as though he'd grabbed the first clothes he'd seen off the discard pile: pants so faded and raveled round the edges that they were a kind of no-color gray; a rope around his middle to hold them up; a formerly plaid shirt with the pocket ripped off, revealing a patch of the original colors. Curran wondered if he too were looking for visions, another of your mental travelers.

For only a few days before, another fellow had turned up and wandered around Rina's garden seeking instruction. That fellow was lean and tanned, with the grace of a panther, and he was deep into the mysteries of vibrations and dowsing and out-of-body experiences. He wanted Rina to tell him which herbs might further his efforts. And for several mornings Curran had watched him kneeling over the clumps of greens in various herb beds with a look of concentration and perhaps inspiration, a bandana tied around his head, black hair curling out from beneath, the picture of health in his dark blue Bermuda shorts and white socks. He claimed to be a full-blooded Blackfoot Indian. After several days of Rina's instruction, and with a basket full of various herbs, he had climbed back into his Chrysler and driven off.

But this fellow looked as though he needed a good meal more than anything else. Otherwise he might be out of his body soon enough and for good. He hunkered down holding Rina's basket while she bent over her herbs, picking off dead leaves, watering them, talking to them like children. "Ah, my beauty, you've come a long way. Keep up the good work." Soon her basket would be piled high with vegetables and herbs of one sort or another to contribute their flavors to one of her salads—fresh dill and basil and thyme, a dash of nasturtium to give a bit of tang to the palate, all of it topped by red and yellow nasturtiums, brilliant as a celebration, a work of art.

Curran watched the two of them till they wandered out of hearing. Then, slipping down from the chair, making sure the door of his room was locked, he dug out a bound book from the bottom of his bureau, settled himself at his desk and opened it.

It was a secret, this book. He had bought it several years before in a bookstore in Truth or Consequences, New Mexico—a volume of plain white pages with a leather cover. *Write your own book,* the advertisement had invited. He had intended to keep a running account of their travels, for he had a tendency to forget where they had been from one year to the next. Everything ran together like melted ice cream, and the unreliability of memory had led him and Donovan into furious quarrels, in which Donovan always claimed victory. What Curran wanted were the facts, so that in the midst of one of these embranglements, he could produce the notebook with a triumphant flourish. "Hah, look at that." And the giant would be quashed with a few strokes of the pen.

Indeed, he had made a noble, if short-lived, effort. Several pages at the beginning listed towns and cities, the dates and lengths of their gigs, brief mentions of accidents along the way, and a few comments about the size of the crowds and the success of the act. The last entry had been in Trinidad, Colorado, which they had reached by the Raton Pass, wondering if their brakes would hold out long enough to take them through the mountains. He had written nothing for over a year.

But something had happened to him. In some ways, it had come from what he had known all along, from being with Dusty and Alta and the others who had come and gone: Carnaby the Great, Sam the animal trainer, Eva the belly dancer, Lila the Fat Woman—all those who had been bent into a certain shape and destined, it seemed, to live in a certain way. This was the mystery that lay behind the idiosyncrasy that beckoned to him now. He had, in a sense, experienced a kind of inspiration. If he had traveled to its source, he might have said it came from his night of dread and uncertainty in the sculpture garden. The images that had held him uneasily in thrall, evoking sensations he had never experienced before and could not define afterwards, had created a hollow space, as though a window had been thrown open to a new set of susceptibilities. And what he had dimly recognized in the past was now connected to what was going on in the present. He was particularly struck by the scene in the square: the so-called Reverend Hoskins striking his pose, giving his word. But maybe even more by the kid standing there watching him.

An idea had been born: everything was peculiar. And from that foundation came the flow of his speculations. Primo: Life threw you into a body, gave you certain equipment with instructions for use and thus all creatures were made peculiar by their form. A cow was not a mouse, nor was a cockroach a hummingbird. And to be any of these things was to be immediately marked by its peculiarity. So with birds and fishes and plants. All this he had stated by way of introduction. And thus the experiences of the tiger were marked by their peculiarity, as seen, for instance, by a hummingbird, who would find those predatory interests freakish, and could never appreciate the joys of the hunt. Likewise the boredom of the tiger with a grain of mustard seed. All of this was, of course, obvious—merely a prologue to his real subject.

With human beings the issue became much more complex. Take himself, for example. In physical terms he was defined as peculiar by his stature. As he looked back on it, his efforts to measure the parts of his body, to identify himself as a midget instead of a dwarf, were laughable. No, he had been entirely on the wrong track, though in fact, at the beginning, he had made several notations on physical peculiarities. One of the locals had exhibited the largest ears with the most pendulous lobes he had ever seen. And he had frequently observed the size and frequency and coloration of the moles on Donovan's back. But these were incidentals.

The larger truth, he had come to believe, was that every man was a hidden source of peculiarity, delivering itself sometimes obviously, but more often in the odd corner and the barely submerged tip, in the sudden opening and the startling projection. Only forget the shared semblance in the human form, which was more a matter of abstraction and arithmetic, and there it was: each man his own freak. And it had been given to him to record the nature of the specimens he came upon—to open up the subject for the edification of the public, to bring the collective mind to an enlarged vision.

Thus his book: *The Book of Fascinations*. Subtitled: *An Inquiry into the Nature of the Peculiar.*

He was pleased with the title. He was struck with humble satisfaction by what had been given to him to do. He would take pains. He would work with the diligence of the scientist, the philosopher's passion for truth. He would celebrate his own peculiarity along with others'. He acknowledged that Ripley had been a pioneer in the field, offering his collection of oddities for the sake of public belief. Now it remained to discover the various avenues and manifestations, repetitions and variations, permutations and combinations. He had set down two large divisions of mankind: of the body and out of the body. Rina belonged to the first; the Indian to the second. Both plant types. There were bird types and fish types. Each with their unique organs of sensibility.

Rina. Plant type: distinguished by keenness of nose, tongue and fingertips. Mental life: scent of woodbine, lemon balm, verbena. Taste of chamomile and hibiscus, the soothing sweet—all the way to nasturtium and garlic. A tough old weed herself, more in touch with the virtues of plants, the essences of vegetables than most.

Alta and Dusty were bird types. Wanted to fly high on the wing. In the body. Had begun like hawks; now grounded like chickens.

About himself he was not yet quite clear. Bird type, maybe: small and quick, in and out. But peering into dark comers. More like a mole, maybe, smelling out the hidden, digging into the depths, feeling his way through some other sense—the vision of the blind.

While he worked, the light was increasing to a soft splendor, bringing the lilies and geraniums in the stone patio to the full intensity of their color. From the kitchen in the other wing came the sounds of preparations for lunch. Rina and Leftheris had spent the morning making little pies filled with spinach and cheese, empanadas with meat inside, and a large pot of beans. Now it was time for lunch. Time to see what specimens had washed up on the shore, so to speak. For lunchtime, and evenings as well, brought in not only those who lived or squatted in the houses around, but those who might be wandering through.

Time to quit. He closed the book and went to put it away in the lower drawer of his bureau. For a moment he stood with the book in his hands, imagining the pages filled with his words. He could imagine the words printed, published, brought to the attention of a grateful world. Reviews. Advertisements. Interviews. Talk shows. Lectures. Symposia. Debates. Awards and citations. Honorary degrees. He could see the billing: THE MIGHTY MITE—WORLD's FIRST MIDGET PHILOSOPHER.

♦

When Curran entered the lunch room, he looked around for the fellow he'd seen out in the garden, but was disappointed. He had to make do with a passing tour of cyclists—shorts and T-shirts, tanned arms and muscled thighs—and two young women with their children, whom he had already seen. The women had watched the cyclists come in, staring at them with the boldness of local folks looking over strangers, and then with the candid interest of women looking over men. One in particular drew their attention, and their eyes roved over his body as they admired him. They leaned forward, exchanged their findings in audible whispers: "What a build . . . have you ever seen such a nice ass? . . . I like them thin."

One of the children was making a mess with her soup. The other, an energetic boy of ten, was telling his mother's friend about Kenny Paissac's birthday party, the highlight of which had been a hair- pulling fight between Kenny's mother and Rita Veronica. It had started when Kenny and Mickey got into an argument about whose dad could beat whom. The parents were sitting around drinking beer. Kenny's mother and Rita Veronica also wanted the men to prove who could beat whom, and settled on an arm-wrestling contest. Kenny's father won. Rita Veronica claimed foul play. The men went off to drink beer by themselves. The women shouted insults. Then charged. Pulled each other's hair. Fell to the ground. Rolled around. The men separated them.

Curran sat reflecting over his lunch. Alcohol raised the peculiar to its next stage: greater volatility. The body types became more physical, the others more ethereal. He made a note on his paper napkin. He'd seen it happen in the bar—that great observatory of human behavior. He noticed, looking up, that one of the women could raise one eyebrow without affecting the other, like a golden retriever. Good for the quizzical, for the sad, the skeptical. He noted this as well.

The adventures of the birthday party were not yet over. While the fight was in progress, Kenny took the bow and arrow he'd gotten as a present and shot into the air. The arrow came to earth in Mrs. Polansky's chicken coop and killed a rooster. Mrs. P entering upon the scene with dead chicken. Yelling. Curses and accusations flying like arrows. Kenny hiding in the bushes. Mrs. P demanding payment for the chicken. Suggestion from somewhere of chicken soup. Agreed. End of altercation. End of birthday party.

The two mothers went on to Rita Veronia. A wild woman. Had set the place on fire once. Nearly burned it to the ground. Always drunk. Been a Buddhist, then a New Seeker. Once a model in Laguna Beach (before she got fat). A psychic told her she had been a holy woman in another life. The Reverend Hoskins was trying to convince her to become one in the here-and-now. They didn't trust the Reverend. He was up to something, they were convinced of it. Wanted control. Was sending round rumors about the lesbians, about how they were corrupting the population. Wanted to run them out. A nasty man.

Maybe it was true, and maybe it wasn't. Or part of it was true and part made up. You never knew. Curran found it impossible to judge. There weren't all that many people around, and every day they had to see each other and find out about each other: what had happened during the day or night and where their lives were now. They had to keep track of each other like they'd lose something of themselves if they didn't. And if a newcomer happened on the scene, that was a great thing. For he could add a new ingredient to the stew. Till his story had been taken in with the rest, become familiar and therefore dull, bleached out with telling like an old piece of cloth. Until something else happened. And if it didn't, Curran had observed, and the dullness went on, then people said things as if they *had* happened. And there was hardly a one walking around who didn't have some piece of life attached to him he didn't know he'd lived.

Just then he saw Donovan, his great bulk blocking the doorway for a moment before he strode in, looking neither left nor right. Ignoring him. Something on his mind. He went over and sat at the counter. Wanted to be alone. Which was okay by him, Curran decided, though he felt just a bit miffed. He reminded himself of his task.

Peculiar business going on, he was sure of it. For over a week he'd watched Donovan poking around in Rina's garden. And Curran knew the reason. Just from a casual remark Rina had made that a number of familiar herbs and common vegetables were aphrodisiacs. Donovan had never shown any interest in herbs and vegetables. For all the years Curran had known him he'd been essentially a meat-and-potatoes man. Now he ate salads choked with tomatoes and onions; plates piled with beans; thyme, basil and rosemary by the handfuls. And eggs, lots of eggs.

In the evenings he tended to disappear.

Body type, Curran noted—with a vengeance. No wonder: he had more of it than anybody else.

His pencil tore the paper napkin, and he had run out of space. He'd have to give Donovan at least a page in his book, he decided.

◆

That evening when Curran came into the bar, he carried a small notebook in his pocket. He would've liked to sit at the bar, but perched on a stool he felt vulnerable, precarious—particularly since even a little alcohol went quickly to his head. A shot of bourbon sent him reeling; gin was his demise. Usually he ordered a beer and drank half, for beer tended to make him feel bloated. He chose a table where he could see everything but remain unobtrusive, where the light was dimmer, where he could sneak out his notebook without drawing inquisitive and, very likely, contemptuous notice: Say, what are you writing there? Another *Gone with the Wind?* Hah, you'll be famous yet! Let them snicker—he'd get his.

For now he was the small bird darting in and out, noticing, picking up bits of incident like seed, recording. Himself too small to be noticed. They would see and dismiss him. But he would soak them up like a sponge. Observe like a child observing the adult world, seeing more than they knew.

The first part of the evening was always the same: Leftheris setting up the bar, wiping glasses and ashtrays, counting change for the cash register, setting out bowls of popcorn. When things got going, he worked hard, mixing drinks, setting them up, rushing around serving, refilling glasses. Then, towards the end of the evening, people had to get up and make their own drinks as he sat laughing and joking with his *compadres.* He loved company, and the girls—wasn't he one for the girls. He loved to tease and flirt, while voices assailed him from all sides:

"Quit flirting with the girls, Leftheris—I'm dry as a bone."

"Get us a drink before you break all their hearts."

"If we don't get drunk, you'll never get rich."

"And we'll never get poor."

"Don't count on it—he might get richer if we didn't get drunk."

"Speak for yourself."

"Can't you see I'm busy—my eyes, my heart."

"Your jaw—that's the only thing working overtime."

"Too busy for boozing! My boozing, that is. Is this how you run the joint? Get us a drink, Leftheris."

But before it reached this point of the evening, Reynaldo and Chico would wander in with their guitars, for they were fond of singing, and people bought them drinks in exchange for songs. Both were revolutionaries and dreamed of utopia, and each had his own intensely held convictions. Curran had listened more than once to Reynaldo, who had leaned toward him, a solid tower, small mouth solemn in his square face, as he told him that civilization was one great big con. Curran was much intrigued by that line of argument, as he admired Reynaldo's sideburns and dark beard.

"And do you know why," Reynaldo had asked him. "It is because of being right-handed. Yes, they get everybody to be right-handed and then they can control you. It is control, not freedom." He clenched his fists, gritted his teeth.

"The world, the whole world, is set up for right-handed people," he went on. "They have them all conned. And they never know it. While they are children, too young to protest, they start in—everything on the right. Which means everything that is right. And then, you see, they march along like robots, never questioning. One two, one two." And he bent from side to side to demonstrate.

"But there are left-handed people," Curran had objected one evening.

Reynaldo threw up his hands in exasperation. (Volatile: body type on the verge of flying off.) "Oh, they can let a few," he said. "But don't you see, see with your very eyes—" pulling down the corners of his eyelids, exposing the blood-shot whites, leaning forward right into Curran's face so that the midget was nearly overcome by his beery breath. "That's to fool us, it's part of the con."

But in the new world—ah, the new world—no one would be forced, no one made to deny his birthright. And everyone would be *free*.

"And in the New World—" This time it was Chico's voice, which was soft, almost feathery, almost too ethereal for speech—"prostitutes would not be illegal. For do you know why they are illegal?" Curran hazarded a guess, pulled it out of the blue: "To keep the police busy."

"You're on to something, friend."

"Otherwise they'd make too much money."

"Of course—exactly right. Now they must hand it over to the pimps, to the cops. Cheated out of free enterprise—you see it also. Ah, friend, you are one of us. In this capitalist society, all the wealth would go to the prostitutes if there were no control. And that is the big secret no one wants to admit, but which every capitalist and politician knows."

After they had discussed the evils and injustices, they would sing one of their songs of tender longing, of lovers kept separated by stony-hearted parents, of the brutality of war and the cruelty of the elements. And always in voices rich with melancholy, Reynaldo's a rumble like distant thunder, Chico's insistent as a soft rain, they sang:

O Corazon, mi Corazon
Tu me has desechado,
Tu me has matado

Y mis huesos blanqueados
Brillan en la noche
Debajo la luna.

Then Captain Valor, whose level of mescal by this time admitted something of the pugnacious into his silence, would bring down his fist on the bar. "Goddamn that cat's yodel. It's enough to take the fight right out of a man." And then he'd sing a song of his own.

Curran sat drumming the table with his fingers while the Captain waved his glass and sang:

I wish that all girls were whales
In the ocean
And if I were a seaweed
I'd show them all the motion.

He downed the liquor and launched into the refrain:

Oh, roll your leg over
Oh, roll your leg over
Oh, roll your leg over
The man in the moon.

By the time he was growing hoarse with his third song, everyone had turned back to his own drink and conversation. Reynaldo and Chico again took up their guitars and started "*O Corazon, mi corazon,*" perhaps in protest.

Curran was bored. Bored with social theories and dirty songs and idiot laughter—the camaraderie of the bar stool. People with their ideas loose: sprouting them like cabbages, sprouting them like geysers, swinging from them like monkeys in the liana. He was bored with all of it. He saw Dusty come in and take his place alongside the Captain. Buddies. Big guns set to get drunk and disgusting together. Leftheris would have to cart both of them off to bed, two great awkward sacks, two moaning swell-guts.

Half his beer drunk, bored out his mind, Curran was just about to leave when he saw the scarecrow, the stick who'd been in Rina's garden that morning. He stood looking over the scene as though it were populated with strange beings who, though not of his kind, might offer a certain entertainment. He didn't seem uncertain, but unabashedly curious. Friendly enough, he appeared to Curran, almost mindlessly harmless—possibly a danger to himself. Curran motioned for him to come over and sit at his table.

The fellow gave a little jerk of his head and a wave of the hand, as though Curran's was the very sign he had been waiting for, and came over and sat down like an old friend. "Quite a crowd they be having here," he said.

"Haven't seen you in here before," Curran observed. "Care for something to drink? I've had half of this beer and that's my fill." "You be no-going to drink it? Shamely to be letting it go to waste," he said, looking wistfully at the can.

Curran pushed the can in his direction. It came to him that here was a man who could not afford to waste anything. Curran watched as he tilted back his head and drank with pleasure.

"Where do you live," Curran asked, trying to figure out what spot of earth had bred the strange speech he was hearing, the strange presence before him.

"Over by the Hill of Holies there be a shed abandoned. It be a good place," he said. "Nor leaking be the roof nor rats hold sway. It do no-take much to live. See these clothes mine? Thawn away in the trash. Somebody thinking they be wored out. But me they fit. And food that otherway be going to waste. Bread people be calling stale, fruit going soft with spots. I live so as wasting no to be." He leaned forward eagerly: "Do you no be thinking that there be terrible waste in the world?"

"Yes," Curran agreed.

"Think if all be small like you," the young man said, "the more little food we all be eating."

This was the first time his stature had been an object of admiration. Curran was enchanted. He signaled for another beer, another glass, to further their communion.

"There be waste everywhere," his friend continued. "Once I be living in Ventura City on what the stores thawn away: fine fruits with only a few dark spots, leaves of lettuce only a little browning, cans of dented sides, meat with odors. All good to eat." Indeed he might have been describing a feast.

And though the fellow was certainly skinny, he looked healthy enough. And cheerful. His life seemed to agree with him. Though Curran had heard often enough of people forced by poverty to live in such a fashion, he'd never known anyone who'd chosen to make it a way of life.

"There be waste everywhere," his companion went on. "What do we use a bedroom for? To be asleep in. Think of a bed that be all the day lying empty, of no use, no one to lie in it. Or a house of which the people be going away from it all the day long. It be standing there, collecting only mortgage payments and rents and repairs. All its maybes sifting off in the wind."

Curran agreed. Except for the trailer he and Donovan traveled in, he'd never owned anything to speak of. Except his suits—he was a bit vain about his suits. Never wanted anything, he told himself. Though perhaps only out of sour grapes, because there seemed for him nothing in life worth having. He had no debts, and supposed that was a good thing.

He saw Billy Bigelow headed toward them with a glass of beer in hand. He hoped Billy wouldn't interfere with the conversation. But as Billy sat down his companion simply nodded and went on. He seemed to have gotten up a head of steam and another presence meant another listener.

"And to pay the rent you be needing a job, and to have a job, you be needing a car. I be seeing it all in Ventura City," he said and then, in a voice that carried the ring of prophecy, "and more and worse be coming to pass."

"You think so?" Billy said. "Will we all be going up in a cloud of smoke?"

The stranger shook his head, gazing at him as at a man of limited imagination. Curran was utterly absorbed—he wished he could be writing it all down in his notebook.

"Bad it be that civilization be destructing itself in its own wasteliness. Food and water and air. But worse-more—" He leaned forward as though not to be overheard: "We be using up the gravity as well."

"The gravity?" Billy said, full of wonder.

The stranger nodded solemnly. "Weaker every year."

"How do you explain that," Curran asked.

"Many and many the skyscrapers pulling against the earth," he said, raising his hands to indicate the multitude. "Many and many the jet planes. And the rockets," he went on. "Each time one goes up, it be like pulling the stopper from the bathtub. Gravity be nearly exhausted."

"How do you *know?*" Billy demanded.

Curran suppressed a grin. A famous first: Billy trying to catch up with somebody a leap ahead of him.

"Already New York do no-exist longer."

"New York no longer exists?" Billy said. "I've been thinking so for a long time. But tell me how you know."

"Once I be going to New York. But I be no-able to get there. The plane be no-going."

"They cancelled the flight," Curran asked.

He nodded. "All flights. And be taking us to Buffalo."

"Because of the weather?"

"That be the claim. But planes be no-going the next day. And my suitcase they be sending to Baltimore."

"But flights are frequently cancelled because of weather."

"The old sayso—the official this-so and that-so, which all adds up to no-so."

"You have a good way of putting things," Billy said, "but all you've told us is you couldn't get there."

"But you be meeting people who say they live in New York. And you know how they be, smiling and embarrassed or puffed up like politicians. They shrink or they swagger."

"So?"

"It be because they can no-tell the truth. It be the great secret they be swearing to no-tell. Or there be panic of the populace. They do no-live in New York, because New York where it be, only a hole remains, sometimes covered with snow."

"And where did it go," Billy asked.

"Up," the stranger said, gesturing in the direction of the clouds. "The earth could no-hold it longer, gravity be so weak there."

"But the newspaper articles. The politicians running for office," Curran objected. "Wall Street stocks and banks and all the stores and businesses." It excited him to imagine their non-existence.

"Business!" he said, with a snort. "My friend onetime be sending me a check on a New York bank—big bank. No funds. And the politicians. Do you no-see? They be lining their pockets, all the time claiming the funds be going to New York. Then every now and then a newspaper be writing that the city be going bankrupt, so nobody be asking questions."

"And the arts and culture?" Curran ventured.

The stranger shook his head. "That be the final proof."

Billy and Curran exchanged looks. "The whole thing up in space," Billy said, going along with it. "Think of that."

"Los Angeles be next," the stranger predicted. "If the St. Andreas Fault no-be first. And Chicago no-far behind. First the buildings begin to loosen like old teeth in their sockets. And the roots of the trees let go. All being sucked up. Even the very tombstones and all the dead lying under the ground," he said with a gleam in his eye. He seemed to be looking off into space, seeing whole cities.

Nor was he distracted by the lively song Reynaldo and Chico had launched into, strumming their guitars with gusto. A few drinks had released them from the hopelessness of their love. Inspired by their example, the Captain also had launched into another of his bawdy songs, and their voices clashed in drunken abandon.

"Meanwhile, it might help me in my business," Billy reflected. "An up without a down. Send things up and away they go."

"Then it wouldn't be magic anymore," Curran reminded him. "You'd have to concentrate on *down.*"

"It'd be a challenge," Billy said.

"Soon it be needful to be wearing shoes of iron," their companion went on, and down-chain the houses at the comers. It be the coming of the new Iron Age. Before it be too late the skyscrapers must come down and the rockets and the jets abandoned."

Curran was fascinated, and itching to get to his pencil and notebook. He had come across one of his finest specimens to date. Then it occurred to him that though they'd been sitting together for half the evening, he had no idea who the fellow was.

"Tell me your name," he said.

"Do you be having a piece of paper?"

Curran pulled out his notebook and opened it to a blank page. He handed it to him with his pencil and watched the fellow print his name with intense concentration. When he handed him back the notebook, Curran looked down and saw written there:

Quam' bukqueau

"How do you pronounce it?" Curran had the sense to ask.

"Buck," he said, "for Buck Rogers."

"The spelling of the future?" Billy said, taking his turn to look at it.

"Something of it," said Quam'bukqueau. "Being now time for departure," he said, standing up, shaking hands with both of them. "Being that you come to visit me, I be telling you of my work. The old shed," he reminded Curran, "by the Hill of Holies." He wove his way through the tables, turned, waved, and abiding by his own laws of gravity, took off into the night.

♦

From where he sat in the garden, Donovan could tell that Curran was spying on him. Every now and then he could see the curtain move, and once he caught a glimpse of the midget's shadow. Knowing that he was being watched, Donovan stretched luxuriously in the chaise lounge. He'd give him a good show if that's what he wanted. If he excited envy, so much the better. Let the little shrimp eat his heart out. He wondered what the little schemer was up to. Then he let out a laugh: he should care. Great God! He'd never had it so good, now that he'd been taken up by the Angelic Hostesses.

This was a commune that had taken over some of the empty houses on the edge of town, a group of women who had modeled themselves upon the principles of Gurdjieff. Some were lesbians who, wishing to have babies, practiced their own artificial insemination. Others were widows and other lonely women seeking companionship and sharing a dedication to social service. For the women took in travelers who needed shelter, nursed the sick and took care of an elderly couple who had spent their lives in the town.

Among the women, Donovan had found three—two widowed and one recently divorced—who not only adored him but also loved to cook. One was a redhead; one a succulent little blonde; the third a tall, elegant woman with dark hair that flowed down her back. The redhead was magnificent with pastries, but always had terrible luck with her pie crusts. The blonde had no patience with anything made of yeast, but the range of her pies was formidable: chocolate cream, French apple, pecan, even green tomato. And her meringues stood at least four inches high.

Today, however, belonged to Dolores, and he had requested a chocolate cake. A rich devil's food, with waves and little peaks of marshmallow icing. As he envisioned the pleasure of it, and that of Dolores herself, he lay watching the hotel's calico cat sneaking through the garden. For a moment she hid in a shrub, then came leaping out as if to attack an unsuspecting bird or rodent. Then she crept among the plants, springing out here, concealing herself there. Stretching like a cat himself, allowing himself an indolent yawn, Donovan watched her while the sunlight played on the leaves.

Meanwhile Curran was watching. Suppose, he thought, each kind of creature invented itself out of some little hotbed of activity. Maybe it all began with the head, he decided, the point that exchanged greetings with the world—the essential thing . . .

"Hello-o."

Donovan sat up, blinking. There she was, and the cake she held was beyond all expectation. "Why, it's a masterpiece!" he said.

"Three layers," she said with pride. "Dark and rich, from real German chocolate and black coffee. And a whole pound of walnuts ground as fine as you can get them. And whipping cream for the second layer. And a fudge icing on top."

"Just the thought of it makes my mouth water. But come sit down here under the umbrella. Would you like coffee or tea or lemonade to drink with this luscious creation?"

But there would have to be, Curran was thinking as he looked enviously at the cake, a system to keep the head alive. He pictured a creature shaped rather like a bowling pin or a cello, with a place for food to come in and go out—the abdomen like a large bowl, the chest shaped like a cover. The head—on guard, looking over a chocolate cake perhaps. It may be that the whole thing had begun with a stomach, trying to keep itself alive; the head representing nature in her most advanced technology.

Donovan went into the kitchen and returned with a tray with cups and coffee pot, plates, knives and forks. He and Dolores sat down cozily at the umbrella table, and while he looked on expectantly she cut the cake and gave him a generous slice. Though she was more than a foot shorter than he was, she was still a tall woman, and in some ways his favorite. He liked to have a woman he could talk to in bed. She smiled at him as she handed him the plate.

"It was George's favorite," she said. "The icing is a special secret. Can you taste the rum?"

"Ummm."

Yes, Curran thought, the alimentary canal. It was all being stuffed with chocolate cake. The head was definitely an afterthought. Donovan would've been happy in his present state even without arms and legs. Curran wondered if he was looking at a throwback in the evolutionary process. Just as, he postulated, the fellow who sometimes wandered into the hotel might be the wave of the future. People, in fact, referred to him as The Head, for he had become so fascinated with the workings of his own mind that the rest of his body seemed only an accessory to keep it afloat. He had dropped acid and done mescaline and peyote, and the whirl of images had fascinated him, like a movie running all day: sound, color, shape, meeting and merging so that sounds made colors in his mind and the colors formed patterns, figures in the flood, some monstrous and others appealing. He said he thought the mind was a sorcerer's well, a conjuring trick, a ring around the rosy, a gigantic flea circus, the tail of a comet chasing itself among the fractious sparks and particles of burning blast, each *smithereen* a particle in a silver spray that bloomed and flared flowers, vines and blossoms and trees and leaves climbing into the skies, where there were worlds beyond worlds: all caught up. In the dark whirlwind, unutterable—a flash: a color of mind, a sky of mind, a sound ringing a silver bell, silver—a cloud silver, with the lining shining in a coil of snaky light, glowing in bands circling and madly whirling back on itself, back and down and around until poof! you went out in a little flaming flicker, a quick sizzling, then nothing at all.

Curran had listened fascinated. That was The Head; Donovan, The Stomach.

Now as Curran looked down to where Dolores, smiling up at Donovan, was about to cut him another fat slab of cake, the midget thought he saw trouble coming.

"Well, here you are."

Startled, Donovan looked up. Vernie—carrying a pie. His little blonde. Dolores, too, was obviously surprised.

"What are you doing here?" Vernie wanted to know, taking in the two of them, the chocolate cake between.

"What rudeness!" Dolores protested. "I could ask you the same question— butting in where you have no business."

"Come join us," Donovan suggested. "Have a piece of cake," he added fatuously.

"What do you mean?" Vernie demanded. "I go to all the trouble of making my mocha brandy chiffon pie and what do I find?" Her chin was quivering. "This, this—chocolate cake."

"It's Tuesday," Donovan said, in a low voice. "It's not your day."

"What are you implying about my chocolate cake," Dolores said testily, standing up.

"And it's light as a feather too," Vernie was saying, in tears now. "And the best meringue I've made in my whole life."

"It's probably all starch," Dolores accused her.

"Better than that bomb you created."

"Have some," Dolores said, digging out a chunk and throwing it at her.

"Be my guest," Vernie said, scooping a handful of pie and flinging it in her face.

"Now, Vernie," Donovan said, coming to comfort her, though he felt pulled in two directions at once. Caught.

"Don't you sweet talk me, you two-timer." She flung a handful of mocha brandy chiffon pie up in his face.

Donovan wiped a bit of pie off his cheek, at the same time licking off a bit at the comer of his mouth. "Lovely pie," he said. Then he was struck by a piece of chocolate cake. "Look, girls, we can all be friends." Cake and pie both flew at him.

"Heel! Two-timer!"

Donovan drew himself up to his full height. Curran had seen him in that pose before: If it was all over, he would at least acquit himself with dignity. "At least you may as well get your arithmetic straight," he said. "I'm a three-timer. But really, girls, isn't there enough of me for—"

"You want to brag too."

"Cad! Blackguard!" The two women set upon him then, tearing at his shirt, pulling at his pants, their hands everywhere. As soon as he extricated himself from one, the other came at him in a fury. "Ladies," he protested. "*Please*, ladies." But the placating tone of his voice seemed to madden them even more. Pushing them both away, momentarily freed, he ducked as best he could a final barrage of pastry and fled into the hotel.

Curran now was writing. *At some point there is an urge for mobility —for reaching out.* To his cello-shaped figure he added two sticks for arms. He paused to reflect. Was there not yearning in this gesture? Cake. Pie. Even in the sky. And was there not a need, too, for changing the scenery? He drew two more sticks at the base of the cello. There he was: *homo mobilis.*

When he looked up for a moment, chewing speculatively on his pencil, he saw that the two women were still in the yard. They were clucking at one another in accents of comfort, straightening their hair and clothes, picking up dishes. A moment later they left arm-in-arm. Raven and snakes. Raven perched on the boy's shoulder, head cocked, beady eyes taking it all in. No doubt had seen too much, knew too much. Snakes twined around Grace's hips and shoulders. A piece of observation for you.

Bird type—Curran made a mental note—of the darker sort. A matter of discrimination. Same with snake types: different kinds: belly-on-the-ground types. Creepy, crawling. Secret, underhanded. Deadly. Deceptive beauty of snake types. Primarily movement. The S-shape. Insinuating. Sinuous. Sensuous. As for Grace . . .

. . .

Stage presence. Dusty had to hand it to her. Talent was nothing without it. The use of creatures in an act—good touch. Put the performer beyond the reach of the audience. In a class by himself. One-upmanship, the name of the game in show biz. He knew a thing or two. The old eye wasn't dead yet. If he could only—he downed the rest of his mescal.

. . .

Grace at the top. Bouquets in her dressing room. One huge basket of red roses with a golden horseshoe in a glittering curve across. The card: "From an admirer." And the man who came back to the dressing room—tall, lithe but well-built. Thick blond hair. A prince. A famous trial lawyer, a man who not only played the violin and wrote poetry in his spare time but also kept a stable of horses and his own private plane. "You don't have to play in these one-horse towns," he said, politely removing his hat. "And I'm here to help you, beyond your wildest dreams." Alta sighed.

. . .

Beautiful all right. Oh, yes. And you couldn't help getting caught up, Billy thought. For her body was terribly exciting. The way she moved her hips, her torso, her arms, as though movement itself were being bor. Powerful stuff. The beat of the rhythm of the blood, the wang-bang down-below where the heat of generation had its living pulse. Where the light, a single cell, created itself out of the dark.

. . .

As usual in the evening, Donovan was present by his absence.

For everyone save him had gathered with the various folks who had wandered into the bar. Who had gotten tired of Chico and Reynaldo, tired of the usual. Here was Grace to generate a little interest. As she shimmered in the center of the room, their eyes were painted all over her like a design.
But this time the boy was also in the act. At first he stood by with the raven perched on his shoulder while she danced to the accompaniment of Reynaldo's guitar. Slowly at first, then turning more rapidly in a rush of sound till, the music subsiding, she stood swaying her hips, undulating her arms. Then, as though at some invisible sign that had passed between them, his eyes directed at a point somewhere beyond the audience, the boy began to sing:

Delight was the name of Liria
Wandering in the valleys
And she did love, and she did love
Liria, Liria O.

Billy was surprised by the note of husky tenderness in the voice and by the voice itself, for it was enough to fill the room. He looked at the boy again, as though to make sure he was the same one he knew. Perhaps Grace had cast a spell on him, had taken him into her world, he couldn't be sure. And yet he sang as she moved, as from a single source and motive:

> *She wanted nothing gold would buy*
> *As she sat among the flowers*
> *For she did love, and she did love*
> *O my Liria.*
>
> *In her sleep she was awake*
> *And crossed the dark borders*
> *There she budded in the night*
> *Liria, Liria O*

Foolishness and nonsense. Roses and horseshoes. Your name in lights. But what was there to want anyway? Was there anything you could call by the name of delight? But she'd felt it once long ago. And love. As for Grace . . . she signaled Leftheris for another whiskey.

. . .

Backers. You got to have backers. If he had it all to do over—at least there were the comforts of mescal. This was going to go on and on, what the Captain called "cat's yodel." Mescal to shut it out, blunt the edges. But there was a different note creeping in. A change of rhythm. Pajarito: a raven full of devilment, wanting everything, ravenous. Well, he knew a thing or two about that. Always being punished. But trying to keep an eye out, watch out for himself. Nobody's fool, maybe. Praying to the gods, he'd been changed into man. But with a raven's heart:

> *Pajarito envious stood*
> *As she slept among the flowers.*
> *Hated the one that she did love*
> *Liria, Liria O.*

The Romans, Curran remembered, had taught a raven to say, "Hail Caesar." A nice touch. He recalled also that some reptiles had made it into birds. Came up in life, made something of themselves, so to speak. Changed their element from earth to air. He needed to think about elements.

Yes, this was more of the kid he knew. Really warming to the song now. Could the other feeling have been there too—or was he deceiving himself? Billy listened. It was a dark place, down there below. Where all things were conceived and generated. That's the thing, Billy thought, watching Grace, her movements hinting of what was shadowy and dangerous. She fits any idea you have of her. From the mud flat on up. Some never got their eyes off the mud flat:

> To drain the springs of her delight
> Was his consuming passion:
> The flash of darkness in his head
> At the thought of Liria.

> You're on the earth to torment me
> To tear my heart away
> And feed it to the slavering curs.
> Cursed be Liria.

It figured: fly in the ointment somewhere. Jealous. Couldn't bear for a woman to have anything. Killjoys. Show a little spark and they had to stamp it out. Take it out on you because they couldn't be happy themselves. Bring everything down to their level.

. . .

There was an interaction between certain creatures and elements not their own. Even snakes could swim. As a boy, Curran had caught harmless garden snakes and thrown them into the lake. As soon as they hit the water, they struck for shore like the lash of a whip, a lightning zigzag. A snake was not a happy creature in water. *He took to it like a snake to water*—how was that for a comparison?

> Then he took his long keen blade
> Stabbed his rival in the heart
> I'll never part from Liria
> Never from Liria.

O why have you killed my only love
Cried Liria, Liria O
Knife, speak the blood of two
I'll go with him below.

Movement and alimentation in their particular milieu. Bats and spiders, frogs and mice, beetles and lice. Feeling their way around in it, sensing the presence of food. Snakes. Grace gathering eyes as she moves through space. What hunger and desire feed on. He did not want to look at the boy. A darkness was gathering. What element was this?

He was the sun, he was my light
The beating heart of stars
His the name of all delight
Cried Liria.

So now it was all over with her. Well, more's the pity. She looked over at Dusty, long gone—in his cups.

. . .

He was back in the sculpture garden shaking in his shoes. It was the boy who had done it, put him back in front of that little stone figure, who stood in a dark and violent place. There in all his ugliness. Was the peculiar simply part of the ugly? He wanted to turn his back on all of it. He had drunk half his beer. Without a word he got up and stalked out the door.

Peculiar, Billy thought, watching him go. Moody. A creature of moods. He wondered if it had anything to do with his being a midget. Probably no more than anything else. And secretive. In-dwelling.

. . .

The ballad had broken off like a snapped stem. And Grace's movements had died with it. Now she held the raven. It sat on the wrist of the hand she held out for it.

◆

After breakfast in the morning, or just before dusk in the evening, these were the times Billy Bigelow most enjoyed walking the streets of the town. He liked to look at the mountains then, their peaks and rocky crests cut out sharply against the sky, the dusky pink-brown slopes spotted with clumps of sagebrush. And the town fresh in the morning light, the adobe houses and stone walls freshly visited, the clumps of sunflowers in the alleys, the tin cans with geraniums in the windows, the lines of wash hanging in the backyards. All the colors and textures. Or else he liked to go out just before sunset when the slanting rays caught the clouds, edged them with the glow of rose and smoke or caught the underbellies and floated them in gold. Then the light pulling away, leaving a brilliant edge on a gray dome, while the mountains played with light and shadow. And the sky deepening with subtle gradations of blue paling in the west till just on the horizon an intense orange glow came like a fire behind the mountains—and the sun was gone. The lights came on then and he could look into windows through curtains still open. He looked most shamelessly. He liked to see the way people lived. The town belonged mostly to children at both those times of day, and to cats and dogs. They knew him now, the children, and even the cats and dogs. And sometimes when he was out walking, the kids ran up to him, begging. "Billy, Billy, show us a trick." And he would pull out a deck of cards and lay them out on a stoop, or make nickels disappear. And before he knew it, a little crowd had gathered around him. After he finished one of his tricks, always a voice piped up. "One more, Billy, just one more." And at times it was hard work to pry himself away.

This morning he hoped he would not be waylaid, for he had something on his mind, was greatly troubled, in fact. Downright stumped, you could say. He passed a couple of boys playing marbles in a vacant lot, walked round a kid sitting out in the middle of a sidewalk. He had drawn an airplane with chalk on the pavement, and was dropping pebbles on it and making the sounds of explosions. He was so deep in his game he didn't look up as Billy passed. Then Billy saw Mimi, a favorite of his, who was running a stick along a fence. They walked side by side for over a block without saying a word. He could see she was bound to a serious task, of hitting everything with her stick and making it yield its sound: fence, tree, barrel, sides of a tin shed, paint bucket, chain-link fence. Nothing must be missed, nothing left out. Or the world might collapse. Or your mother break her back.

Once upon a time
The goose drank wine

The monkey spit tobacco
On the streetcar line
The streetcar broke
The monkey choked
And they all went to heaven
In a little green boat.

Somehow he found that in his mind, from God knows how long ago, from the dusk of summer evenings when he'd played hide-and- seek and night trot, wandering all over the neighborhood, leaving clues so that he and the other kids might be trailed and then slip away from those who followed. And he remembered the elaborate systems of roads he had made for his cars around the roots of trees, and how much trouble he had taken trying to learn to whittle, and how many trees he had climbed and how all the days were filled with running and jumping and fighting and laughing and crying. And he remembered the smell of the A & P store and the noise of the Saturday matinee and the baseball games played endlessly in the vacant lot.

He remembered those things, and felt sick at heart. For the source of his trouble was a boy who had never been a child. Who had been robbed of his childhood, as of a birthright. Mother abandoning him after having given birth, so Grace had told Billy. Leaving him on the doorstep with a note: "You begot him—now you got him." Priam Gillespie with a son. Then she'd left town. For a time there was an old Mexican woman, half senile, who'd taken care of him—taught him a few songs, though half the time she didn't remember to change his clothes. After the first two grades he refused to stay in school, and nobody bothered about him. Grace hadn't had a whole lot of time to devote to him; if it hadn't been for her, they'd have starved to death.

Priam Gillespie with a son—Billy considered it. No mother to give him the suggestion of tenderness. No, he might as well have been left exposed to the dark whirl of atoms, the cold emptiness of space. Perhaps he was capable of living where no other mortal could survive, on some cold planet with nothing but a coating of algae.

Or the desert. Where the earth was hard with minerals. The ancient seas having receded to leave room for the mountains that would be heaved up in another age; then the heaving earth, the terrible pressures, the unimaginable heat, lava flowing everywhere—the agonies of matter. And now spines of cactus and thistle; horned toad and lizard and snake. The cold-blooded leftovers of the Pleistocene Age. Spiny plants; armored animals; the starved and twisted forms. Learn to be human in *that* setting. The kid had learned to throw stones.

And wanted to learn more. Though Billy had discovered that a while ago, he'd somehow let go of it, maybe thinking he'd be spared having to trouble over it. But the kid was deadly serious. Wouldn't let go. Billy had found him at one of his magic books. Found him in a state of unusual emotion: eyes full of violet light, pupils dilated, looking almost mad with wonder. Then his eyes narrowed like a cat's, grew canny.

A little later, the kid came to him and said. "I want to learn magic. Like you."

Billy had looked at him. The little bugger meant it. He wanted to laugh. He had an apprentice. But there was something else in the eyes —furtive, not quite truthful. Billy had a flash of memory: the kid standing there in the circle, carrying out his little ritual. No, it was for real, as he'd suspected. The kid wanted the genuine article, the power to change reality itself. He picked up the book and read, where it fell open, about the magician who'd killed all his enemies by making a house fall on them. "Kill him! Kill him!" And Billy had been the one to mention that in the first place. It was certainly an advance over throwing a few stones.

A powerful ambition, he thought, as he wandered along the street, paying no attention to where he was going. Powerful and deadly. The desire to hold people in thrall, to work them like puppets, to cure and to kill or, maybe, only to kill. The violence that was in him, there from the very beginning, Billy was convinced. Wanted to learn magic all right. Billy had to admit he was afraid, for what he was being asked to do. He had been called upon to take that mass of hatred or confusion or simple, pure chaos and do something with it. You couldn't get rid of it, that was for sure, couldn't sit around hoping it would go away: Does the leopard change his spots? And what were you supposed to do with it? He couldn't pacify him with a few card tricks either.

No, he'd have to pretend to more than he knew, and just hope and pray he'd not be exposed by the other's canny, instinctive intelligence. For that was a considerable weapon: it had got the kid where he was. It looked like Billy was going to have to live a lie, one of his larger efforts: the lie that is more than a trick of movement or even a trick of belief. Live a lie and hope for—what? Not the truth. That was too much to ask for.

♦

"First you have to choose a name," Billy said to the kid.

Which would be quite a feat. Since his arrival, the only appellation that had been thrown in his direction was "Kid." When Billy had asked Grace what the boy's name was, she'd said, "Well, I 'spose he has one. We've just always called him Kid." And it was hard to imagine him as anything else. The way you get to calling a cat "Kitty." By that time it's too late for a proper name—even the cat won't stand for it. And trying to stick a name on him like Johnny or Eddie or Dan wouldn't have worked at all, a label without any glue. For there was about him something that wouldn't fit inside the edges of your ordinary name.

"Every magician has got his own special name," Billy explained. "But it can be a motto that expresses what you're trying to achieve. *Kill him, kill him* snagged Billy's thought.

"What sort of name?" Kid said.

"Something impressive. You only use it when you're working magic." And he tried reeling off all the impressive names he could think of: "Lodovico, Leonardo, Antonio, Alonzo," he chanted. "Alexander, Theodophilos, Napoleon, Chesterfield, Seigismundo, Maracaibo, Geronimo." He racked his brain for more. "Philipus, Gregorio, Hercules, Excelsior," he said, giving out.

But after each one the boy shook his head.

"Well, how about a motto?" Billy said. "You can do one of those instead—what you're trying to achieve."

The boy shrugged.

"They're supposed to show what you're trying to do as a magician," Billy explained. "Like *I will prevail* or *To the top of the mountain*. Generally they're in Latin—according to the book. My Latin's a little thin, owing to the passage of time: *E Pluribus Unum, non compos mentis* and *ex post facto*. That's about it: *one of many, crazy in the head* and *after the fact*.

"What comes after the fact," Kid asked.

He was about to explain, then changed his mind. "Why, there's no telling," he said. "It's the unknown quantity, the condition of possibility. Anything can happen."

"I'll try that one," Kid said.

"Good idea," Billy said. "I was never much for facts myself. You need a few of 'em to stay alive, but what's around and underneath and after is much more interesting. Get past the facts and you get to the magic."

There was an eagerness in the boy's expression.

"Hold it—just thought of another. *Ecce Homo.* "

"What's that mean?"

"It means, Look at the guy. "

"Could you put them together? *Ex post facto, ecce homo?"* "Terrific. Get the facts out of the way and see what a fellow's really got. Also, the name contains the secret of the *Ex,* which not only marks the spot, but is also the sign of the unknown. A significant place, because what can be more significant than something you don't know is there."

After the kid had passed this, the first step of his initiation, Billy explained what he'd need by way of equipment. And the next morning the boy went out at dawn to find, if he could, a wand that he could cut with the first stroke of his knife. There were no hazel trees around, so he'd have to make do with cottonwood or scrub oak.

◆

There was a great to-do in town, and as a consequence a sudden abnormal flurry of activity. Ordinarily the houses sat sleepily under the sun, and dogs and cats curled lazily outdoors in spots of shade. Except for an occasional outburst of exuberance, bad temper or momentary violence, people lived quietly, practicing yoga or the flute, eating vegetables, tending gardens, painting landscapes, designing jewelry, cooking exotic meals, reading obscure philosophers, speculating on various political schemes, making love, having babies, and gossiping. That had been the usual order of things.

Several years before, as more people began to settle in the town, they had elected a mayor. In the first year he did little except to organize a volunteer fire department, which served for all kinds of emergencies. If anyone was seriously ill, he was taken to the hospital in Atlantia, a hundred miles away. The mayor had also designated a patch of land outside the town as a city dump. Then a group of parents met to talk about starting a school, also to be run on a volunteer basis. And so things continued in the town: if a problem came up, if a sudden need arose, people tended to it as the occasion demanded.

The mayor, a genial, balding man in his mid-fifties who had left a thriving insurance business to settle here and bake the town's bread, was always addressed by his title and was in danger of having his name forgotten altogether. Perhaps because there was not a great deal for the mayor to do, his title had become weighty as an honorific and thus had stuck to him.

Now, considering that things had gone smoothly enough having been allowed to go their own way, all kinds of people having been taken into the community, it seemed ironic that the source of their present trouble was a fellow who had come with the signal intention of doing them good.

It became clear almost at once that the Reverend Hoskins was a visionary. There were other visionaries in the town, but these, having escaped being branded as too wild or crazy to live without being locked up, kept their visions to themselves; or if they revealed them, it was to the like-minded or else to those who were prepared to hear and dismiss any vision except their own. But the Reverend, through the power of his personality, as well as his appeal to something familiar and not easily pushed aside, drew people into the light of his intense conviction where, dazzled with the desire to serve it, they tried to pull in everybody else too. All his adobe bricks, piled atop one another, now formed into walls, were conspiring to create an oasis there in the desert, a giant oasis with gas pumps and prayer stops and hymns piped into the restaurant, along with a daily uplifting message served with the first cup of coffee.

"I had my first misgivings when I saw the billboards going up," the Mayor was saying as he sat eating lunch in the hotel with his wife, Isabel, and Hazel, an old woman who kept a grocery.

These signs now stood at both sides of town where the highway divided: TIGHTEN YOUR LOOSE LIVING HERE. LOVE IS YOUR BIGGEST WHEEL. TRUCK YOUR WAY TO GLORY.

"Eyesores," Hazel said. "I thought that was one thing we came here to escape."

"Signs and portents of things to come," the Mayor said wryly, "though I'm sure they think they're making progress with the godless lot over here." He rubbed the side of his nose reflectively. "Maybe we should've had an ordinance—it just never came up before."

"Nobody ever lost money overestimating the appeal of a free ride to Paradise," Isabel said.

"Now we got all those folks pouring in, all fired up to leave their troubles behind. And I don't blame them, I suppose," the Mayor said.

"You can hardly do that," his wife agreed, "considering what brought the two of us here."

"I just prefer my own brand of escapism, if that's what it is." "But who ever figured he'd want to take over the whole joint," Hazel asked.

"That's not so hard," the Mayor said. "Not if he's got the answer." "But what'll we do now?" Isabel added. "It's no joke. While we've been sitting here minding our little affairs, he's got in thick with all the politicos."

"But he can't really claim the land, can he?"

"He's claiming the right to buy it, because there's no title."

"But that's New Town. What about us? We've been here longer— the town's been here forever. There must be some sort of title to the land, registered somewhere in the capital."

"But this is the capital," the Mayor said. "That is, the first capital —way back when. I've written to the Office of Records in Ventura City, but they don't know anything."

"They can't just take us over, can they?

"That's what has me worried," the Mayor said. "Right now I'm stumped."

Leftheris had paused to listen as he served them coffee. "The town's been here for over a hundred years," he said with feeling. "Old Town and New Town. It's tradition. Gold miners and prospectors, wanderers, even a few horse thieves and outlaws. That was Old Town. If you didn't like it, you went across the river. But it's two towns. If it was one town, there'd be only six cities of Cibola."

"Tradition is one thing," the Mayor said, "politics is another." "What is all this I hear," asked Alexos, having come in from repairing the front stoop.

"The crazy preacher wants to take us over," Leftheris said. "And he's got a petition going round to get rid of the Angelic Hostesses, because what they're doing is illegal."

"You mean having babies?" Hazel said with a laugh. "We've been doing that since Adam grabbed Eve.

"Not the way they're doing it," the Mayor said. "If you happen to care about such things."

"I hear that in his place they don't even have doors on the rooms." "In his place," Isabel said with a snort, "you probably wouldn't need them."

"This isn't helping," the Mayor said. "You better take him seriously."

"Why can't we just leave each other alone?" Hazel wanted to know.

"There's always something," said Alta, who was eating lunch at the next table. "Just when you think you got a place you can stay for a while, take a little rest, you got somebody trying to crash in the walls."

"What do you expect?" Dusty said sharply. "You so in love with the place that you want to stay forever?" He snorted with disgust. "Not that I give a shit. One hole's just like any other." He sat drumming the table with his fingers. "Wish he'd get done yapping," he said, with a glance toward Leftheris, "and bring me some more coffee."

Alta looked at him. "When would you have time to find out what hole you were in?" she snapped. She couldn't see Billy's expression as he sat playing with a piece of cellophane wrapper. Probably thinking she ought to let up on Dusty.

But she couldn't help it, not when she had to think about how he spent every night getting drunk, staggering up or having to be carried up to bed; how after he finally woke up, he eased a hangover till noon. From then on, he spent a few hours of boredom till the next round.

"What about you, Gus?" she said to change the conversation. "You getting tired of this place?"

"Hell, no," Donovan said. "Having the time of my life. Haven't exhausted the resources by any means."

"I'll bet you haven't, you old rascal." She looked around. "Where's Eddie, anyway? Practically never see him during the day any more. What's he up to?"

"I think he's gone peculiar," Donovan said. "Not that he didn't always have a touch. Only now—" He shook his head. "Always muttering to himself. Locked up in his room most of the time, or else wandering around the street."

"Maybe he's got a woman," Dusty suggested without interest.

"That'd be the day," Donovan said. "Woman hater from the day he was born."

"There's always a first time."

"Give me a break," Alta said. "Wait—I want to hear this," she said, listening again to the other conversation.

"Besides, that's not the reason he's got the petition against the women," the Mayor was saying.

"Why then?"

"To intimidate them. Then he can control them."

"Do you mean with the election business?"

"Exactly. They deal with him or the authorities, and he'll call them in."

"So now they'll vote like he wants. To take us over."

"So what do we do?" Hazel said.

"Pray."

"We could organize and incorporate ourselves."

Alexos stood, frowning, as though trying hard to get something clear. "They say possession is three-fourths of the law," he said. "We've been here for over a hundred years."

"We need a legal opinion."

"Delay them as long as possible."

"We've got to have a meeting," the Mayor said. "The whole town."

"A campaign," someone suggested.

"What a mess," Alta said. "Even if we packed up and went, where would we go?"

"There are other cities," Donovan said, "if you feel that way."

"You mean another hole," Dusty said, "only bigger?"

"You really want to go," Billy asked.

"I don't know. I'm just tired of trouble."

"Then you must be tired of living, sweetie." Dusty turned to see if Leftheris was going to remember him. "Damn—I need some more coffee."

"Then get it," Alta suggested. "You got two good legs. What about you, Billy—you for staying?"

"Well, I like the folks here. And I'd feel bad just pulling out right when they've got trouble. They've been good to us."

Alta sighed. "But what can we do?" she wanted to know. "I don't know a rat turd about politics."

"Maybe we could give a benefit performance," Billy said.

"Whose benefit," Dusty asked.

"I could paint them some signs," Billy said. "I haven't done that in a while."

"Sure," Dusty said, "You can compete with the Reverend, TRY OUR PARADISE CHEAPER RATES."

"They say it's all a state of mind," Donovan said.

"Tell me about it," Dusty answered.

♦

A few days after the townspeople had met, Billy's signs were all over the town, FREEDOM, they demanded, OLD TOWN FOREVER, they maintained, DOWN WITH TYRANNY. "The Revolution has finally come!" Chico and Reynaldo declared, with great satisfaction. They left off singing "O Corazon, mi Corazon," and launched into songs of revolutionary fervor.

Curran had followed the whole campaign, though from a distance. He didn't intend to participate, and everyone had too much on his mind to pay any attention to him. This suited him to a T. He was able to gather a great deal of material, though politics as such had no interest for him. No, it was all the movement of the hive: the clash of soldier ants, the hanging on of drones. Man was a political animal. But Curran had settled on the individual as his source of inspiration. And for the moment he was doubly preoccupied.

Since the evening when the boy had sung the ballad of Pajarito, he was somehow always running into him. They passed each other on the way to their rooms, they found themselves side by side at dinner. Every time, Curran wanted to draw away, as though the kid smelled bad. He always gave you the feeling he was up to no good, had that glint of surprised hostility in the eye that made you think you'd caught him in the act. It wasn't guilt—Curran was sure of that much: the kid was beyond guilt.

One morning Curran wasn't able to sleep and got out of bed just before sun-up, strolled through the garden and out to the arroyo behind it. And there he came across the kid standing inside a circle drawn in the dirt. A metal cup, a band of feathers and some other trash lay inside the circle, and the kid was chanting some sort of mumbo-jumbo. The intensity of will and effort was what caught him short. Curran slipped off before he was seen. He didn't want the kid looking at him, boring through him with his eyes with their odd violet color. Wanted no part of it. He had the strange feeling that one day he would be trapped into looking the kid straight in the eye, and felt an unreasoning terror. He was, after all, just a kid.

And part of the time he behaved like you'd expect. All during the campaign, he was right in the middle of things, all excited and eager, running errands all over town. He'd helped Billy with all the signs, had sat there painting the big letters in red and blue. Though you couldn't help wondering how he knew how to hold a brush or could do more than dab on a few savage splotches. And once, while Curran was watching, the kid did something that struck him as odd. A blob of paint had spilled on the edge of a little scrap of wood. And the kid sat there playing with it. Making it into a little figure. Got so fascinated that he'd forgotten all about what he was doing. Billy had looked over at him, smiled and left him alone. And there the kid sat, dipping the brush and adding other figures. Curran couldn't tell exactly what they were doing, but they appeared to be running and leaping. Then the kid noticed Curran watching, quickly dipped his brush, crossed it all out, pushed the board away almost angrily, got up and left.

Now, though, Curran was quite sure the kid was up to tricks, having caught him in the lobby. He'd been behind the desk near the cubbyholes where the keys to the rooms were hung on hooks, and this time a clearly guilty look had crossed his features when Curran came up. Well, he'd let Billy worry about that, though he was curious. He might find out something useful for his book if he kept an eye peeled.

Meanwhile, though, he was on his way to plenty of material.

◆

Quam'bukqueau lived in a small shed that had survived the fire that razed the house, known as Noah's church, to which it had belonged. No one knew any longer whether the church was named for the man who had started it and who was, by all recollection, its only member, or whether its religious feeling had been inspired by the Flood. In any event, he had built it on the slope of the Hill of Holies, so called because it had once been a sacred spot of the Indians.

Now the shed stood alone under the onslaughts of wind and rain, the boards, all silver-gray, shrinking under the sun. The knotholes and the spaces between the boards had been stuffed with rags and old newspapers and the wadded pages of magazines Quam'bukqueau had scavenged. Fortunately the shed was small and served him in much the same way as a shell its snail. When the weather was fine, he opened up the door and sat on the stoop working on his project, letting the sun shine on him and the cats. At night he drew back into a pile of bedding and slept.

During the day he made his rounds: to the hotel kitchen, to the bakery, to the trash pile behind the grocery. There he collected whatever scraps, unsold rolls or bread, and partially spoiled fruit he could find. If he found more than he could use himself, he shared it with the cats and dogs. On days of scarcity, he did odd jobs for people in exchange for food, but this didn't happen often. He wanted no money: money was enslavement.

At first Curran thought him simple-minded. But in the past he had lived much like anybody else. He had worked in a factory making ball-point pens, had rented an apartment, was making payments on a car, and owned a stereo and a television. "It no be good," he told Curran, shaking his head. He had slipped out of it all in order, he said, to live more deliberately. His ingenuousness appealed greatly to Curran. Whereas the kid was wilder than an animal, this fellow seemed simpler than a child.

Beginning with his name. Which was, as he explained it, the written form of "This be Buk," the *c* being unnecessary, because the sound was performed by the *k*. It was one of those arbitrary and wasteful elements he was working to get rid of in the language. The *queau* was a silent syllable. For every creature deserved a respectful silence after his name had been announced and himself introduced. Though Mr., Mrs., Ms., etc., had been set up as titles of respect, these were merely forms of social respect and missed the point altogether.

The first and last syllables were of equal significance. As for the *Quam'*, this was a step forward from the usual statement, "I am," which Quam'bukqueau felt to be one of the most pernicious influences in the language. It was everyone standing around saying "I am this, I am that" that led to much of the evil of the world. Everyone was imprisoned in the *I am.*

His effort to free himself had led him to one of his first tasks, straightening out the verb *be.* Its irregularity, shedding its baleful influence, had led to greater irregularities, the knots and twists of the spirit—separating each man from his neighbor, puffing him up with self-importance, isolating him in his self-concern and personal aggrandizement, clouding his vision and hardening his heart.

One of the first necessary reforms, Quam'bukqueau felt, was to eliminate the *I am* altogether. He was working on a more advanced form, though he was still not satisfied:

Qua'be	*Wit be*
Thee be	*Thees be*
Hit be	*They be*

Thus the grammatical form would subtly alter the spirit of the language, perhaps one day bringing something new to birth. And here he ducked his head shyly. For now, he was merely making a small pioneer effort.

Although he had only begun the task and had not yet made much headway, he was trying to get rid of the element of time as well, to change all verbs to the present tense. This he had already done with *be.*

"But things do happen and have an ending," Curran had objected on his previous visit. "Day and night go by and other things begin."

"That be the way you think about them," Quam'bukqueau answered. "The past and the future live in the present as soon as you no longer think about them. Nothing be divided from anything else."

"The world would fall apart," Curran insisted. "You couldn't tell anybody where you'd be tomorrow or what you'd been doing yesterday."

"Men be slaves to the world of time," Quam'bukqueau said mildly. "Children live in the world of today—in the moment."

Curran saw everything running together in a blur of color.

"Some people can never get out of words," Quam'bukqueau said.

Was that his aim, Curran wondered. To escape from words completely, to rise from the gravity of language and escape, floating freely. The idea had appealed to him once.

But, Quam'bukqueau went on to explain, he wasn't really trying to dispense with language; he wanted instead to create a language for the New Age.

The language now had been so mutilmediated that it was all but ruined. And he described how certain politicians and generals had so paradoxed their auditioners by abnormaling their responds that verbs were nouned and nouns verbed and adjectives adverbalized in a way that was enough to uncertain everyone. Even the Russians were thrown for a loop. He was sure that this form of impenetrabling would end up with the world being smithereened.

This is where Curran's previous visits had taken him. When he arrived at the shed this morning, he found Quam'bukqueau deep in thought, pencil poised above his notebook.

"I hope I'm not disturbing you," Curran said.

"It be pleasing to see you," Quam'bukqueau said. "Time for a rest."

"You've been working?"

"Very hard. All the day-night. Working so hard as to be swallowed up in no-time."

Out of body type, Curran was thinking. Without a worry in his head.

"Have you thought about what's going on in town?" Curran asked him. "There might not be a town any more. Doesn't that bother you? Haven't you seen the signs?" Not, he thought, that he had any right to question anyone's zeal.

"Yes," Quam'bukqueau. "It be a great trouble, a sore distress. And the signs be very good: FREEDOM, DOWN WITH TYRANNY. And we be struggling with the same words, locked in the same battles. It be the chains of the mind," he said, touching his temple, "to be sundered and broken. Look," he said, riffling through the pages of his notebook till he found what he wanted. Curran read the word *freeliness.*

"A word for the New Age," Quam'bukqueau announced with modest pride. "Think of it. Frr-eee-liness," he said, throwing open his arms to indicate what the word gave on to. "No more hedgings, grudgings and qualms. These be the moles and blemishes on the face of action."

"Yes," Curran agreed. It did have a certain merit, though he wasn't sure he himself had any faith in a New Age.

"Oh, I know," Quam'bukqueau was saying, as though he had read his thoughts, "you be skeptical. And with good reason. Man of the present is a creature in chains. It be doing no good to slide past, to be blinding his eyes to where he *is.* " And he turned to another page of his notebook and passed it to Curran.

Upon which Curran read a list of qualities of the Man of the Present:

Courage like a dish of goose grease
Culture like the mother on a vinegar vat
Intellectual Powers like slugs crawling out of a strawberry patch
Willpower like three screws in a dice-box
Discretion like a forklift in a cemetery
Expressiveness like a fart in a bucket
Decisiveness like a helicopter in a sandstorm
Cosmic ease like a dog shitting peach pits

"Well," Curran said. "It looks like you've got a job cut out for yourself."

Quam'bukqueau nodded gravely.

◆

Where am I now, Alta wondered. And where am I going from here? She was sitting in a chair on the balcony, looking out over the town, while she waited for Dusty to wake up. The day had too much sun and glory in it for such a question, light shaping the morning with a bright hand—making brilliant planes on the sides of houses, sliding down the red-tile roofs, playing with the leaves of palm trees, falling in brilliant shards on the ground. Always with the help of shadow. But all the while it was light in control. Light having awakened things again, calling them back from the dark, touching them into form and tones and colors, fingering them into presence: Come on, come on now. Allowing spaces to become peopled and filled, housed and flowered and treed, making distances and nearnesses, heights and levels, hills and valleys. Come, come. Vividly. (Whether valiantly or vainly, it was too soon to tell.) And then calling the eye: Only see. Come and see.

But Alta, morosely chain-smoking, was considering the irony that they had been married on this day twenty-five years ago. And there was Dusty, sleeping off his drunk, about to collide with his hangover. And the question for her—What was left when you got past the deceptions and betrayals that met you on every side, when it wasn't even a question of that anymore? When you'd hit the sand trap? Soon as you tried to lift a foot or even a finger, something moved in to slap you down.

Even if she said she owed it all to Dusty, said he'd put them where they were. Him and his farfetched ideas. Then what? What did that prove? Not that wanting something was wrong; no, she'd gone along with that. Even felt enthusiastic for a time. But somehow things had got warped. Had become something only for himself, or so it looked to her now. The way he had used people, made big promises, lied so long and outrageously that he'd convinced himself every word was the truth. Everything sacrificed for the sake of his dream—till he'd stepped over the edge.

So now what? She turned to look at Dusty, who had one arm over his head, the other flung out over the pillow. He had a good buzz saw going too, sleeping the day away, lying there trying to forget the fact he'd not only done it all wrong, he'd been a bastard while he was at it. He and the Captain going to hell on a worm's back: drinking the nasty stuff it floated around in. She could see it there in the bottle. One look at it ought to turn a sensible man into a teetotaler.

She could undo him, of course. It wouldn't take much now. Just remind him at least once a day how much he'd let her down, *and* everybody else. Keep digging her claws into his back. Probably spend the rest of his life on the bottle—till his liver gave out or he fell into a hole some dark night and froze to death. She shuddered. This was the man she'd lived with for twenty-five years. And once, somewhere along the line . . . she knew him. It had been given to her to see him at his worst, to look down in the direction he was pointed at and see the pit, crawling with all the lower forms of life, all the disgusting things you could think of: the silverfish under the stump, dung beetles and worms, things dead and rotting and fed upon by scavengers. They stirred something in her too; first hatred, then the desire for cruelty. Fire to ice: the burning cold, the freezing heat. No, it wouldn't take much to split him all the way open. She had not been above revenge. She liked the feeling of her own claws. Or had.

She lit another cigarette.

Carnival for the Gods—what an idea! What gods? And who were *they* to think of entertaining them? A bunch of freaks entertaining the gods with their freakishness. As if that was what the gods wanted. As if there *were* gods.

But then just what and where would they be without the carnival? What sort of lives would they have? Grace and Billy and the others? And herself? She'd grow bored stiff in any little town and go mad in any city before very long. To accommodate herself to any settled life wasn't in her nature. She should've been a nomad. This was the longest she'd been in any spot since can't remember when. And she liked it, only. . . And Curran and Donovan—what would they do anywhere else? Be shunned or ridiculed. The only one who might manage was Billy Bigelow. He could always find enough work as a carpenter or electrician to keep his hide sleek. Be better off than here. But like everybody else he had a perverse streak. Had to have, to stick around.

And she thought of all their years together, different acts coming and going, the excitement of opening in a new place, and talking afterwards about how it went, and striking the tents and booths and rides and going on to the next place. A few fat years, the many lean; good times and bad. She thought of the meals they'd eaten together in the trailer, cups of coffee drunk, sandwiches grabbed on the run, nights of Dusty talking about the next run, the next show, the next town. All filled with enthusiasm. There were things she'd want to remember, maybe only because it was her life. Only now the fire had gone out of it, the spirit, the sense that tomorrow something wonderful might happen.

Well, if something's going to be done about it, one of those voices that pops up in your head was telling her, *you're going to have to be the one to do it.*

Screw that, she thought. *I've had it up to here.*

You got any better offers?

Here was a point. *Only to do something, you have to believe in it.*

Sometimes you have to do it anyway.

Bug off, it's my anniversary. We're gonna celebrate if I have to wring his neck.

"Dusty," she yelled.

"Wha-what?"

"Wake up," she insisted, going inside to stand over him while he blinked sleepily. Then she went downstairs to the kitchen and ordered breakfast sent up. She brought back with her a pot of strong black coffee, and found that Dusty was at least sitting up in bed, though hunched over, hands at his temples.

"You know what day this is," she asked.

"*Is* it a day? You positive?"

"Unless they've invented something else after night. Come to think of it, there's room for improvement. And if I were you, I'd have the first crack at it. Here's coffee," she said, handing him a cup by way of consolation.

"You're a pal, Alta—a true-blue sweetie."

"That's your hangover speaking."

"There's more of my true voice in that hangover right now than anywhere else. But since you brought it up, what day is it?"

"You don't remember?" Not that she'd expected him to.

"To tell the honest-to-God's truth, I've lost all track of time. I don't even know what month it is."

"It's our anniversary. Twenty-five years."

"What d'you know," he said. "What d'you know." He stirred his coffee reflectively, then looked at her. "I s'pose you'd like to throw it all out and start over somewhere else."

"Is that what you think?"

"Hell, Alta, I don't know. My head isn't in any shape to answer any high falutin' questions. Not that it ever was much."

She shrugged. "I figure all the receipts aren't in yet. Anyway, I feel like celebrating. That's why I'm having breakfast sent up. We can eat out on the balcony."

"Okay by me. Better let me have some more of that coffee first. God what a head!"

Some minutes later he roused himself out of bed and went into the bathroom, and she could hear him splashing water onto his face. The breakfast tray arrived. When he emerged, he put on a bathrobe and the two of them went out on the balcony. Alta set the tray on the little round metal table, and they sat down.

"That light sure hits you in the eyes," he said, squinting. He lifted his glass of orange juice. "Well, happy anniversary." They clinked glasses.

"You remember—" they both started to say, and laughed.

"Bet I know what you're going to say."

"You could have had that other guy—what was his name? Owens. Yeah, Leland Owens. He had a real thing for you."

"Yeah, but who'd want it? Nice one minute, then stab you in the back the next."

"I didn't know that though. He was my competition—and he had all the advantage."

"So it looked like. Put on a real display, I will say that for him. Flowers all over the place, always pestering around."

"And I was working hard as I could just to catch your eye." "Well, I was looking your direction. Is that why you proposed in midair?"

"Figured I wouldn't get a better chance."

"Wonder you didn't kill yourself and me both. 'Marry me'—and then you go swinging past. Nearly upset my timing."

"A true test of your performance. I figured nothing could flap you," he said, touching her hand. "You were too good. Only when you swung by and said 'yes,' I was more rattled than anything."

"Were you happy?"

"What a question. Were you?"

"Well, I don't regret any of it," she said. To her surprise, it came out that way. "I just wanted you to know."

He sat quiet for a while.

"The thing is," she said, pressing her advantage. "We've gone this far, we can't pull out of it now."

"What do you mean?" he said, looking at her.

"I mean, we've got to pull things together, do our business. There's Billy and Grace and even the kid, and Curran and Donovan. They're depending on us."

"Alta," he said, "have the sense to know when you're washed up."

"But you can't let them down now," she said. "This is their life. They've gone too far and sacrificed too much."

"Listen," he said, "you're out of your mind. Where do you begin? You can't make something out of nothing. What can we do—here?"

"It isn't nothing," she countered, almost angrily. "There's us. There's talent. And even in this place, you can put on a show. There are people here, they need something to pass the time. And maybe now's the best time to do it. There's a lot of bad feeling leaking out just now. Maybe they need a distraction. Take their minds off things, so they can think straight."

"I'm tired," Dusty said irritably. "I'm worn out."

"So what are you going to do—drink away your life? You still got the rest of it, you know."

"Christ, woman, you're enough to drive a man to the bottle—from either direction."

"And what does that mean?" she persisted, glad at least to get a rise out of him.

"Because you're never satisfied. From the direction of hope or the direction of despair."

"Well, I learned all that from you," she said.

"You're hard on a man, babe."

"You married me. Took the dare—and in mid-air at that."

"True, I did."

"You sorry?"

He was looking down at his hands, twisting the ring on his finger. "Remember when I bought this, that time in Kansas City?"

"Sure, I remember. We were drinking champagne then."

"The real French stuff. High on the hog. And the show just rolled sweet as sugar." He shook his head. "It was going to be my luck," he said. He pulled it off his finger and bounced it lightly in his palm. "Should've thrown it in the river years ago for all the good it's done me. Here," he said, handing it to her. "An anniversary present. And here's luck. I mean it."

"Maybe it'll bring some," she said, taking it, regarding the little ivory head. "Maybe it's gonna come out of a dry spell." She got up then, went inside and rummaged around till she found a gold chain in her jewelry box and put the ring on it.

"I'll wear it," she said, slipping the chain over her neck as she came back out on the balcony. "Your luck is mine and mine is yours, one way or another."

There was a knock on the door, and when she opened it Billy Bigelow stood in the hallway. He bowed and handed her a single rose. "Happy Anniversary," he said. "No magic to it," he added. "I stole it from the garden. Tonight I'll buy you a drink, for the sake of a quarter of a century."

"Well," she said, smelling the rose, "here's somebody that remembered— how about that." Then she thought, I shouldn't have said that. I'm not trying to get in any licks. In fact, she had another idea. She went back to the balcony after putting Billy's rose in a glass of water. She went up behind Dusty and put her arms around him. "I feel like going back to bed," she said, "maybe lazing around for a little while. And since it's our anniversary . . ."

"It's a nice idea, babe, but you're barking up the wrong tree. If you think I'm not good for much, you're right."

"A little snuggling never hurt anybody."

"Babe, you can't get blood out of a stone," he said, standing up.

"You can give me a run for it," she said. "If I catch you and tackle you, you can drag me off to bed."

"Babe—" he protested.

"Look, I'm not asking for anything. I just want your arms around me.

He looked at her. "Can't argue with that," he said.

◆

Curran's book changed its direction before his very eyes. One morning as he stood on his chair to see what might turn up in the garden, and having discovered only the calico cat stalking butterflies, he had a sudden glimpse of himself standing there. As if he were standing outside himself and had come upon a man the size of a child, hiding behind a curtain peeking out at the world. He was shaken. He wanted to laugh at his own peculiarity, and at the same time wanted to have a temper tantrum. He wanted to go out and wring the cat's neck. He wanted to say something especially insulting to Donovan, a withering remark. He wanted to turn people to stone with a very look—and he remembered he had done that once, or very nearly.

He felt humbled and ashamed, baffled and belligerent, pulled in so many directions that he got down off the chair and sat doodling with his pencil for half an hour. His subject matter, like a great undigested bolus, had been tossed into his lap: if he was looking for peculiarity, he might as well start with himself, without pretensions or disguises. He might as well stand bare-assed naked. He wasn't prepared for essays, or attempts. No, he would have to back up a few paces—turn things inside out. And suddenly he knew the nature of his inquiry. It would be like turning your pockets inside out to see what was inside.

On a blank page in his notebook he wrote:

RENVERSAYS
QU'AI-JE
(What have I got?)

It didn't seem like much. Given what it took to be human, he'd been scanted by nearly two feet, though he'd been given all the right parts. Yet he'd never *quite* made it up to the human: he'd always been standing in a pit, even though he prided himself on being cleverer than other people. And what did that mean? A foolish and empty boast, an elevator shoe for self-esteem.

Suppose you took things back to the beginning, to the first cell, a cell stamped with intention, a set of possibilities, an idea for the future. For that's what a cell was. He had been the result of nature thinking small. And he thought about the ways other people had started out in life. Or had it been mere inadvertence, a mistake, a momentary lapse of attention—the gods reaching for the wrong screwdriver?

Possibly it had been the same with the fellow he'd read about who could read five languages but couldn't understand any of them; or the fellow who sang his own operas when he was asleep but was nothing more than a short-order cook when he was awake; or the genius of an inventor who had designed a magnificent automobile engine, big as a house, as well as a battery-run mouse trap. Or anybody else who spent his life on one little trick—being buried alive for days or training fleas to walk a tightrope, or swallowing goldfish. Perhaps all these were lapses, inadvertencies, like the great reptiles with webbed feet and heads like violins, like mastodons with very tiny brains. There was always a chap who thought he could fly if he just put his mind to it, with or without wings. And those who thought they themselves could be gods if they grabbed enough, hoarded enough, bossed enough people around, slaughtered enough.

And what did it all amount to? Nothing, so far as he could determine, except that anyone could start out a far piece from being human, and maybe never get there at all. Possibly he had been haunted all along, fearful that because he was small he also lacked in other ways, and that circumstances would dwarf him as well.

What were his chances in the world? His parents had hired a special tutor for him, and he could browse to his heart's content among the shelves of a good library, but as for his future . . . He had no skill with horses, so he couldn't make it as a jockey. He read about one job opportunity that had momentarily intrigued him: it would have given him the chance to see London. For the entertainment of his clientele, the owner of a casino in Mayfair, had ornamented his staircase with dwarfs, had wild animals roaming through the rooms and acrobats hanging from the chandeliers. But it wouldn't have suited Curran's temperament or sensibility, standing around as a droll object. From a very early age he had been stage-struck. But what roles could he have played besides a Munchkin in "The Wizard of Oz?" There were plenty of children around for the role of a child. A midget was not a child. And off he went to join the carnival.

But of those who started life with everything one could ask, how many came to grief or drink, wasted their talents, threw themselves away? Wealth, talent, opportunity: gone in a puff of smoke. He had seen it happen. Even in the carnival.

In the midst of a sentence, he found himself dreaming of his youth. Dreaming about Elise. Young, then—such a lovely girl. The acrobat. Lean and lithe and limber as a salamander. And light. Nothing dark or heavy could live in her.

He had loved her. At the risk of being ridiculous, he had followed her around. Brought her chocolate when the act was over and she was back in the dressing room. Saw she got to bed at a decent hour and roused her in time from her catnaps to put on her costume and get ready for her act. Little Elise.

"And what would I do without you?" she'd say to him. "I'd never survive." And she would bend over to kiss him on the forehead. For his part, he thought of P. T. Barnum's midget, who had been kissed by over two million ladies, including the queens of England, France, Spain and Belgium, because he was so sweet. And he ground his teeth. "What would I ever do without you?"

He wanted her to mean it. But it was debatable whether she would ever *see* him or continue to think of him as one of the props. But though she had her crushes here and there and sometimes went out on dates, all this was short-lived.

Until Orlando the Juggler. A tall man with muscles that rippled like a cat's, who tossed cups and plates and ninepins into the air and balanced chairs on the end of sticks and stacks of cups on these, and held the whole up on his chin. He couldn't miss, not in anything. Toss it in the air and he caught it behind his back on the heel of his left foot, did somersaults in the air and came down in time to catch whatever was falling. And the audience ate it up. When Curran watched, he ground his teeth. He was so full of himself. Curran hated the way he milked the audience, made them clap till their hands were sore. Or maybe he was jealous—of that too.

But mostly he was watching Elise watching him. Her eyes went to the juggler, and he treated her as if she were only his due. The way she looked at him... Curran could have throttled the joker. And the world wouldn't have been any the worse. For he could see what would happen to any woman. The sort of slavery she would enter. "Stand there and admire me." It was all he had to say: Admire me. Admire me. He swam in a sea of applause—it was his element. There was no room for anyone else.

They were married, of course. Even stayed with the show for a couple of years. Elise was still lovely to watch, though it seemed to Curran that her husband was jealous of every little bit of applause she got. Then she was pregnant, and after a few months they went their own way. Curran wasn't sorry to see them go. Out of sight, out of mind.

He saw her maybe six or seven years later. She and Orlando had gone to Europe: he had worked with all the big circuses there. A triumphant tour. And she—she had her son. He was a decent enough little tad, Curran supposed. She had brought him along to meet her old friend. She no longer had an act. She'd gone heavy in the hip and thigh, and she didn't look happy. All she had were clippings about her wonderful Orlando.

Curran looked at these while she went off to get a coke for the kid, who'd been whining for one. Meanwhile the kid went round poking into things, picking up ends of rope, standing on boxes. He was standing on one when he said, "I'm taller than you."

The sort of thing kids say. Curran gave a little grimace meant to be a smile.

Then the kid got down, came over, planted himself right in front of him and said, "And I'm as tall as you are now."

Something hit Curran then. And he gave the boy so savage a look that he seemed nearly paralyzed. Curran meant it, wanted something to change inside the kid and never be the same. He wanted to trample something. Suddenly the kid shook himself and ran off with a howl.

"I've got your coke," Elise called, coming back into the tent. "Come, I'll give it to you." But he would not be persuaded to return.

"What's got into him?" Elise said, glancing around the tent. Nervous, she looked around again, as if she'd best go after him. "Kids— you never know with them. Such a worry sometimes. Sometimes," she said, wistfully, "I wish I could have it all back again. I loved to perform. You know, there are things you feel in your body . . . I can't explain: Something flows through you. You forget where you are. You don't even know what it is. I wonder sometimes, is there any other way you can know that feeling? Do you know what I mean?"

"It's just an act," Curran said, "a way to feed your face."

He watched her expression grow blank. "You think so?" she said, looking at him intently.

"You haven't lost anything," he told her. "It's a hell of a life. All this moving around. And what happens when you get older—get a touch of rheumatism and all that? It's no picnic."

Yes, he thought now, he had taken his revenge all right. He could be proud of himself. And what did he have? Only his smallness.

♦

Of all the people affected by the division and trouble in the town, Alexos seemed to react the most strangely. As if he were touched in the head, had sat on a pin or been startled out of his skin by a gadfly. Ordinarily a quiet man, good with his hands, able to repair what looked to be hopelessly fallen apart, he rose early in the morning and worked all day around the hotel. He never hurried, always took his time, saw what needed to be done, laid out his tools and materials carefully and went to work. He saved everything—little pieces of wood, bent nails, used screws and bolts, worn-out sheets, old rages, parts of motors, old spark plugs and lengths of twine. You never knew when you might need something in a pinch. He squirreled everything away in carefully labeled, drawers, boxes and jars.

Though quiet, he was not unsociable. He loved a good meal, his glass of brandy afterwards, good company and good talk. And he was passionately devoted to his family and friends. In the evenings after dinner, he took his brandy in the bar, smoked a cigar, talked to his friends, then went off to read the classics.

Suddenly restless and preoccupied, he barely touched his food and ignored his friends, left off reading his favorite authors, neglected his family, and instead climbed the stairs to the attic, where he remained so long that he was groggy and sleepy in the morning and for most of the day. Elena knew something was wrong.

"Alexos," she entreated him, "what is it? You have eaten nothing of your supper, and tonight it is wonderful lamb I have cooked in a sauce with tomatoes and onions, and delicious green beans the way you like and little carrots sweet from the ground and rice with raisins and nuts, and good bread with a thick crust, and all with a most lovely wine. And oh, Alexos, what is wrong? And why do you spend so many hours away from us? And what are you doing up there in that dusty attic while I lie in bed waiting and waiting for you and growing sleepy when you do not come. Have you grown weary of me and no longer even like my cooking?"

So Elena made her complaint, with numerous variations, some caressing and pleading, some bordering on petulance, with sighs and grimaces and tears and downcast eyes. For she was convinced he must be going mad. She had no idea what to do. Nor was she reassured by Alexos' response:

"Please, please—you must let me be. I must find what I am looking for."

In the attic? In the dust and cobwebs a hundred years had created? In light that would ruin his eyes? She knew what was up there. Old clothes worn by the ancestors of both families, all stored away in trunks: ancient silks and shawls, and tortoise-shell combs, and cuff links and collars. And old love letters and bills of sale and marriage licenses and birth certificates and bundles of newspapers and documents . . .

Documents. After a week he emerged one evening dusty and triumphant, waving a wad of them in his hand. It was a rather noisy evening in the bar. Captain Valor had outdone himself on mescal and roared from one table to the next trying to pick a fight; since no one paid him any attention, he ended up cursing and swearing and singing at the top of his lungs. Meanwhile Chico and Reynaldo, at the height of revolutionary fervor, and above the interference of the Captain, were angrily attacking their guitars. At this point Alexos appeared in the doorway. One of the women shrieked, apparently mistaking him for a ghost. Suddenly the room became quiet.

"Alexos!" the captain called. "Come have a brandy. What are you doing, standing there in the doorway?"

"My friends," he announced. "Here is what we have been looking for. The deed to the land, the articles incorporating the town. They are here—in my hand."

For a moment there was a stunned silence, as the news penetrated the fog of drink. Then a sudden shouting, cheering, stomping, clapping, everyone talking at once.

People crowded around him. "Give him room. Make way," someone yelled. "Don't suffocate the man."

They moved back then. He held up his hand for silence. Carefully he unfolded a piece of yellowed parchment, motes of dust filtering into the air. "Listen, my friends, to the proof:

Know Ye, that the Governor of the Territories of Cibola, by the mutual agreement of the Governments of Mexico and the United States in accordance with the Treaty for the Pacification of Borders, does hereby grant, give, bargain, sell and convey unto Demosthenes Kalandropolis the tract of land extending from the route known as La Via de los Almas Perdidos south as far as La Colina Santa, in extent three hundred and sixty acres.

To have and to hold the aforegranted and bargained premises, with all the privileges and appurtenances thereof, to the said Demosthenes Kalandropolis' heirs and assigns forever.

Know ye furthermore and moreover that said tract shall henceforth be known as Old Town, and that henceforth, by the powers vested in me, reposing special trust in the integrity, ability and discretion of said Demosthenes Kalandropolis, I do hereby appoint him to be Mayor.

I, therefore, authorize him to fulfill the duties of that office according to law; to cause to be kept the Laws and Ordinances made for the good and peace and conservation of the same; and to hold that office together with all of the powers, privileges and emoluments of that office for the term of Seven Years, if he so long behaves himself well in that office.

Thomas S. Coward
Governor

"Those are the most beautiful words I ever heard," Elena exclaimed.

There was more. Alexos explained that another document, drawn up a few years later, stated that the town *was* a town as long as the hotel stood. For in the beginning it was postal and telegraph office, town hall and hostelry—indeed, the only building there, a stagecoach stop, a pause for rest and refreshment and a change of horses for the long journey on the Via de los Almas Perdidos, so called because so many never found their way back. Later, as more people arrived and the old man sold bits of land to incoming settlers and a town had grown up, there was a real city hall, long since burned down. Alexos produced an old photograph of the town in those days. But after the silver petered out and all the excitement and activity came to an end, the buildings mostly abandoned and the town mostly gone, all the official documents were brought back to the hotel and stored in the attic.

By now Alexos was ready to sit down and rest his bones, but after a burst of applause Captain Valor called "Speech! Speech!"

Though ordinarily a man of few words, but seeing perhaps that the moment had fallen to him as to those who had come before, pushing himself forward into the spotlight, Alexos drew himself up and spoke in the manner of Pericles delivering the funeral oration. First he called to mind the achievements of his forebears, who together with Elena's had been given land, still occupied by their descendants. He gave special homage to Elena's grandfather, who had created their inheritance by building the hotel and serving as Mayor of the town; then to his father, who in spite of reverses had maintained the tradition of a place where all might come to spend a night and find good cheer as well. And walk the streets of the town, though still unpaved, free men with their heads held in pride. "There is no exclusiveness in our public life, and in our private intercourse we are not suspicious of one another, nor angry with our neighbor if he does what he likes; we do not put on sour looks at him, which though harmless are not pleasant." Thus he quoted Thucydides, and concluded by saying that the threat from the other faction had now been met, and henceforth all should live together in peace and freedom, sharing the bounty that had been made possible by generous laws and men of good will.

It was a noble speech, delivered with great passion. And everyone listening as Alexos stood in the doorway, occasionally gesturing with the hand that held the documents, knew he was present at one of the great moments in Old Town's history. The tears ran unashamedly down Captain Valor's cheeks, and when the speech was finished he unglued himself from the bar stool and made his way—supported by several hands held out when he threatened to reel over backwards—to where Alexos was standing and seized his hands. "Spoken like a man," he said, as the others cheered and shouted "Hear! Hear!" and "Old Town forever!"

Elena then ran up and embraced her husband, led him to a table and brought him a steaming plateful of delicately seasoned lamb and a glass of mellow red wine.

There were drinks all around, the celebration racing far into the night. Word spread between friends and neighbors, and before the night was over everyone in both towns knew what had happened. Some wondered what the Reverend Hoskins would do and a few were in favor of running him out with pitchforks for good measure: Several, overcome with whiskey and excitement, had to be carried home.

To herself Alta said, "We ought to have a real celebration. It's the perfect moment." As far as she was concerned, the discovery coincided perfectly with her efforts to get Dusty out of the bar and back to work. As Alexos said, it was the *kairos:* things had come together in the perfection of the moment. A show would be the crowning touch. Nothing big or fantastic, but from those few still left, a band of survivors, you might say, a showing of their best.

♦

"How about it?" she said to Dusty. "You got any better offers?"

"God, woman, you bug me."

"They deserve it—and what are you doing except going to fat? You got to do what you're cut out to do. Otherwise you rot. Come on."

"The work," he groaned. "We're out of practice. Timing's all shot. It'd be like starting from scratch."

"Never hindered you before. You've started from less than nothing, climbed out of a hole to do a show—in debt on all sides. Come on—they're counting on you."

"Nonsense. Half the people in town have been drunk ever since the news came out. They're perfectly capable of doing their own celebrating. And so am I, for that matter."

"What about the rest of us?" Alta continued. "Eddie spooks around till he gets on my nerves, then hides in his room for hours. I think he's going ape. And Gus is even worse—chasing everything on two feet. And Billy's got his hands full with that kid. None of the lot is up to any good, I tell you. They need something to occupy them."

"Okay, okay. You'll be on me till I'm half crazy. First you're on me for trying to do a show; then you're on me for not doing one. But we'll put on one performance, if that'll satisfy you. At least I'll have a little peace for five minutes."

She was triumphant. They all went to work. Now, when the spirit of the town was running high, was the time to make the most of things, before the excitement flagged. They'd have to rehearse the acts, sell the tickets, find a decent set-up. After discussions with Alexos and the Mayor and anyone else who had an opinion, they decided to have the show right in the hotel, in the old ballroom that was added during the boom and which, except for a couple of special occasions, had been closed up for years.

Once the news of the carnival spread, there was no lack of people who either wanted to be in it or around the edges. A young fellow brought out a unicycle from somewhere, and a juggler of some skill, as well as dancers and musicians, appeared. Dusty began to imagine a carnival of some dimension, no great magnitude but not so piddling as it looked from the outset. He was getting back to his old self— issuing orders, everywhere at once, acting with authority. A crowd of kids lolled about watching them rehearse out-of-doors. The actual performance would be inside the great ballroom, with the audience sitting on three sides.

Meanwhile the ballroom was getting a thorough refurbishing. The doors were thrown open and a crowd had descended with mops and buckets and brooms, sweeping and washing windows and mopping floors. Several of the men put up ladders to take down the pendants from the old crystal chandeliers, which were washed and replaced, casting their rainbow colors to the windows. Others filled in holes and repainted where the plaster had cracked. There was liveliness in all these activities. The men teasing the girls about not being able to paint a wall properly, and the girls giving their tormentors back as good as they got. Alexos was pleased. Nothing like a fresh coat of paint to lift the spirits. New life. A future.

Alta and two other women went through the costumes. Nearly all of them needed washing and cleaning; many were torn and bedraggled. Since they had acquired new performers, they had to come up with something quickly. The women went through their clothes and boxes of material for bits of finery, hats and the like, and there were days of fitting and sewing. The costume made for Quam'bukqueau, who was to be a clown, was a masterpiece—one orange and one blue sleeve, the same colors in reverse for the legs.

There were posters and festoons all over the hotel and throughout the town. Booths were set up outside the hotel so that during and after the carnival, folks could wander among them and buy popcorn and candied apples and shoot at targets and knock down bottles with balls and toss coins into rings. They could buy beer and soft drinks and hamburgers and hot dogs and sit and play bingo. Once the carnival was over, everything was to be cleared away and a dance held in the ballroom until the wee hours, music provided by three of the town's musicians, a fiddler, a trumpet player and a man on the piano.

For the occasion, Billy, with the help of the boy, had executed what he considered his masterpiece. On a board three feet high and ten feet long, he set out the letters for CARNIVAL FOR THE GODS in a special script he invented called "the flying serif," each letter so heavily ornamented with serifs that it took an exuberant leap before the eyes. These were painted in red and yellow. Then the boy took over. At the bottom he added wild and flaming vegetation, plants shooting up, exploding into blossom. At the two ends, these plants were elaborate vines all in flower, winged figures swinging from them. Other figures were climbing the sides of the letters, sitting astride them or dancing over the tops.

"Looks pretty classy," Billy said to the boy.

The boy didn't look at him directly, but from the hunch of his shoulders Billy could tell he was pleased with his work. Billy watched him add one more touch—unnecessary, he thought—to the tip of a plant.

That afternoon Billy and Alexos hung the sign above the doorway of the hotel. Then they stood and watched people admire it as they walked by.

"Where'd you learn to do all that," Billy asked the boy. Surely it hadn't come to him out of the blue.

"Here and there," he said.

Not giving anything away, was he. Always carrying around something secret—a whole bundle, most likely.

"But mostly here," Billy thought he heard the boy say under his breath.

◆

Curran had put away his notebook with the feeling that he'd put it away forever. For a couple of days he and Donovan spent hours in the garden talking about their routine, trying out different positions and movements. Though neither would admit it, they were having a wonderful time.

"We've been sitting in our own fat too long," Donovan said.

For once, Curran agreed with him.

They had a new comedy routine. The two of them are walking under a ledge. Both are hit on the head by a flower pot. When they recover from the blow, the giant thinks he's a midget and the midget, a giant. The giant speaks in a small high-pitched voice, the midget in a baritone. They went over the routine so many times, adding new incidents and trying out new lines, that there were moments that they lay back in their chairs weak with laughter.

◆

There was only one hitch before the actual performance. The night before, at their final rehearsal, when all the costumes had been fitted, all had gathered in the ballroom except Quam'bukqueau. "Where is he," Dusty wanted to know, but no one had any idea. It wasn't like him to be late. After a few minutes, Dusty wanted to begin without him, he had a lot to do.

Then Quam'bukqueau appeared, looking somewhat dazed and disoriented, a large bruise on the side of his head. He couldn't give a coherent account of what had happened, except that something had hit him hard on the side of the head and knocked him out. But what was worse, when he had come to and had gone back to his shed, he found it a pile of smoking cinders.

"Why would anybody do that?" Alta said, aghast, though it was, she knew, a pointless question. But why would anyone take the trouble over a simple, harmless fellow? Maybe because he was.

"What'll we do?" Elena said.

Indeed, no one seemed to know. There was a good deal of milling about, as Quam'bukqueau stood shaking his head as though he'd awakened and found himself in a strange world.

"Proceed as usual," Dusty yelled. "We're not going to let one little thing scuttle the whole works, are we?"

"Of course not," Donovan yelled back. "If anybody wants a fight, they can come pick on me."

"Well, not on me," Curran said to general laughter.

"Come on," Dusty said. "We got work to do."

The incident reminded them, though, that not everyone would be coming to the show, that some might look on it as a slap in the face, though Alta's intention was to put some good feeling back into Old Town, to make people forget their hostilities.

But the next day a large crowd was on hand anyway, even some from New Town. The ballroom was gleaming. A temporary stage had been erected at the center; lights mounted on poles in the comers— each a serviceable if crude spotlight. A curtain screened the performers at the back. Ringing the stage were cushions for people to sit on. A tattoo of drums started the show, and Dusty mounted the stage, resplendent in top hat and tails and a red-sequined vest.

"Ladies and gentlemen," he announced. "We present to you not the Greatest Show on Earth, but the Carnival for the Gods. For all —great and small. This is the place, now is the time to forget all your troubles and have the time of your life. We'll dazzle your eyes and amaze your wit. There's magic—there's laughter. Juggling and clowns. Great acts—the greatest. All kinds of wonders. Not to mention the greatest wonder of them all, our own Amazing Grace. And now, ladies and gentlemen, on with the show."

While he was bowing from left to right, Curran tackled him at the knees, Donovan caught him and carried him off. And the show began.

Donovan and Curran started off with their bit, but they were in and out between the different acts, buying time for prop and costume changes, providing a thread of continuity. After the juggling and an acrobatic routine, Billy did his magic, inviting the children from the audience to come up on the stage while he produced a live rabbit from his hat and created a pile of scarves at their feet. Then he blew up balloons and twisted them into elephants and dogs and kangaroos and let them sail off into the air. Then the midget stole his rabbit. To great applause, Billy produced another.

When the act was over and Billy had taken his bows and slipped behind the curtain, he found Grace ready to take her turn. A snake was draped about her shoulders and another around her waist.

"Do you smell smoke," she asked, turning back to him just as she was about to walk through the curtain.

"I'm not sure," Billy said.

Dusty had finished announcing her act, and she walked out on to the stage.

"*I* smell it," Donovan said. "Where's it coming from?"

Then someone yelled "Fire!" and they could hear a sudden turmoil in the audience. Everyone went wild, shrieking and yelling and pushing to get out.

All the performers made a mad scramble into the audience. Grace was standing confusedly on stage while people stampeded toward the door. She was trying to calm the snakes that were weaving nervously around her. The end of the ballroom was a wall of flame, the old wood crackling and burning like paper.

Billy leapt up onto the stage. "Come on," he yelled, trying to grab her. "We've got to get out of here."

"Billy," she cried, "what are you doing?"

His frantic reach had the gesture of a threat. Before he knew what happened, one of the snakes had struck him on the hand.

6

The miles were rolling away in great circles of darkness. He could feel the landscape roaring past, and felt himself hurtling through the great quiet. He could feel the solitude of the landscape, of the desert closed off by the darkness. But he found no rest there, as though the darkness were boiling away from him as he lay heavy and leaden, his body a molten center pouring out heat. The heat had dried out his blood till his veins were hot wires, as the water broke out on his forehead—all but his hand, which they had put in ice. That source of heat and confusion, the reason for their hurtling through darkness, lay numb and unfeeling, a part of him that no longer belonged to him. There were the faces, the eyes of those around him, watching over him, glued with concern to his face. But he could not look at them. He closed his eyes and was tom away down into the dark, the dark of himself and of earth. Fear moved over him, clutched at his chest, and some dim force struggled to survive.

He lay somewhere back in the extinct beginnings, eons ago when the earth was trying itself out, discovering rain and soil and inventing it wasn't quite sure what. He was a creature of the sea, that maker of forms, and had stumbled upon sentience and awakened with an obscure appetite. Appetite that pushed and moved him till it roused him from the depths and from its obscure beginnings, until it crawled out of the sea and clung to earth; tried to shed the scaly, fishy armor of its great hunger. What heaviness. And perhaps always heavy in its struggle, its effort in a world always ten steps ahead because forty steps behind— asleep in the great inertia of matter.

He emerged as reptile—as salamander, as lizard and horned toad, as dinosaur and brontosaurus. He was armored body and great claws and jaws and teeth—rows and rows of teeth. Instinct and violence and very little brain. But he was huge. He was monstrous. He wore a great horn on his head. He had a great dagger for a thumb. He moved among plants and blundered through swamps. He was stolid and immovable as an eater of grass; he was rapacious in his hunger for meat and clawed and tore his way through muscle and nerve to the bone. He shuffled his way through eons, while nature invented and discarded parts and tried out the grotesque: webbed feet, gigantic snouts, great dorsal fins and wings. Then suddenly, as if by accident: Reptile with ambition. And yearning. You could understand it: flat on the ground without so much as a neck to take the eyes from the heaviness of earth. Even before the take-off, the urge for a new career: took off its skin and new, crept naked.

But mostly he remembered pursuit and flight and the tearing of flesh, the joy of claws and the rows of teeth. The cold reptilian eye.

He could see all of earth, but mostly the desert, where the great blundering forms gave up the struggle and left their bones to the future. While the plants struggled on with their weapons and armor: the thorny cactus and the spiked Joshua tree and the yucca and the century plant. There was an atmosphere of expectancy, of waiting, as though in some obscure corner lay another secret to be revealed. There in the desert, as they all stood at attention, the latest upstart arrived, rising and blundering like the rest, ready for rackety times. Discovering his legs, struggling to stand on his feet, falling in love with his thumb. Maybe the queerest offspring yet, who would tear and rip flesh with the best: clash his battleships like dinosaurs; fly over the earth like birds of prey with leather wings; sulk in the deeps like electric eels and sharks and rays. Nature's greatest plaything. Till he would seize hold of the tools himself and take on the greatest game. Imagine thinking up the brain, that toy of possibilities, winding it up and letting it go. What madness. For as he tossed restless, he seemed pursued by the dark reptilian dream: the cold eye, sluggish, hardened in its prejudices, sunk into its rituals, haunting him even as he woke as man.

He slept and woke again and was himself, born into his own darkness, the darkness of ignorance, and into his own struggle. And how is it that at first, as a child, you are the darling of the world? He had rambled in the woods, picking berries, collecting odd bits of moss. He'd caught garter snakes and taken them home in his pockets. Watched them whip through the brush. Creatures of the earth. Like him. Caught up in his own motion: running and climbing, falling down and picking himself up again. Whooping and yelling and coming in tired to the bone, letting the screen door clatter behind him and, hands barely clean, dirt still under the nails, sit down to stuff his mouth with home-baked bread thick with butter. His appetite devouring him.

And what was he—a cell too, stamped with intention like a maple seed? But not knowing what it was. Struggling, struggling, trying on forms: sign painter and electrician and magician, husband and lover, and a father without knowing it. He'd tried them all. Watched things come and go, rise and fall, appear and disappear. Wife running off with a salesman of fertilizers and weed-killers, carrying a child that he would never see. Now rolling through the darkness, it seemed all of it had been a struggle, as it was now—trying to stay alive.

"You just hold on there," he heard Alta say. "We'll get you there." And she sponged his forehead with a cold cloth. But it soothed him only for as long as she did it.

He was alone. The heat pouring through him fell away. It was cold and numbing where he stood, no longer on the edge of the desert but at its very heart, and the cold and the dark stretched away to the borders of the world. A chill passed through him and he shivered all over. Eons and eons it had taken to create the desert: the stretches of white gypsum, the great caves of limestone stalactites and stalagmites, one drop at a time, at the base of which the water lay in green pools, and opaque fish, fragile-looking as china, swam with sightless eyes. And where was he in all this vastness? If he cried out, who would hear him?

"We're all here, Billy," Alta was saying to him. "You just hold on.

"I got bit by a snake once," Grace said. "And when I got over it, I was never afraid anymore." She squeezed his hand.

But their voices strained in his ears. There was nothing to hold onto. He was there alone, on the naked shingles of the void. All his efforts in vain. Once more the carnival had failed, and this time he had fallen too, struck down. And what had his life been worth? The cold had got him, the numbing poison. In the night on the desert he lay where unknown, killing forces clashed and had their way, wind striking rock, water tearing away earth, and drought without end. Dearth and dryness. This was the dream of earth: night on the desert, earth without heat. The cold planet. The sting of the serpent.

♦

Lord, he was done for—there underwater. Drowning among the drowned. Had he been washed away in the flood? Swept away like old Jonas Liverpool at his baptism? Ducked under the water. Thought it might do him some good to be washed in the blood of the Lamb. But the current had caught him like a leaf. Staggering, falling down drunk, then drowned. Caught in the flood of the Lamb. Water mingling with his whiskey-soaked breath. Old reprobate, giving up his ghost to water. What a way for a man to go!

As for him, surely he'd clung to earth in his fear, held on for all he was worth. Desert was bad enough, let alone the nightmare fear of water. Must have been chased. Must have been trying to escape, taking his life in his arms and running breathless. And Holly Moses, he'd fallen in, to feed the fish. Or maybe the sun had just plain fizzled out like last year's sparkler and he'd run to seek the last lights in the depths. He couldn't remember.

How was it he wasn't drowned? Seemed to be breathing under water. He moved his arms, then hung there stilled with wonder at the great fish approaching him. So hello and who are you? As the fish hovered closer, a wave of terror went through him, then left him drained of emotion. When you've gone this far, you may as well forget to worry: nobody's going to steal your wallet. The fish hung there barely moving, though its tail undulated like folds of cloth. Goldfish did that. Mostly he thought of fish as slabs, flat and stiff, the eyes gone blank, the scales dulled to indifference. But down here, alive in their element, they rode the waterways. This one had its lights on: flashes of red and blue and green and gold, coming at him in points of fire. All the while, the mouth working, a cavern into the dark. It could swallow him. Go ahead then. He gave himself up, closed his eyes. But when he opened them again, the fish was gone.

Had he gone beyond memory—beyond the time he'd come to the water's edge with line and sinker, to where the creek made deep pools and he took corn and worms and marshmallows to catch the trout that hid under the shelves of rock? But the old Negro who came to fish with bread crumbs had better luck and laughed softly and held up the string of fish that he'd take home and clean, throwing the guts to the cats.

He headed home too, rooms opening along the corridors of the town: the hardware store and the old market, with pickles in barrels and herring in brine and wheels of cheese and fig newtons in the cookie case and bags of rice and flour in printed sacks. And here came the fishmonger with his wagon and scales and smell, and the egg lady and the old farmer with his wagonload of strawberries and his mother in her blue house-dress, her hair uncombed, in her usual rush of eagerness and dismay, as she tried to buy the day's supper without spending a cent more than she had to.

And the old soda fountain with magazines along the walls, candy cases full of fudge and chocolate-covered mints and nougats and divinity, kids looking at comic books and jabbering over their cokes and sodas and arm-wrestling and flirting and popping gum and looking wise and acting smart.

But it was gone. Turned under the soil. The printing plant where the *Evening Star* emerged every afternoon with all the news of Gnaw Bone, Stone's Crossing, Shiloh, Mount Pleasant and Stony Lonesome —on the front page with the obituaries. Gone with the old feed store, the green sign with its fading letters above the doorway. And the two thin old men in their green aprons, proprietors of sacks of feed, bins of tulip bulbs and onion sets, racks of seed packets, and flats of tomato plants, petunias and marigolds. The old men fading away with the store, taking with them the smell of feed and seed and old wood. Till now: observing him from their steel-rimmed glasses, hair waving like milkweed, as they stood under the sign, Grissom's Feed Co. Gone, but it all came floating back.

He could look down to the depths, to the sea floor, where the fish teemed among the sea anemones and banks of coral. Fish that could have swum in the dreams of his most distant ancestor. And strange spiny creatures that could have battled the porcupine and taken over the desert. He almost got sucked into a whirlpool pulling down the fish and turtles and jellyfish, big and little. Till they reached the waving heads, the opening and closing jaws of two gigantic serpents. He flailed his arms, escaped. All paths led to destruction: pursuit and flight and the tearing of flesh.

He swam over the debris: hulls of broken ships and skulls of drowned sailors, over cannons half buried in the muck. The great dump. Rusted bed springs and fallen timbers. All the remains sunken to the depths, never to rise again or to wash ashore with shells and sand dollars and bits of glass to hint of exhausted life. But even so, what you tried to get rid of came back at you, to make a dump in your own back yard. Or else try to slough it off, throw it down, and here comes Old Mrs. Monday to pick it up and cart it off to her shack at the edge of town, where she lives amid stacks of newspapers and piles of rags and old calendars, in the clutter of bottles and sacks and broken furniture and worn-out toys. Till she's dead herself and food for worms. Dead of trying to hold onto everything till it crumbles in the hand and stinks of decay. Holding on to what comes back one way or another.

He drifted farther, beyond the town, beyond these depths, and saw in the distance a shelf of broken continent. He watched giants ten and twelve feet tall, and pygmies they could have squashed underfoot. And creatures with bodies as fluid as the water, moving before his eyes like color floating. Their thoughts floated too, shaping their forms, shaping speech without words. Some winners, Billy thought, some losers. You could make a world anywhere.

He was down in the great lost and found, whirling among shapes and forms, all that could've been dreams on the way to the sleeper. Trees were growing with roots in the sky and stars lay scattered over the ground. Would he rise, would he wake, or simply drown in the deep. The waves were streaming past with sand and shells, the roar of water in his ears. The coolness touched his brow. Then looking into Alta's eyes, struggling to the surface, a gurgle in his ears, he emerged.

♦

The letters flamed red and gold: CARNIVAL FOR THE GODS. And within the flames the letters were formed by acrobats, standing on their heads, curving their bodies backwards and forwards, standing on each other's feet, extending themselves out from each other's shoulders—flames dancing around them till they went leaping and somersaulting, flying into the air.

It would have made a great act, Dusty. You could make a fire that wouldn't bum. Should be easy, considering where the hottest fires burned. Old Dusty: heat of ambition, flame of desire.

Now the spotlight came on and Alta walked to the center of the ring, a white cape around her shoulders. She took off her cape, assumed a ballet pose, then began to climb the rope, pulling herself up hand over hand. Strong like a man, and robust, but her arms and legs were finely shaped. A marvel as he watched her pull herself up the eighty feet of rope, then swing around a hundred and fifty times by her wrist, her sequined blue suit a dizzying flash of sparks. And when it was over her wrist was a raw red wound, and it was a wonder she never got blood-poisoning. She still carried the scar.

You had courage, Dream Girl. Endurance. And what was it like when you were young and the lights were on you and you went flashing through the air for Dusty to catch you and let you hang there by your wrists?

It was like I was in another world. Carried along like a rocket or a shooting star. Just a flash. Like I didn't have a body.

Seems like when I watched, I was up there with you. But with my heart in my mouth. Saw you miss your timing that once when Dusty caught you in his knees. And you went back for the evening show. My knees were all water.

You have to be crazy... Ah, but those years. It was like ... It was like the best time you've ever had in bed. Oh, God it was lovely. Is that what birds know, just in their common everyday—zinging through the air, doing the trip from branch to branch?

Sometimes they sit in the pelting rain, freezing on the wires.

*I've done that too. Champagne and shrimp cocktail and filet mignon when you're
up. The heat turned off when you're down. But you know all about that.*

Ups and downs? Why, that's a magician's stock-in-trade.

And once it had all come together, and they looked as if they'd sail into the blue
beyond. Back past the money troubles and the fights, the efforts and the failu-
res, to the days of dancing horses and the juggler who juggled three flaming
torches, throwing them up so it looked as though they'd catch the top of the
tent on fire; and the magnificent Carlini, who had mastered the triple somer-
sault on the trapeze; and the genius of the high-wire and his family, who threw
themselves with every performance into the teeth of death.

The hot glare of lights and the whirl of pink purple red orange yellow green
blue; the flash of spangles and the glitter of sequins; the leaping soaring jumping flying whirling of the human body; the smells of animals—acrid cat smell
of lions and tigers, muffled dust smell of elephants, reek of bears and earth-
smell of horses, pungency of man sweat. Animals and men. Giants and midgets. Antics of clowns. A dozen of them emerging from one ancient Ford: tall
and short and fat and lean. Each one raising one more degree the laughter of
the crowd till it sounded in his ears a mighty roar, a great wave rolling over him.

"Hold on, Billy," Alta was saying. "You want a drink of water?"

He was still there, rolling through the dark. Rolling on and holding on.

O roll on, Billy. Don't you roll so slow.
O how can I roll, when the wheels don't go?

And where was the magic now? He tried to remember. Was it in a pack of cards
from which he was sneaking out the queen, or in a pile of colored scarves?
Where was it? He had to find it before it was too late.

Billy, Billy, it's time for your act.

Already? Time for me to go on?

But perhaps first you'd like to say a few words to the audience.

Ladies and gentlemen—fellow spectators.

Yay, Billy!

Thank you, little girl.

*All of you who have followed my career, aided and abetted me, applauded my
efforts . . .*

(Applause.)

Thank you, one and all. And now on the verge of the greatest disappearing act of my career—up without a down—I'd like to give some accounting of myself...

(Expectant pause.)

Give it to 'em, Billy!

In my long career, I have taken 9,473 rabbits out of hats, not counting those that multiplied while they were inside.

You're a genius, Billy.

I have made as much money disappear as I spent—no one can beat that record.

Hey, Billy! I done that much with a hole in my pocket!

And I have danced illusion for the sake of wonder in the eyes of forty thousand children.

But Billy, what will you leave behind?

Calm yourself, Madam. Kindly do not spill your soda down the neck of the gentleman in front of you.

(Laughter.)

My legacy, you mean? To Alta and Dusty? Donovan and Curran? Grace and the boy? The fire in the heart, Madam. My little bag of tricks. Had he forgotten anything? He thought of the boy.

"Alta," he said, raising up. "My cape's here somewhere. Here, I'm lying on it."

"Take it easy, Billy."

"And now, kid," he said to the boy, who'd been hanging over the bed, a wildness in his eyes, "this is yours. You got to take up where I left off."

"Don't leave us, Billy," Alta wept. "We need your magic."

"There'll be more," he promised. He could see acrobats leaping into the flames, dissolving, leaping out again. And he joined them, leaping into the air.

7

She didn't care about anything—that's what Alta said to herself: didn't care anymore how she got from one day to the next, dragging her weary bones through the hours; didn't care what she put in her mouth, it all tasted of wormwood and ashes; didn't know where she was going or why—except that to keep moving was better than standing still. Standing still, she'd turn into a mummy. She could've stayed in the city for its offering of conveniences and comforts, even for the adventure of being there, at the doorway to the future, so to speak. But she had no palate for enjoyment. She just wanted to get off on her own. She told the others to stay, she didn't want anybody fussing over her. But they wouldn't let her go alone—they'd come too, even though the city was a marvel. It could have been a miracle for Billy had they got him there in time, if they could've hired one of the helicopters kept in readiness to fly people in from all over the territory. For the city was the site of all that the most advanced scientific and humanitarian thinking could produce—the great hope for the future: Atlantia. And all of them had marveled at the clean sweep of the thoroughfares, the domes carefully designed and built to serve both need and desire, all sun-heated, air-cooled, surrounded with plants and trees and decorated with murals and marble columns.

An oasis in the desert. The Corps of Engineers had created a dam and reservoir and flooded much of the surrounding land, displacing various small ranchers and submerging the native flora and fauna. Various agencies, however, were trying to relocate the ranchers and remedy the damage to the environment. Meanwhile the arable land was being farmed in cotton, pecans and chili peppers, and a number of the inhabitants had become prosperous.

But Alta's only interest had been in the hospital, where they had arrived too late. They had tried to revive Billy with every possible means. But now it didn't matter to her that it was the most advanced hospital of its kind, equipped not only to do operations by means of light rays but also prepared to make use of all the known agencies of nature, whether plant or mineral, and all human skills scientifically applied to alleviate any sickness of body or mind.

Alta had no interest—fat lot of good it had done. Nor could she work up any enthusiasm for the apartment complexes that were small neighborhoods in themselves, with their own nurseries, gardens, playgrounds and baseball teams. Nor for the research center, with its observatory and labs. For the few days they were in the city, the others having followed them in the trailers, Dusty having returned to the hotel for their possessions and to pay the bill, Donovan had been lost in sheer fascination with what the latest and most advanced thinking had been able to create. He'd never seen anything like it.

"Too bad Billy couldn't have seen it. He'd have been impressed."

"Didn't do him any good, did it?" Then, thinking better of it, Alta said, "Why don't you stay here?"

"What would happen to the carnival?"

"What do you mean?" she said, angrily, as though she were being mocked. "There isn't any carnival." Dazed though she was, full of anguish, they gave her no peace. She seemed to have been pushed to the center once more and, even though she didn't care about anything, put in charge of their fates. Dusty, who had been roused for that one brief, dazed effort, was again adrift. Indeed, they all seemed to be circling the same spot—the void left by Billy's death, a void at the very center of their lives, and they were stricken, disoriented, undone. Perhaps they had never expected to be without him, or hadn't really known what his presence had meant. Or maybe this was the final blow, coming when they had been weakened by too many disasters, so that now the whole structure of their existence was undermined. They avoided talking to one another, seemed embarrassed in each other's presence; as though they might have to confess something about themselves they couldn't bear to say. The boy looked eerie, his skin almost translucent, and he seemed more withdrawn than he'd ever been. Billy's cape over his shoulders, a dark blue cape with lavender silk lining, he sat and played solitaire by the hour.

Alta had no desire to go back to Old Town. That was a time gone forever, a place where she'd almost been happy, if you ever knew what happy was, and Billy had belonged to it. No, if she went back, she would be continually reminded of him, pricked by hot needles. Add to that her worry over Grace. As if they hadn't enough troubles, here came Dusty with another letter from Priam Gillespie. He was on his way to the Territory, looking for Grace, going to take her back by force if not by consent.

"The old bastard," Grace said, after she'd read his latest missive. "Can't even add. Probably thinks I'm still under age. Though he was willing to lie quick enough when he could get money for it. Let him try to take me back—I'll rip his balls off."

"You'll have help," Alta assured her, even though she didn't know him from Adam's off-ox. She'd stand there like an old she-bear protecting her cub. But in truth, the meanness had gone out of her with everything else; there was no fight left in her.

No, there was no carnival—it didn't exist. There was nothing. When she reached down inside herself, it was only to find herself falling in the dark. Falling and falling. If she hit bottom, it seemed to her, she'd be blown out like a match. But maybe there wasn't any bottom and she'd go on plummeting forever, plunging down through the universe like a scrap from a comet's tail. And that thought was even more terrifying. But one night as she was falling, she came to a pause at some point of her downward spiral, and there was Billy just in front of her. Her eyes filled with tears, she couldn't see him and could only hear his voice: *It's carnival time. Come now, come.* She didn't want to hear it. Anyway, she didn't believe in the voice. But try as she might to shut it out, it wouldn't let her alone—till she wanted to weep and tear her hair. Yet as soon as her attention lapsed, as soon as she took her eyes away from what she was doing, it spoke to her, insistent as a steady breeze, a whisper of summer air, teasing her: *carnival time.*

◆

She couldn't remember the flight over the mountains. High mountains, she was told, rocky and barren. But she didn't remember, it was only the telling that gave the image to her mind. Though she kept with her the sensation of flight, like a great swing across the tent—the motion after the fact. Or maybe they hadn't flown at all, but had simply been drawn over the mountains by Billy's voice, the beckoning of his hand. She couldn't think, drew a blank. No questions please. Out to lunch until further notice.

Dusty: "What is this fiesta, anyway? Why are we going?"

Alta: "To be going. That's all the reason you're going to get."

Donovan: "You think they got anything for us?"

Alta: "It never crossed my mind."

Curran: "When will we be coming back?"

The torment of questions. Never any peace. I'm just an old windbag, she thought, trying to pretend I still got some real stuffing inside. She wanted—what did she want? To get out of herself, to get rid of the stale old rind that she was; to be put out of her misery, get past it somehow. But she didn't have any faith that she would. She was moving in the dark, blindly, just moving. The torment of questions: everybody came into the world half-cocked, having all of the questions and none of the answers. You spent your life hanging on a question mark, a little fish on a big hook. As if she knew, as if she wanted to come back at all ... But she wasn't going to think about the future. Leave it alone. Let it take care of itself. She was going to keep her eyes on the one little square of ground right there in front of her. If she did come back, she'd hightail it through this part of the country as fast as she could, head on back to the States. At least it was a big enough place to move around in for as long as her legs could carry her. Or if there was some way to get to Mexico City, she'd do that, then figure out where to go from there. If there was any place worth being—without Billy. Why is it, she mourned, that you never know how much you really love somebody till it's too late. She said this even though she knew she'd loved him all along. Yet she couldn't help thinking she'd let him down somehow.

What had driven her over the mountains after all—the torment of questions? Or Billy's presence? What else was there in the dark beyond the mountains?

Carnival, that's what. Seemed like she'd been hearing of it all night long in her dreams. Woke with the buzz of talk in her ears, the stir of motion in the countryside. And when she looked down from the window of the inn, the whole countryside was on the move, people streaming in towards the city, in wagons and on foot, by horse, on donkey-back. And on boats all down the river. Storytellers and musicians and vendors and players. Whole families with tents and cooking pots. She could look down and see them one after another, the boats all decked with flowers and flags and streamers, leaving the landing still thronged with people and floating toward the city, its sun-baked roofs somewhere in the distance. And music, faint at first. Coming more strongly: fiddles playing something lively. And when that subsided, the notes of a flute. But she couldn't hear the melody, there was so much noise on the landing.

But will there be a boat to take us? She looked around, trying not to lose the others, as if they all weren't lost already. Donovan— couldn't lose him. Take that one comfort.

"Here, here." A woman thrust a handful of coins into her palm. "Throw them to the musicians. For luck," she said. "It's supposed to bring luck."

She couldn't think, not in that throng around the landing, pouring in an out of the tent that had been put up, waiting to board the boats. "Here," she said, to the boy, pressing the coins into his hand. And watched him pitch the coins as though he'd been waiting to do it all his life. For luck, she thought, and remembered Dusty's ring she still wore on the chain around her neck. Hadn't done much for her either. Her hands were empty, but when she looked down her hands were filled with fruit and little pies that came from the trays of the vendors as they passed through the crowd. And she couldn't remember how she had paid for them. She was eating hungrily, tasting the cold chicken, the flaky crust, the juicy peaches. People pressed around her, and her ears were full of noise: of children shrieking with excitement, pulling at their mothers, wanting to see, whining for something to eat, darting about impatient with waiting; of babies crying and their mothers hushing them; of men joking and drinking beer. And with all that, the musicians playing, pausing, tuning their instruments, warming up for another tune, as the vendors cried their food and drink and the boatmen cursed and swore.

"Curran, Dusty—Kid, Grace," she called out, like a mother herself. "Keep close." Where would they end up if they got separated? Everything was such a struggle.

Next to her two burly young men, one of them already flushed with drink, were comparing their experiences of the previous year.

"I was a gorilla last time," the tipsy one was saying. "Scared all the girls in the park. You should have heard the peacocks too."

"But if you scare them," the other said, "they run away."

"Then you chase them." Shaking his head, rocking with laughter.

"What's so funny?"

"You know," the fellow said, nudging him. "Come on, you know."

"Where's the boat?" Curran demanded irritably, the line of his vision drawn at everybody's waist. "I can't see a thing."

"You'll have to wait your turn, sonny," an old woman chided him.

"What can you see, Gus?" Alta called to the only one who could see over the heads of the crowd.

"They've just filled a boat," he said. "There's another coming up." She closed her eyes for a moment, as though trying to put herself past the noise and confusion, the smell of sweating men and women mingled with the odors of food and flowers. The voices blended with the other sounds, making one great din in her ears, a meaningless buzz. Oh God, she groaned inwardly. Would she ever enjoy anything again? She looked over at the boy standing in his own silence. She almost expected something suppressed and savage to speak through him again, maybe stronger than ever, strong enough to drive everybody away. But now he, too, seemed completely drained, nothing there at all—clean as water.

What next? For a time he seemed to be softening at the edges. Billy, she thought, you shouldn't have left us.

The crowd suddenly moved forward and left a clear space, through which she saw for a flash of a second, across the river, a white horse with a slender girl standing on its back, a pale blue figure. The horse dashed by, its tail a white plume. How lovely, she thought, wondering if the others had seen it. Her eyes stung with sudden tears.

Then they were on the boat, even managed to find a place to sit. Some of the young men sat at the back, trailing their feet in the water. We've made it, she thought. This far, anyway, even though she had no idea where they were going. Afloat, she didn't have to think about anything, just let herself go ...

... floating out there on the river. How smooth it was, the air gentle on her face, a sheen of light sliding along the water. Clouds piled high above her. Everything light and genial and easy. Voices gathered her in, the murmur of talk, someone singing. Bottles of wine were being passed back and forth. She drank and the wine tingled in her head, rich and fruity, and she felt warmed, given release. Oh, how long it had been since she'd seen a day like this. All bright on the water, a mirror with cloud and sky and leaves reflecting, merging on its surface, silvering ahead in the shimmer of light. And oh, the flowers. She hadn't known there would be flowers. Gardens that extended to the river's edge full of roses and bougainvillea and flowering cacti and palm trees and jacaranda and mimosa and orange and lemon. No wonder it was called The City of Gardens, this city of the valley— Mecharlinda.

The slopes of the distant hills were green, heavily forested. And beyond them? She didn't care. For right now the wine was flowing freely. She was being carried along on the water and lifted up by the wine. Now and then a flower would land in the boat, and always she looked too late to see who had thrown it. But it was enough just to look around and let it all happen, this sudden bounty falling upon her. Where it came from didn't matter. Call it manna from heaven, it was all the same to her.

A silence fell. Startling in the midst of all the hubbub: the singing and shrieking and roaring and laughing stopped in a silence deep as a well. Even the children hushed. Had they been expecting something and known just then that it would happen? And now came the flute, the notes rising like the call of a bird, haunting and pure, filling the silence, flowing through it to the other side. Flowing through her. Then she saw the flute player sitting on a rock, paying no attention to them, perhaps aware only of what was in his head, making a tune out of everything around him, the river and hills, the flowing water and the boats filled with revelers. For a moment everything seemed silvery, like life turned to legend, nothing sharp or distracting, but relieved of all clutter and dismay, transformed into what the notes created. It was—she couldn't say what it was, but she would have been glad to sit there forever, listening with every pore. But in a moment the melody entered the silence and mingled with the renewed laughter and talk of those on the barge. Even after it was gone, she continued to listen, hoping it might come again, though she knew it wouldn't. Alta couldn't tell if the melody was joyful or melancholy, but it seemed that if she could stay inside it, she'd be put out of her misery. Only now even that didn't seem to matter either. There's nothing you can hold onto, she thought. Nothing at all.

"There, see! There it is," a little girl shouted, pointing. For a moment Alta couldn't see anything. Then she caught the outline of roofs, red-tile roofs, then the walls of the emerging town. She didn't want to leave the boat. Let it just go on and on, flowing with the river. And wouldn't that be a fine thing, she thought. Nothing to do but wave to the folks on shore and hug the bottle and catch a flower now and then: that's the life. They were approaching the landing, a cluster of people already gathering at the side, already eager to be off, ashore. The ropes were being thrown, the boat pulled in. Having gathered their bundles and children, the crowd thronged ashore and went their ways. Alta looked this way and that—"Here! Over here, Grace,"— till they were all together, intact, on the way into the town, over the bridge, and onto the cobbled streets that led off in various directions.

There were people everywhere, on the streets and in the tents and booths. The town was ringed with tents, some with families that had come for the festivities, others with acrobats, jugglers, clowns, musicians and storytellers who had come to entertain. There were booths with food and drink, great pots of meat stew and chilies, *caldillo,* sausages and *fajitas,* and crusty little pies filled with meat or cheese or vegetables. Donovan stopped in his tracks, took in the assorted smells. "My God," he said, "a dog would go out of his mind." "Speak for yourself," Curran said.

Other families without tents were sleeping in the parks, having brought their own cooking pots and firewood on carts. People stood in clusters here and there, eating and drinking at the booths, crowding the streets, spying at the tents to see what the performers were doing, joining their cronies, the old men joking with their friends, their wives exchanging gossip, the young flirting and bantering. In the hullabaloo dogs were barking, horses neighing. There was a great boom as a cannon went off somewhere. "Just look at this, will you?" Dusty said. "Wonder who they got in charge."

"Well, he probably won't need any help," Alta said. She was feeling a bit befuddled by all the noise and color as it joined the wine she had drunk on the boat. Decorations everywhere, the town one great huge festoon: pots of geraniums and petunias and fuchsia hanging from the lamp posts, balloons and crepe paper on balconies, banners and flags on the public buildings.

"What're we supposed to do now?" said Curran, looking over his shoulder.

"What's the matter?" Donovan gigged him. "Afraid of getting trampled? Don't worry," he said, in a tone of exaggerated nobility, "I'll protect you."

"Thanks a lot." Curran ground his teeth, not wanting to admit he was terrified of getting left behind.

"Look," said Alta, "people are lining up all along the streets. Can't you hear the band?"

"It's not for half an hour yet," a woman explained. "Everyone's trying to find a good spot."

"We better find a place to stay," Alta suggested, "in case we get separated. You know a good place?" she asked the woman.

"The hotel and the inns are all full. Maybe there's room in one of the tents. But don't miss the parade."

"The parade's starting," someone yelled.

"No, that's just the band warming up."

"How'll we ever see anything? So many people." They tried working their way along the street through the crowd, Donovan pausing at one of the stands for meat pies and sausages and a pile of little honey cakes topped with nuts. He handed round the food, and himself ate three rounds of everything.

"Friends! Down there." Someone was calling to them, waving from a balcony, an old man, almost entirely bald, with a round, smooth face like an ancient Chinaman's. They stood looking up at him, quizzically, unable, in the noise, to comprehend a word he was saying. "Come up," they finally made out. He was offering them a chance to see the parade from his balcony. Indeed, a great many people were already on the balconies, on roofs of houses, or standing on benches in order to see. One small boy, having climbed a statue of some general or patriot, had joined him in mid-gallop on his horse's back.

Donovan preferred to remain below, since he could see over the heads of the crowd, but the others climbed the stairs to where the old man waited. "You've come at the right moment," he said, smiling. "For you must see," he said to the boy, as though he were the most important person, "how the animals move—the elephants and tigers, the lions and bears. All wild, with nothing lost—"

"Here?" Dusty said. "Elephants here?"

"From the world over—all the animals. To the hilt and limit."

Dusty couldn't help feeling a trace of envy through his anticipation. What does all this mean? He approved of celebrations, had been a carnival man all his life. And he'd mounted acts with the best: animals and freaks and folks that could use their bodies like musical instruments. But this promised to go beyond anything he ever imagined doing. That was the trouble in the world: somebody was always one up on you, trying to beat you at your own game. There were too many ideas, he thought. Too many sets of intentions. But he was impatient for the elephants. He liked their solid slow-moving bulk, their patient animality, their hugeness.

A parade, Alta thought. A parade. The music was in her blood. And she could feel the kid beside her, his attention straining forward; he was leaning so far over the railing trying to see up the street that she feared he would fall off. She exchanged a look with Grace, and decided he'd be all right.

A burst of trumpets filled the air. Then music. And there appeared a figure in the center of the street, dressed in motley, waving a scepter, his face all clown's smirk. "The Prince of Folly," the old man pointed out, putting his hand on the boy's shoulder. "You can't have a carnival without him."

And there he comes. Doing flips, running to the crowd, making faces, sticking out his tongue, making obscene gestures.

Then the elephants. Slow and ponderous, swinging their trunks from side to side. Red blankets on their backs, red velvet squares with gold tassels on their heads. Young boys standing on their backs, guiding them, encouraging them forward. In the middle of the square they pause, standing on their hind legs, forelegs on each other's backs. Four sets of them in all, forming a square.

"Look at that!" Dusty said. "A dozen of them. I could never manage more than four."

A parade of animals following. All kinds of wild animals: leopards and lions and panthers and tigers; zebras and gazelles and ibexes; dromedaries and llamas. They walk without chains or muzzles, their trainers behind them.

"How can they do that?" Curran said.

"It's all in the training," Dusty said. "Sam oughta be here—he's really missed a bet. The only fellow I ever knew really had the knack."

"I've never seen so many animals in one place," Alta said. "And there they are just marching along, minding their own business, not trying to run into the crowd."

The old man listened to them, smiled as though he had himself waved a hand and made it all appear. For now come chariots and carriages, musicians and dancers and Indians on horseback; dozens of clowns on tricycle and unicycle, on donkey and pogo-stick, others on foot, turning somersaults and cavorting, bouncing and tossing balls; then great papier-mâché figures of animals and legendary figures, giants and heroes; mermaids and fairies; animated figures of the zodiac—all come pouring through the streets in splashes of color and music.

Then, at the center of the parade, preceded by those acrobats doing their leaps and backward curves on the backs of horses, more advance, leaping through rings of fire, their red costumes decorated with suns and moons. Though the music and spectacle had burst upon Alta with a wonderful sense of surprise, it was the acrobats that overwhelmed her.

"Look!" she cried. "Aren't they wonderful!"

Backward leaps through the rings of flame. From one to the other. It *was* like that, she thought. It really was—even without the flaming rings. Lost in all that. Because you could see in your mind that you could leap like that, you made yourself into a flame, an arrow— everything concentrated, pure.

"What's the matter," Grace asked her.

"Nothing. Nothing," she said, suddenly realizing there were tears in her eyes, on her cheeks. "I can't bear to see it end."

◆

Though he had seen Alta waving to him from the balcony, trying to get his attention, Donovan had ignored her. He wanted to be left alone to enjoy the spectacle. Then he noticed they were gone, the whole kit and caboodle. Well, he was glad of it, he had to admit, glad to be shut of them for a little while. Especially Curran, who was getting on his nerves again. He was going to indulge himself, live it up to the hilt, as long as he had the opportunity: eat, sleep and play. There were women around, likely looking girls. One had already promised to meet him down by the river. She'd show him a place where they could spend the night. The hell with the tent. Better out in the open with some beauty in your arms than listening to Curran snore.

But the question was how to get out of the clutches of the old woman who was dragging him along. As the crowd had started to disperse, she'd come up and bade him welcome in a kindly if authoritative manner. She was a slender, statuesque woman with high cheekbones and a high forehead. Queenly. Had she been younger, it was a brow he'd have loved to nuzzle. And her mouth had been fine, he could tell. Something remained to suggest her sensuousness. He thanked her for her welcome.

"And now I'll take you to get your costume," she said.

"Well, that won't be necessary, ma'am," he said. "I'm really just a spectator."

"Everyone who comes must put on a costume," she told him. "It is one of the rules. Otherwise there is a penalty."

"Sounds like you all make it a serious business," he said. "Well, a costume it is then. I wouldn't want to be breaking any rules." Still, he hoped to give her the slip, and if anybody jumped on him about it, he'd make an excuse: he was a stranger, didn't know the rules, etc. He wasn't in the mood for nonsense. He'd been in costume all his life for that matter, and for once he'd like a little relief, just be allowed to watch the show. He was tired of his life—in fact, fed up. But he couldn't conceive of any other. Nor was he able to give the old girl the slip; she had her eye right on him, might as well have had him handcuffed.

They had arrived at the arena and he had been given a number and told to wait until it was called. He thought he was free now, but still the old woman clung to him. Finally he was given his costume and, after he'd changed into it, led to a seat inside. Seems you had to go out in the center right under a spotlight and listen to somebody tell you who you were. He chafed with impatience at the whole idea, sitting there watching one, then another go out into the circle of light while a voice read out a fortune-cookie description. He watched with minor interest as a young man in a gorilla suit went cavorting about.

The old woman, sitting beside Donovan, shook her head. "Same old thing," she said. "I've seen him in that suit the last two years."

"I thought you had to take what they gave you."

"That's the custom, but if you insist, sometimes they let you have your way. Not always, but I guess he won out. He's harmless enough, just likes to scare the kids and chase the girls."

"Sounds all right to me," Donovan said, dressed only in a loincloth and a pair of sandals. "Seems like they couldn't find much to fit me."

The old woman smiled. "If you don't like that costume, you can come back tomorrow for another."

"If I don't freeze to death first," he said. Unless the girl had a pile of blankets, he could give up any thought of a night by the river.

Now it was the turn of the fellow sitting next to him. A small, rather droop-ing youth. Out in the spotlight he was told that he was a connoisseur—a taster of wine, of good food, a lover of beauty. Lucky stiff, Donovan thought. I'm *that* already—just let me at it. And unless he imagined it, he thought he saw a gleam of sudden imagination enter the eye of the lucky fellow; at least the news affected the set of his shoulders. Connoisseur, eh? He could teach the kid a thing or two.

Then the old woman was nudging him, and he took his bare chest, his exposed thighs out into the spotlight. A disembodied voice moved down around him: "A warrior once, but captured now and turned into a slave. Man-acles around your wrists and ankles, you sleep in chains, work out your days in the heaviness of labor under the scorching sun."

For a moment after the voice had ceased, he was unable to move. As though a sentence had been pronounced upon him. All thought of celebration fled his mind. Once he was in the street, he couldn't even remember how he had gotten there, only that he was suddenly outside the arena. The town hardly existed for him. The old woman had vanished, and he seemed to be in a strange place, a bare stretch of desert under the glare of a pitiless sun. For a time he had been yoked to a plough, pulling it like one of the oxen across his master's fields. The sting of the lash had stitched his back. Now he was pulling and hauling great blocks of stone being lifted into place with pulleys. All day he spent at this labor, grateful only that he could be above the ground instead of digging in the mines. The thirst that tore at him was terrible, his hunger insatiable, for he never had enough to eat. And always he was weary to the bone.

In flickers of memory he recalled his strength, the time when he went about pillaging cities, taking silver vessels and precious stones and gold coin, captur-ing women and young boys, selling them, holding them for ransom. And though a remnant of that strength returned to him each morning, offered again by the abused limbs and bruised body, the weight of his life he carried like one of the huge stones he was helping to lift to build a house for the dead.

The carnival swirled around him on the periphery of his vision, now and then a face like a gargoyle's leering out at him. He stumbled around, not know-ing where he was going. It was beginning to get dark. He wished someone would find him, Grace or Alta, even Curran. But he saw no sign of them. He followed the flare of torches along the darkened streets, which suddenly seemed surprisingly empty, though he caught the sounds of merriment, perhaps from along the river. All the fun was going on somewhere without him. The old woman had cast a spell on him; he had been singled out and cursed, separated from his friends, estranged from himself. He was ready to weep with anguish and frustration. Once he thought he saw someone he knew, only to find himself in a nest of shadows. And then the town too was gone. He looked back to see the winking of its lights, the dark shapes against the darkness, but he was out somewhere in the open fields, no one else around him.

Hunger gnawed at him, and his mouth was dry with thirst. Dimly he remembered the booths with everything imaginable to eat. Now he would be glad to eat anything. He caught the image of a red-cheeked boy throwing part of his sausage to the little spaniel begging at his feet. Having snapped up the tidbit, the dog went hunting among the stands, nose busy, trying to find another morsel. Donovan could almost anticipate how he might have fed on the richness of smell alone. The steam from cooking stew. The odor of frying sausage and hot meat pies. Ah! Oh! Food. Water.

His legs gave out. He could go no farther. There was nothing to put between himself and the ground, not even dry leaves. He sank down, weary to death, not caring if he woke again. He lay down, closed his eyes, then opened them. He was looking up at a sky full of stars thick as an outbreak of measles. Distant and brilliant, the Milky Way stretched across the sky. But he was fading out of the picture. Laid low. A great mound of flesh, a battleground for hunger and thirst, and every other desire imaginable. Well, they could have his carcass. He was too weak for any desire, even the desire to stay alive, and fell asleep.

◆

At one point, when Curran had watched Donovan wandering along the street, a head taller than anyone else in the crowd, he wanted to find his way to him, run up and seize his hand. They would be together. He would be protected. For crowds had always terrified him. He was safe only when he was part of an act, dignified by the price of a ticket and having thereby struck a bargain with the audience. The ring was a magic circle. Inside he was safe—special, even. They could watch him do his stuff. But now he was even more disoriented than usual. And he had the sense he was alone: nowhere could he look for any salvation. Even the giant looked vulnerable in his sandals and loincloth.

He had no explanation for anything going on, as if his existence had been predicated on a throw of the dice and after that he'd been left entirely to chance. Though the old man had taken all of them to the arena together, in a curious way, they'd become separated once they got there, as though that had been maneuvered too. One by one they'd entered the spotlight, taken the cue from the disembodied voice that seemed to be reading out their separate fates. His: "You are a child. You can't escape childish things."

His fate? Or an insult? Before he had entered the spot light, he had felt exposed and ridiculous in beanie and knickers and knee socks, an old song in his head mocking him: *I'm just a kid again, doing what I did again . . .* He'd always hated that pumping tune, the childishly sentimental words. They had singled him out, he felt sure, just because of his size. And he felt uniquely impotent: not only had he been forced to leave his clothes behind, but also his notebook. The carnival had aroused in him a powerful curiosity. And he had again experienced the urge to record. In the crowd he could've wandered around again, the distant observer—looking down in a way, instead of being made, as always, to look up. But he had been deprived of this support—his talisman.

As soon as he went outside, Curran was surrounded by a gaggle of kids, who didn't appear to notice anything different about him.

"Hey, you want to come with us? Come on." One grabbed him by the elbow, and the whole bunch went tearing along breathlessly down the street. Then threading among the crowd, crawling around and under and through, bent on their own purpose, whatever it was, going their own way. He had no idea where they were going. At least they weren't like the kids who had jumped him back in Ventura City. Breathless, he finally found himself in a square with a fountain in the center. It was mobbed with kids. On one side was a little stage with a curtain, a puppet theater featuring a performance of Punch and Judy, the obstreperous Punch beating his wife, beating up the doctor, killing a policeman. The children roared with approval, cheering him on. Curran discovered he was yelling along with the rest. And felt a curious release.

When it was over, three of the kids he had come with raced through the booths looking for something to eat, considering buns full of nuts and raisins, *fajitas* stuffed with meat, honey balls. The odors of food hit him from every side, his nose suddenly so attentive it took away all his thought, his mouth watering. He ate a sausage so voraciously, it was gone in an instant; he wolfed down several little pies. He loved the intensity of his hunger. He moved from there to thirst as if from one great experience to another. Then the three of them gave themselves to the games—ring toss, horse races, darts.

Weary, finally, they sat around one of the fountains, licking ice cream cones. The whole day had gone, Curran didn't know where. He had skipped from one thing to the next without noticing the time. And now the fatigue he sat in was almost a stupor. He had run himself out, looked and touched, smelled and tasted, yelled himself hoarse. He hadn't felt this tired since—when . . . ?

He got up, bade his companions goodbye and walked slowly in the direction of the river, listening to the crickets and the subdued sounds of voices. The hush of evening was settling over the town. The birds were quieting. He stared at the water, at the outlines of the houses and the shapes of the fields, at the cattle grazing in the distance, at the clouds, one moment melting into the next. Then the moon rose, nearly full, and he threw bits of stick into the water and watched them drift away.

Floating away slowly, they entered a pool of ghostly light that seemed to hold and draw him like a spell. Just for an instant, then it was gone. A glow, as though a gaze had been turned in his direction, an eye casting a benign glance, then withdrawing. Someone was there, someone he knew. The hair rose on the back of his neck. He listened, straining ears and eyes. A dog began to bay at the moon. There was nothing but the water lapping gently against the bank, the moon shimmering on the surface. Only that.

◆

Considering how the others had come out, Dusty had done right well by himself. Something about a uniform did things for a man. And he couldn't help being impressed with himself as he looked in the mirror. Yes, it did him proud: gold buttons on the chest, stars on a high collar. He found himself standing straighter than he'd stood for a while, shoulders back, stomach in. Just a bit of a pot, going to have to do something about the drinking. Nothing serious, mind you. Nothing like a few of the paunches he'd seen around. But he'd have to look into it. For the rest, not bad. Even the gray at his temples was a plus: lent a certain distinction, announced that he'd been in the world awhile, knew a thing or two. And with the sword at his side—the real thing, a heavy reminder of the pact between duty and bloodshed—he felt he'd been given a certain favored position. At the forefront. . .

He knew better, of course, but couldn't help himself. He was used to costumes. He knew their power: robes and vestments, gowns and crowns, capes and wigs, swords and codpieces. The codpiece was mightier than the sword. He'd have to think about that one. Or maybe they went hand in hand, so to speak. Depend on the women to run after both. Say what they would, they all liked that part of a man: the old bloodlust, the look in the eye they thought was meant for them. As he walked through the crowd, he felt the eyes of the women upon him, maybe a jealous glint from the men. Yesiree, he did all right by a uniform. Maybe he'd been born a hundred and fifty years too late. As he approached a woman in an elaborate wig and brocaded gown, she smiled at him so winningly he bowed and kissed her hand.

"I hope, Major," she said, "we will meet other than on the field of battle."

"I am at your command, Madam," he said, tickled by the sound of his gallantry. He could play that part, all right.

"Then tonight you must sign my dance card."

Tonight. Of course. Fancy costume ball at the arena. How long since he'd been on a dance floor. He'd give it a whirl. What was a carnival for? "You may depend on it, my beauty."

The costume seemed to determine everything that happened to you. He thought of Alta, wandering around as a gypsy. If that had been reality, they'd never have met. And would that have been for better or worse? A life becomes a costume for another age, a conch shell becomes a decoration. The thought left him in a kind of void. He wondered where the others had got off to, whether they would find their way back to their tent, perhaps eat supper together.

The streets confused him, and it was impossible to make sense of anybody's directions. The crowds moved and pressed around him, oblivious in their merrymaking. Whistles and noisemakers shrilled and banged in his ear, firecrackers made him jump. When he reached one of the sections of tents it was dark, and he couldn't tell if theirs was among them. The smell of cooking meat tore at his appetite. There were people sitting around fires, eating and drinking, talking with light laughter. The people had grown quiet, perhaps building up for a burst of merriment later on, once they'd eaten and got their second wind.

"Here, sir," a voice called out from near one of the campfires, "come and join us." He might've been wandering among the fires of bivouacking troupes. He went over to where three young men sat, a musician, a Venetian merchant and a sailor. "You hungry," the sailor asked, and spooned up a plate of stew and gave him a glass of beer.

He ate the food gratefully, even greedily, then sat smoking with his companions, trying to catch something of their faces in the firelight. The musician was a large, rather soft-looking young man who sat dreaming as though carrying on a conversation with his guitar. He didn't seem to be listening at all to the conversation around him. The lean, dark-bearded merchant was asking the sailor if they'd found anyone yet for King and Queen. Apparently not, for the sailor shook his head. "Some stranger will fall for it," he said. Then they switched their interest to telling jokes.

"What do you get when you cross a donkey with an onion?"

"A bunion."

"A kick in the ass."

"A strong leak."

They ran out of answers. In the outbursts of laughter, Dusty missed the punch line.

Then they launched into the stories of their lives, all but the musician, who sat plucking cords, humming. The sailor had traveled the world, gone to China and Japan, been shipwrecked off Madagascar. Rescued by an English ship, his companions having died of exposure, scurvy and starvation. You could've believed him, Dusty thought, if you didn't know it was all a pack of lies. The merchant had taken a voyage to Spain in order to negotiate the sale of silks and spices, had taken ill with a fever and nearly died. When he returned, he found his house had been seized for debt, and his family in great misery. It was Dusty's turn. But when his time came, to his astonishment, he blurted out: "I didn't want the war." He'd sat there all the time quietly doing his duty while they were at each other's throats in Congress. Did his duty and minded his business. But as soon as it came to war, he knew they'd suspect his loyalties. He resigned his post despite a letter from the commanding officer encouraging him to remain. Went back to the South and joined his family, joined the Confederate cause. But he hadn't wanted any of it. Thought it was a calamity. Didn't think a gun would solve anything. A bad business, all of it, though he took up his post in the army. Even though they had no idea what they were getting into. Watched all that winter while his superiors pleaded for troops and reinforcements. Then found himself with all the rest, confronting a force of such magnitude . . . Told himself he'd known all along. Knew the rest would happen too. Opposition to the General's battle plans, betrayal by a subordinate . . . Delay in the advance. Confusion in orders.

And yet on the day of battle the sun rose in such splendor, the sky was so clear, the air so fresh over the fields of Tennessee that he felt almost joyful. Even in the first rush of battle. Then began the long day, the forces hurling themselves at the Union lines, which held fast, never seemed to give. The air grew stale as the day wore on. Futility and confusion—till he met the ultimate confusion. The neat strategies breaking apart, as the enemy held its ground, punished them with fire. Then the crisis, the moment to be seized. The charge across the valley to take the crest of the hill. The moment on which all things turned. He led the charge of his brigade. His hat was off. He yelled to the troops. His horse raced forward. In the fire the men fell like dummies. But gained the crest. The one spot.

He was there. Horse shot in four places, sole of his boot ripped away by a mine. There—unhurt. Till another blast of fire and he caught a bullet in the leg. No surgeon there. He himself had sent the sawbones off to care for wounded prisoners. He had, in effect, ordered his own death. Confusion and futility.

Dusty, sitting with his head in his hands, watched strategies and battle plans dissolve away. They were the neatly drawn lines of order, lines of light. Broken, erased, smudged—noise and smoke pouring through the gaps. Chaos. His life.

"Forget it, Major," the sailor said. "It's a dream everybody wakes from. It's all for the carnival, you know."

Dusty wasn't quite sure what he meant. Take nothing beyond the face value? All shifting lights and glancing shadows—a play in the mind? He was unable to move. He watched unseeing while the young men gathered up their things and went off in the direction of further celebration. They had thrown another log on the fire; then they were gone.

While he sat, looking up to a figure high in the air: a young man in blue tights, gold sparkling from the threads: Gold Dust. Gold Dust and Dream Girl. Up there in the air. The slender, dark-haired youth with the fierce eyes, the hawk nose. And Alta. His dream. His future. All dissolved into confusion and futility. Come to grief upon the hard recalcitrance of matter. No matter how hard he worked to make things move or come together. Striving, always striving—toward the idea, the great scheme. The moment of sweet glory when the cup runneth over. When you tapped on the rock and the water gushed out. And there you were. *There.*

Now all broken lines and wreckage. Things torn apart. The tent burned and swept away by the wind, the ground covered with scraps of paper and bottle caps, tigers and acrobats groaning in the ashes. He and Alta grown old, time pulling at their faces till their faces fell in folds of flesh, melted away like wax. He'd loved her once and she'd grown old.

What was left, after all? He'd gone on his way, left her behind, to shift for herself. A wave of despair seized him. He took the sword from its scabbard, saw its gleam in the moonlight. That was real, even if the rest was phony.

Alone, all these years. She might as well have been alone.

It could have been his own voice accusing him, but he recognized it even before he looked up.

"You loved her," he said, with sudden knowledge. "All these years."

Standing before him, Billy nodded.

"And she loved you."

He nodded again.

"That's what you came to tell me? That you had an affair?"

Wouldn't have taken me to tell you that.

He brooded for a moment. "Well, she was alone, I grant you. Even when I was there. Always preoccupied. She went along with me.

And you love her, Billy said.

"Love? Haven't looked at her that way since..." Dust and ashes like the carnival.

What are you waiting for? Eternity to bounce on your chest, the sun to burn itself out? Come on, put that damned thing up.

"You got any better ideas?"

Dream, Billy said. *You were always good at that.*

"You shouldn't kick a man when he's down," Dusty said, suddenly angry. But when he looked again, the darkness had re-gathered around him. Then he thought, What else am I supposed to do? Then he said, "Maybe I got one more carnival left in me yet. Hell, why not? The gods willing—and Alta."

♦

The next morning Donovan woke stiff and sore in all his muscles and bones, and with a terrible dream still reverberating in his head. He dreamt that he'd tried to escape, tried to free himself from slavery, but was caught, blinded and, like Samson, put to work turning the mill wheel to crush the grain. His own groans had awakened him.

But he opened his eyes to the sun, to an ordinary day. The dream was so vivid in his mind that it took him a moment to adjust to the reality: the field was deep in grass and daisies, the palm trees and jacarandas against the sky, the houses on the outskirts of the town. And Billy Bigelow.

"Why, hello, Billy old fellow. What're you doing here?"

Couldn't pass up a carnival.

"Too deep in the blood, eh? What I mean is ... having a good time?"

Can't complain.

"Maybe you got a few advantages. See what they got me into?" He plucked at his loincloth. "Dangerous business to put a man into a thing like this. Next thing, he's acting like a slave, thinking like one."

It doesn't take any talent, Billy told him. *There's all kinds of slavery.*

"Can't say I've been unhappy with some of the forms. If you follow your stomach and your parts, life can't be all bad."

What about your head? When are you going to start using that?

His head. What a thought! He'd bumped it often enough on the lintels of doors and low-hanging beams. Couldn't say his head had got him anywhere in particular. Not even in the carnival. Didn't take any brains for that. The other organs had done much better by him. It was something, you know, to be a giant with appetites to match. And they'd led him into some sweet times. He'd have been glad to tell Billy about a few of the recent ones, only Billy probably didn't have the time to listen. And since he wasn't exactly there in the flesh, it might not be in the best of taste, like describing the glories of the sunset to a blind man. Maybe Billy was beyond being interested.

"So what's a fellow supposed to do?"

The head, Billy repeated.

"Is that all?"

Isn't that enough?

He wanted to ask Billy to explain himself, give him something useful and concrete to go on, but Billy had disappeared. Disconcerting when a person could just take himself off like that without satisfying your mind.

He picked himself up from the ground, brushed away bits of straw and dirt, picked the twigs from his hair. He was hungry as a cannibal, and thirsty too. As he was trying to find his way through the outskirts of town, looking for somebody who could give him directions, he caught the smell of breakfast in the air and spotted a young girl putting out scraps for the dog on the front step of her house. She was lovely, he was quick to observe, with a mane of dark hair hanging to her shoulders. He could see she was startled by the sight of him.

"Miss," he said, "do you suppose you could give me a piece of bread?" She was looking at him still in a startled way, like a cat about to skitter up a tree. Indeed, he must've been a strange sight, all eight feet of him standing there in loincloth and sandals, looking altogether the worse for wear. He had to keep talking, trying for gentleness of tone, urbanity. He considered throwing himself at her knees, but was afraid that might offend her. Maybe he should praise her beauty or perhaps, on the other hand, impress her with the desperation of his condition, win her sympathy. All of this crossed his mind in a split second.

"Lovely lady," he ventured, "you see before you an unfortunate man. I have landed in this place, I don't exactly know where, without food and drink, and in this costume. . ." And surely there was more of him to be naked than for most people. "I have lost my bearings, yet I'm so weak from lack of food . . ."

Apparently she had adjusted herself to the sight of him. Nor was she appalled any longer by his presence. "Come inside," she beckoned.

When he finally left her, he had no complaint with the world. A long breakfast had left him in a stupor of satisfaction: sausages and a pile of eggs cooked with tomatoes and chilies, thick slabs of bread and coffee. He was beginning to feel human again. And though he'd have liked to stay and sweet-talk her a bit longer, it was time to get rid of the garments of his dark time.

Where was he going? Billy had left him with a bug in his ear. Wherever it was, he supposed he'd be taking his appetite with him— couldn't just throw it away. Yet a curiosity had seized him. He saw himself back in Atlantia, looking at the buildings. It had excited him to be there, and he'd wanted very much to visit the observatory. Imagine, looking up there at the stars that had hung over his collapse into weariness and sleep. The bright band of the Milky Way. Lying there on his back, he'd been staring up into billions of years ago, maybe staring into the future too. Suppose he did go back to Atlantia, put on the garb of a scientist? But maybe there were already enough of those folks working their brains, putting enough marks on paper to give the next generation a shove beyond the pull of gravity. What would they do, he wondered, with the idea of a carnival? Maybe the jokers needed a touch.

♦

They had told her she could come back and choose her own costume the next time. And now Alta was going to do just that. While she didn't know about the boy, he acted willing enough to come along. He didn't say what he intended to do, though he seemed to be getting along all right. They hadn't even insisted he leave behind Billy's cape, and let him add it to his motley. She had kept him by her, and they had gone off together, the gypsy and the fool, a fitting pair, it seemed to her. Things had not gone badly.

She wanted to do right by the kid, if only she knew how—for Billy's sake if nothing else. And because he'd been left to her, in her charge. Heaven knows, Dusty had enough troubles of his own. And she and the kid, after all, had been struck in the same place.

At first the boy had terrified her. Billy's death had shattered the silence he carried around, that ran from the hostile to the inscrutable and seemed to mellow only in Billy's company—shattered it and let out everything underneath, like the breaking of the earth's crust. He howled like a dog, raged around like the wild thing he was, till it seemed his grief would split him in two. Drove her crazy as well. Because she'd wanted to howl along with him. Don't worry; she'd just about turned herself inside-out as it was. And when she was done, it seemed like she'd never have another tear for anybody or anything. But his wailing reached all the way through her and went beyond anything human, all the way to the edges of the night.

But then, with the kid too, the storm raged itself out like any other act of nature: trees shattered, branches broken and scattered, then the terrible calm. So the aftermath of a great love. And what was left he must've taken in like a color of the mind. And she sensed a certain kinship between them, if only the kinship of loss. He never took off Billy's cape except to go to sleep.

"Tell us a fortune, mother."

A tall lanky young man stood in front of her, dressed like one of Robin Hood's band, a little pointed green cap on his head.

Why not, she thought. A gypsy was supposed to tell fortunes. But the moment she took his palm, she found herself in a place she hadn't been before. She might have stepped into a chamber full of voices that spoke not in words but in moving colors of the mind. She knew this man, knew what lay beneath his costume, behind his face.

"You're in love with two women," she told him, "and you can't make up your mind."

"You said it, mother—you have read me right." He turned to his companion, a genial, heavy-set man with the fuzz of a mustache across his lip. He was dressed as a courtier, and looked on with amused skepticism.

"The blonde is a mermaid and the brunette is a witch."

"That's a frightening choice. What's a man to do?"

"The mermaid will always be a fish below. And a darkness lives in the witch."

"Sounds like I better choose neither."

"Make the dark light."

"Make Barbara bleach her hair," his companion suggested with a little snigger. "It's what gentlemen prefer."

The confused lover poked his friend in the ribs. He was going to ask another question, but she had told him enough. After all, it was his affair. "And now you, friend," she said, seizing the moist, fat hand the courtier seemed reluctant to give her.

"Come on," his friend rallied him. "What are you afraid of?" "There are things you want to hide," Alta said. Ah, his genial face, a bit heavy in the jowl—the covering of flesh did not protect him. "A theft," she said, "from one who trusts you."

He jerked his hand away as from a candle flame and fled into the crowd. His companion looked after him, astonished.

"Well, too late now," Alta said. She was now aware that people were watching her and she was pressed eagerly from all sides by those who wanted their palms read. A bench was brought for her to sit on, but it was too far out in the open. She'd made one mistake: It would not do to broadcast certain things to a bunch of curious onlookers. Since they were on the edge of a park, she went under the shade of some trees near a small fish pond. The boy sat on the grass, listening silently. She didn't mind his presence. She had felt his eyes on her, and it struck her that he knew what she was going to say even before she said it. Could see what was there to be read from a palm—loves and hates, pulsations of the will, the throbbings of desire. Coiled up, still enfolded lives. Could see to the core where thought is born and given shape, the seeds of the unfolding future. What moved in hints and guesses.

What would he do with that burden? She'd thought of him as being empty; but now she saw what could live in him, make him full. And maybe the future would grow out of that. But right now she had no time to think about it. Other fingers were plucking at her hem. What to say? She had to pick and choose. You could give a fellow too much of the future, maybe more than he could use. A little went a long way. And there were those who'd never believe her anyway. That was all right too.

Everything was open, flowing, present. Her life had become as porous as a sponge, everything flowing in and out. She was hardly in the world. Everything she'd lived and done, all she was, was like the jelly inside the eye, every light penetrating it, casting its colors on it. She'd taken it all in—grief, joy and struggle—always risking, suffering, risking all, not holding back. How often she'd lost and failed and come to grief, risking so much and losing all. And suddenly none of that seemed to matter in the least.

There's nothing more I own, she thought. I might as well be a plaything of the wind. I can't even remember straight. It can blow right through me. But something stands in spite of all. She looked around. She was alone now with just the boy. And this boy is here with me— at least for now.

Don't forget me, Billy said.

"Of course," Alta told him. "By this time, I should know better."

She and the boy got up and wandered out of the park. They paused to get ice cream cones, for her throat was dry. Strawberry for her, chocolate for the boy.

Yes, she thought, *I'm really into the spirit of it. I'm going to have myself a ball.* She'd had enough of this fortune-telling bit, even though it was interesting going around and looking into people's secret lives. A little too vicarious, she decided, or just plain snoopy. There must be one thing more, something else for *her* to live. She wanted to try one more costume just for the hell of it. Something really spectacular this time. *I'm going to celebrate,* she thought. Why not? What else was there to do, having come this far? She wanted the right costume for it. The works.

Just at that moment, she caught sight of Grace hurrying past.

"I've just seen Priam Gillespie," she said. "I'd recognize that old crotch-grabber anywhere."

"You mean he's chased us this far?" Alta said. "The old pisspot—what's got into him? As if you were his property. Well, stay close. He'll not lay a hand on you as long as I've got anything to say about it. It's over my dead body, if he tries."

Grace looked at her, then touched her on the arm. "Maybe it's time for me to be moving on. I've caused too much trouble already."

"Don't think of it," Alta said. "What're we here for if we can't stand by each other. We'll take care of you, don't worry. Don't just take off." She felt a terrible pang—and knew the girl would be leaving, maybe not just yet, but soon. She'd be gone and there'd be another empty place in her life. The boy stood in silence. Probably he knew it too. Probably'd take off as well. Nothing lasted forever, carnivals least of all.

"The big celebration's tonight," Alta said. "I'm going to try to find the others. Let's have a little fun before it's over."

Grace put her arm around her. "Well, I'm going to find a nice quiet spot for awhile—maybe walk down by the river and go out in one of the canoes. Bye," she said. "See you later. There's Dusty—I see him down there a ways." And she turned off into one of the side streets, as if certain of the direction in which she wanted to go.

Priam Gillespie. The old dog had a good nose to pick up their scent, though in fact they hadn't made any secret of their whereabouts. A one track mind. Having lost the only good thing he'd ever had, he wanted it back. Squandered his loot and wanted more. And Grace was his gold mine. As though she had no other reason to be alive. The thought made Alta gloomy. She felt uneasy letting the girl go off by herself, wanted to protect her. Then, she thought, *I can't do that anymore.* What then *could* she do?

All this time she'd wanted to give something to the girl, something for the future. Was there anything she had to offer, any kind of legacy? She searched her mind. Only her affection, which came with both warmth and light. In which Grace stood open to her vision as all she was and all she could be—what Alta wanted to see existing in the future, nothing to hinder it or cripple it or beat it into the ground. What else could she give her but the gift of all her mistakes and past misfortunes? And what are they but what you are? That was all she had to offer. Whatever she was. Maybe whatever grew in the future was grounded in that, in this life or any other. And it seemed that only if you could live some different life, step back from your own enough so that it seemed a different life, could you ever learn enough to change the course of things. And would you ever learn enough?

"Well, what'll we do?" she said aloud, not expecting any answer. Just a moment ago she'd felt like she used to feel right before she stepped out in front of a crowd. Where did it go? Seems like you couldn't ever get free of trouble. Like a pack of hounds, always on your track. Maybe that's what it means to be alive, she thought. Something always in the wind.

"Hell," she said, thinking of Billy, "You can't laugh at we serious professionals." The boy was walking ahead of her, kicking at stones, picking up sticks and tossing them into the air. *Well, kid,* she thought. *You got his cape—it's up to you to make a little magic in the world. Your turn.*

She saw the costume she wanted almost immediately. A flowing, shimmering silvery gown with a red mantel embroidered with gold and white pomegranates. The crown was lovely, better than anything she could have put together herself. But she didn't know if she dared to ask for the costume, until the old woman told her she could have any one she wanted.

"And how come nobody's got that one? Because it's the one I want."

"Then it's yours," the old woman told her.

And it became a question she didn't have to answer. Maybe they'd just put it out, or maybe it had been hanging there unwanted all day. Maybe only she thought it was the most splendid costume she'd ever seen. And maybe she had it not because she exhibited any special virtues, but only because she was what she was. At any rate, it was hers.

She was Queen of the Moon. And in that costume she'd have to give the signal for the opening of the reservoir, which would flood the sewers and gutters of the city and carry away everything that had collected in them, at the same time sending streams of water to fill the water gardens and fountains in the parks. Then, at her command, the fireworks would begin. And for all the next day she had to join in the merriment of the city, all day and all night—going from group to group, joining in all the toasts. She might be lying on the ground in a little heap at the end of it, but somehow, she decided, it would be worth it.

"You have to have an escort," the old woman told her. "You can choose anybody you want." And she showed her the king's costume: red silk shirt and breeches, a white mantle and a crown with a blazing sun. King of the Sun and Queen of the Moon. Tonight would be their coronation.

Alta wondered if Dusty would play along. Maybe he'd just laugh at her—he was certainly capable of it. She looked around at the boy, who was waiting for her patiently. He was apparently absorbed in watching people come and go.

"You can get another costume," Alta said, but he gave no sign of having heard. She turned back to the gown. It was really something—she'd never seen material like that before. And it had better fit, she thought. It *will* fit.

Since she had seen Dusty coming along behind her, she expected him to appear momentarily. But when he came up, she found him looking rather more thoughtful than she expected. That is, after a night of playing general or whatever he was, which was no doubt right up his alley.

"I'll be glad to get out of this rig," he said.

"Not suited for the military," she asked. "Seems like you'd be headed for a few conquests." She realized this wasn't the time to banter him, even lightly.

"What's that," he asked, looking at her gown.

"Queen of the Moon." He could laugh if he wanted to. "I get to choose an escort."

"What do you know."

"I'd like to choose somebody who has a taste for the job."

"Wouldn't be me you're thinking of?"

"You never can tell."

"Well, I don't want to unduly influence your choice, but I'd accept. In fact, it would be an honor."

"Well," she said, "in that case I'll consider it."

They looked at each other as if, having been introduced, they were trying to decide whether they might like each other.

"Besides," he added, "I've got nothing better to do."

"You'd better believe it," she said.

They went off to dress. She put on the gown and stood admiring herself in the mirror. *Well, Billy,* she said, *why don't you come on around and admire me. You ought to be proud.* She put on the mantle, which flowed around her in flaming folds. *How about that, Billy? And tonight I'll get the crowning touch. Moon and evening star.* She felt a radiance come over her, and she was sure of his presence. There came a point where there didn't seem much space separating the living from the dead: their messages were always in the air. *Billy, Billy,* she said. *It's all a spectacle. One grand illusion. We're in it for the play.*

And after he had walked all around her, duly admired her, she heard him say, *Go to it, Dream Girl.*

◆

It was true that Priam Gillespie had reached the city, and since his arrival had been on a roll, swept up by a great wave, the water underneath him rolling and swelling and cresting, Priam riding the wave, plummeting forward—and hanging on for dear life and anything else he was worth. Never had he been in a place where the liquor flowed so freely, where there were so many companions to drink with. He shared freely from the bottle he carried with him, and freely shared from whatever jugs and bottles came his way, handed around by others. He lurched happily from one group to another, belching with deep satisfaction, drinking toasts to unknown wives and sweethearts. He'd raised his own glass a number of times to Grace, toasting her in whiskey-saturated breath: "And here's to Grace, the greatest little snatch this side of Bangkok. To my darling Grace—her cup runneth over."

As the whiskey took him in tow, melting him into sentiment, tears came to his eyes: *Ah Grace, my lost and lovely, where will I find your sweet honey pot again?* Then, with more whiskey, his mood shifting toward the bellicose, he drank and shook his fist: "Robbers," he shouted, "who have cheated me of my prize! Lying, meddling, robbing, cheating bastards!"

Having worked himself into a fine frenzy, he waved his arms, shook his fists: "They'll pay for this. Mark my words. The scurvy villains. If Priam Gillespie be not avenged . . ." But his legs began to waver, his knees turning to water, and his mind was suddenly aswirl like a sink when the plug is pulled. "Mark my . . ." And he sank into a stupor.

The next thing he knew he found himself in lavender silk pantaloons and fringed vest and turban, held aloft and carried about on a palanquin. By God, he couldn't believe it. He was a sultan. A bevy of maidens followed after him, feeding him pears, grapes, oranges, nectarines, cashews, currants, passion fruit guavas, bananas, figs, dates, cherries, causing the breezes to play among great fans of ostrich plumes. Can it be, he wondered, that I have died and gone to Paradise? No, he thought—not unless they've changed the entrance requirements.

Or can it be, he speculated further, that I got so drunk I went to the other side of three sheets to the wind and will now stay there forever surrounded by these lovely maids? It was a possibility, but not one you could bank on. Finally he sank back on the silken pillows while a monkey frisked about his head. Why ask questions, he decided, questions that might prick the whole thing like a bubble and you'd wake up back on the cold hillside where you'd been before, right out in the middle of nowhere, perishing of hunger and thirst. No, he'd just go along for the ride, as long as the ride lasted.

"Now tell me, my lovely," he said to a black-haired nymph, dressed enchantingly in a filmy bodice and Turkish trousers, with a beauty spot located charmingly on her rouged cheek, "can you give me a touch of that nectar so pleasing to my glottis and other stops along the length of my esophagus, which at the moment is as dry as a snake's gizzard?" From a carafe she poured him a glass of the foaming wine.

He took it down in a single gulp, smacked his lips appreciatively and wiped his mouth with the back of his hand. With a little giggle, she twined a flower in his hair. He seized her hand and pressed it to his lips. The bristles of his beard were rough against her skin. Could do with a shave, he thought. No, he figured, no time for that.

They made quite a procession through the streets, the crowd making way with great cheering and hooting and wisecracking. He'd been given a bag of pennies to toss, and he threw them down, watching the kids scramble for them. Think I missed my calling, he thought. Should've been one of those oil sheiks, like the fellow who gets his weight in gold every year. *Now let's see, with me weighing around a hundred ninety, and gold over four hundred an ounce* ... He had a try at multiplication. A million, two-hundred-thousand and more. And that was just pin money. By God, fate had done him an unkindness. Only Grace to just barely keep him afloat, and now he was afflicted with the task of getting her back. Only he wasn't going to get much done being carted around. He told his bearers he wanted to take a little stroll, and they set him down in front of the entrance to the park. Here was as good a place as any to begin his search. All the festivities were set there, and if Grace was anywhere to be found, this was likely the spot. To make sure he wouldn't get thirsty, he availed himself of a bottle of wine one of his attendants was carrying.

Quite a showplace, the park. He walked through the entrance in the stone wall along the cobbled way, among pines and palms, along flower beds planted with rose bushes and beds of pansies, alongside ponds and water courses that with this evening's festivities would be freshened again with water. At one side was a small natural waterfall that splashed and zigzagged over rocks until the water spilled into a series of irregular ponds graced with pink water lilies and black and white swans, mallards and other water fowl.

Quite a place, he acknowledged, continuing on—though he'd never been much of a man for the out-of-doors. Liked most of his pleasures inside four walls. All the ones he could think of. But for a park, he thought, scanning his eyes over the variously colored bougainvillea, it had a certain pizzazz. Yes, indeed. He approached a great tree, an ancient hoary tree, with branches as great as the trunk itself. At the center, one huge branch divided into two, which formed a natural arch nearly as wide was the tree was high.

Several peacocks strolled pecking at the ground. One fanned out his tail and let out a cry like the shriek of brass.

The buggers could make a noise all right. He sauntered past the tree and beyond it into an open space with pleasant walks, statues and thick grass. Men and women were sitting on blankets with baskets of food unpacked and spread out in front of them, or else meandering along the paths, disappearing into little groves where the foliage had been allowed its freedom.

My God, he thought, they're all starkers. Buck naked, every one. Some clothes lay discarded on the grass, some draped across the benches. And everywhere he turned beauties, and the men weren't bad-looking either. But it was the women he couldn't take his eyes off —and all without a stitch on. He couldn't believe it.

He watched a youth as he poured some wine for a young girl, the very sight of whom was enough to bring tears to the old man's eyes. She took a sip, then another, then handed the cup back to her companion, who drank deeply. They stood gazing into each other's eyes; they kissed. Then he put his arm around her waist and they walked away slowly.

He watched them disappear into the grove. "My God!" he exclaimed. *They've gone off. He's going to pop her cherry.* He stared after them till his eyes felt as if they'd been stretched on elastic. And here he was, women all around him, and he with his clothes still on. He ducked behind a bush, took off his silk pantaloons, his pointed red slippers and his fringed vest and rolled them all up into a bundle and set them under a bush. Kept the turban on his head, though. To protect his pate from the sun. Barefoot in the grass—for the first time in what seemed a century or more. Grass tickling his feet. He grabbed up his jug, paused to take a swig and scratch his belly. Then he came forward, carrying his great paunch, a few hairs sprouting out at the navel. He looked around, filled his eyes: women, women everywhere. Surely one to spare.

He went hobbling down the path as quickly as he could, for he saw a dark-haired girl, unaccompanied, just ahead of him. He half-rushed, half-staggered after her. "Hey, girlie," he said when he was within reach, a bit breathless.

"Would you like a leetle touch of wine? Though for my taste I could do with a good snort of the sneaky Pete."

She turned toward him, gave a little giggle and ducked into the trees.

"Well, I'm damned," he said. Problem was he didn't have a cup. He ran back.

"Excuse me, ma'am," he said to a woman sitting on a blanket on the grass. "You wouldn't happen to have an extra cup, would you?"

Graciously she smiled and gave him one and he went off happily. "Anyhow," he said, "there's more'n one pebble on the beach." The jug was heavy in his arms and he undertook to lighten it a little. "Maybe I'll just wait for one to come by. See which one'll give me the eye." Meanwhile he drank from the jug. And again. Till the jug was below the halfway mark. And again. A couple of girls were walking toward him, a redhead and a blonde. "I want," he said, thinking of the redhead. "I want ..." he said, pointing, for suddenly speech seemed to desert him. The nipples of their breasts were aimed towards him, ever closer, nipples aiming right for the eyeball. Closer. But no, not steady, sinking, falling away, and he, yearning forward, troubling in the dark to find them again ...

When he came to, the darkness was all around him, but a full moon shone on the trees and shimmered on the water. He could hear noise as from the gathering of a large crowd. The park was empty. He tried to remember where he'd put his clothes and rummaged around under bushes, cursing and swearing. Had there been no moon he'd never have found them. The noise of celebration played in his ears while he scrambled around on all fours. Just as he was about to weep with vexation, he put his hand on one of his slippers, found the pantaloons. He had a hard time figuring out where to put his legs. Got the shirt on, then the vest. Where was the other slipper? Looked under his bush and then the next. Couldn't find it. Looked again. Went round to the other side. No luck. Well, damn. Some mutt had probably carried it off. He'd have to do without.

He went limping along the path. As he walked, he heard water rushing in his direction through the courses of the water gardens. Lights went on, colored lights playing on the water. The fireworks began to go off, great bursts of color blossoming in the sky. Pink and blue and yellow and white. Then he came to the reservoir where the crowds were gathered. On a platform were two figures all dressed in red and white. Squinting, he saw somebody he knew. Grace. Hot damn. Here she was, and he was going to get her.

Then he saw something else, a figure he didn't recognize but whose aspect did not strike him favorably. "Who are you?" he demanded. "You're not one of those mummers, are you ?" But whoever it was, he could see right through him. Yet he was there, no question about it.

Terrified, he dropped to his knees. "Don't haunt me," he pleaded. It was the drink—he'd drunk himself to the DTs. That was it. "I'll give it up," he promised. "Go on the wagon and never touch a drop. S'help me—if you'll just go away. And I'll give up smoking too, you can bet on it." He looked out the corner of one eye. It was still there, un-propitiated, not saying a word, but pointing a finger at him. "And women," he added for good measure. "I'm getting on and . . ." Surely one could ask no more of him. "Oh, don't hurt an old man that wouldn't kill a fly." And he hid his face in his arms, falling forward whimpering and blubbering. How long he lay in that condition he did not know. After a time, he raised his head and looked around. Rockets were breaking into colors above him, illuminating the surrounding trees. He gaped in wonder. He tried to put his lips around a question. This place. Himself. He tried to connect. There before. Seen it once. Dreamed once—gone where? Vanished. He fished around in the fog. Tried to get to the top of his mind. He touched the top of his head, gently, as though he might find a hole where the air came gusting through.

A stranger nearly stumbled over him. He looked up at the man. Tried to say something, put his lips together to make a sound. He babbled a few words that the fellow was unable to make out. He felt himself being helped to his feet, being led off. The city officials tried to speak to him, but he was unable to tell them his name.

After that he spent his days in the park, sunning himself on the bench and feeding the birds. Each year, at a special ceremony, the city gives him a new coat, a new pair of shoes and a supply of shirts, socks and underwear. As the town lunatic, he is considered holy.

◆

The carnival was nearly done. From where she stood, Alta could see the boy wandering off, and she waved to him and called. But he was already beyond her. Comfortable in his motley, the boy had wandered up and down seeing everything. He had watched various people in their costumes—Alta and Dusty and the rest. He had seen them crowned King of the Sun and Queen of the Moon, and he had known how Dusty had felt a kindling of desire and how Alta was swept away in a flood of tenderness. He knew all that. And he had seen Billy whenever he appeared. He saw him rally Dusty and gig Donovan and frighten Priam Gillespie out of his wits. He saw the old man's hair go white with terror. He saw Grace. He didn't know where she was, but he had a vision of her dancing, the snakes forming ribbons of light, the crimson butterfly lifting from her shoulder like a flame and the silver letters of *Amazing* curving like a smile and dissolving.

He saw the crowd spilling through the streets in their revels. He watched the peacocks in the park strutting and fanning their tails. He observed the clouds high above the city changing from towers into battleships into white whales. He watched the water flowing among the rocks, and the light glancing on the water as the flute players made melodies to accompany the revelry. And he decided he wanted no other costume, just this one, and Billy's robe to sleep in when it got cold.

Near where he stood, he saw a man dressed as a pilgrim. Approaching him, he asked, "Do you know where the seventh city of Cibola is?" He'd been wondering about it for days.

"Seventh?" the man said. "Ya ain't joshing me, now? There's only this here, the last of 'em. That's all there is."

"That's a lie," the boy said, outraged. "There's got to be seven." "A long time ago there was this story they used to tell," the fellow said. "Nobody paid any mind 'cause they knew there's only six." "That's impossible," the boy insisted. "There's got to be seven." The fellow looked confused, put his hands out in front of him and backed off. But it didn't matter; the kid refused to believe him. He was quite determined to search for it, and if he didn't find it, to create it in an imagined land.